Altering Me

TETHERED TO YOU, BOOK 2

KRYSTAL KAE

DARK ORCHID PRESS

BEFORE YOU READ

This book contains sexual themes, language, violence including violence against women and brief mention of rape, discussion of past suicide attempt, and references to and depictions of death and murder.

CHAPTER 1

Violet

To say I was in shock would be the understatement of the century.

The very same black eyes I had grown so fond of seeing on Kade were now a part of my own face. Up until this point, I hadn't noticed anything different with my vision. In fact, everything seemed normal. I took a step closer to the mirror, further examining myself. My right hand floated up and my fingertips began pressing the delicate skin around my eyes lightly. I wasn't sure if I was expecting to notice something different or anything else unusual, but my eyes wouldn't be black unless I had become a demon.

So how in the hell had I become one?

"What...?" I couldn't even form my thoughts into words as my heart rate spiked. I didn't even know how to become a demon, and here I was, in Darthou, sans Kade, and wearing a pair of demon eyes. "Is this some sort of trick?"

Sarah, Kade's aunt, who had been at my bedside in the infirmary since I had awoken, stepped into view. I could tell by her expression that she was concerned. Her perfectly shaped eyebrows were pinched as she hugged herself. I whipped around so fast that it startled her out of her pose.

"Where's Kade?" I blurted, heated. By his own admittance, he didn't want this transitioning business for me, and he'd only explained it away by alluding to how dangerous it was. We never got to the nitty-gritty of how such a thing even occurred. My mind jumped to various conclusions, some of which painted Kade in a very negative light. I didn't want to believe they could be true.

"He's with the council." Sarah took a step forward, talking to me as if I were a dog on the loose that she was trying to calm. "But he will be here as soon as he can."

"Where is this council?" I bit back. I had an anger bubbling beneath the surface that I needed to let loose.

How could he possibly leave me at a time like this, and with complete strangers? I felt alone and betrayed, and if I didn't see Kade soon, I might explode. I had been shot, broken, and bleeding, and then I awoke in a new place without him and without any explanation as to what the hell was going on. Kade's apparent betrayal in the matter sunk in deep, and Damian's words flashed through my mind at such a lightning speed that I wanted to hurl something across the room.

Kadriel will steal you away tomorrow. Just wait and see.

He was so sure of himself, telling me point-blank that Kade would do just that. I didn't want his words to be true. I *refused* to believe they could be, and yet here I stood.

And here I'd thought Damian and Brett were the worst of my problems.

"Where?" My voice rose and Sarah's bright eyes widened in fear. I wasn't sure if I'd ever had this effect on anyone in my life before now, but I wasn't going to back down. I wanted to believe that she wasn't here to keep me prisoner, as her petite frame didn't seem all that intimidating, but since I'd been thrust into a world of which I knew nothing, I couldn't be sure of anything.

"Please, I don't think he should be much longer," she pleaded, but I was having none of it. "You've been through a lot. Just sit with me until he returns. I promise you he will be back as soon as he's able."

I shook my head as a strange sensation began to pulsate at my back. I turned to follow its current, eyeing the unusually grand mirror suspiciously. If I was a demon, could I cross through it? I mean, what exactly did I have to lose at the moment? I was trapped in this room with no other way out. I focused my thoughts on Kade, grasping onto the fumes that were threatening to consume me, and I reached out.

Astonishment swept through me when my hand disappeared through the glass, creating a rippling effect. My wrist twisted as I blinked, unbelieving that I had just passed through solid material as if it were nothing but air. I hadn't even felt a change in temperature in doing so.

I was eager to find out what lay on the other side and held my breath.

"Violet, don't!"

Sarah's alarm was evident as I crossed the threshold and entered a brief moment of complete darkness before stepping out into another area that held no familiarity other than the same concrete-style walls. I clenched my fists as I glanced back at the mirror, amazed at my newfound ability to leave the confines of the odd infirmary on my own.

I didn't know why, but I'd half expected to see Sarah following just behind. To my surprise, she was nowhere to be seen. I was an eyesore, and all alone.

My jaw set as I ground my teeth at the sight of my appearance once more. Beneath the robe and the inky black matter, I almost didn't recognize the reflection I was met with. A fire began to ignite within me and take hold. I knew it wouldn't quell until I had answers, and I was hell-bent on finding Kade to get them. He had some serious explaining to do. Saving me, dropping me off in a weird-ass hospital-type place with his aunt, and then running off to this council? Something wasn't adding up.

The stern voice of an older man swept through the dimly lit stone corridor and captured my attention. To my left, the hallway darkened, appearing to wrap around into total darkness. But to my right, I followed the voice as I crept along the pavement-like stones on the balls of my feet. It was a bit medieval looking, as iron torches came into view, affixed to the walls. They became more prominent as I continued to follow the curved path.

"But even *you* are not above the law." Displeasure was evident in the man's voice as his words delivered a deafening silence that had me slowing. I had no idea if I should be retreating, or if I should wait it out to see if I could gather any more intel on what lay ahead. There had to be a reason that I'd found myself here, and I didn't want to leave without knowing whether Kade was here or not.

Another voice chimed in as an opening provided an onslaught of light, pouring into view and almost within arm's reach.

"There are proper steps to be taken, ones you seem to—" His abrupt cutoff caused me to freeze in my place. If I took a few more steps, I would enter whatever room was up ahead and around the corner. So far, I had only heard two separate voices, but I had no idea how many could be present or what kind of audience awaited.

"I believe we have a guest," a third voice said, and I tensed as I backed up against the closest wall. I knew I had been caught. Not a doubt in my mind told me otherwise. "You may show yourself."

I blew out a shaky breath and attempted to harness every ounce of courage I could possibly find. I pushed off and entered the room, straightening my shoulders.

The room that I entered was grand in appearance, its massive ceilings similar to the infirmary but the space at least three times the size. There were bookshelves and tables on the far side of the room, all neat and orderly, and I wondered when the last time was that any of it had been touched. It looked like a museum that should have a *Do Not Touch* sign nearby.

There were no windows, as I glanced about, nothing that could let in light from outside. It was extremely bright in here, though the only things emitting light were the firelit sconces around the room and probably a dozen chandeliers hanging above. They weren't exactly tiny candlesticks up there either—they looked about double the size of my fists.

I felt bad for whoever had to light all of those suckers. That seemed like a chore and a half of punishment.

While I briefly took in the sight of six demon men forming a curved half circle, it was the man they were placed around who truly caught my attention. My previous anger and drive melted away as our eyes met, but his appearance didn't go unnoticed.

Kade's dark hair looked to be a matted mess, and he wore a severe expression, which quickly shifted as he took me in.

The look that he gave, however, didn't sit well. His lips parted and his eyes widened, almost as if he were surprised to see me. Well, maybe more than surprised. Shocked, perhaps, like he was seeing a ghost. Honestly, I had no idea if a ghost would even frighten a demon, but I couldn't think of what else to compare it to.

"Please, join us."

I didn't care who was addressing me, but I used the offer to my advantage and continued my barefoot journey to join Kade at his side. My robe began to feel rigid in spots. Whatever this black stuff was, it was apparently turning the fabric to cardboard and my hair as straight as a board.

"You have been our great topic of debate today," another gruff voice added.

I cared not for who was speaking as I proceeded to join Kade. He wore an all-black number that was extremely formfitting, with weaponry at his sides, around his legs, and upon his back, as if he was dressed for battle. He had left me to face Damian, and seeing him in this garb would have been appealing any other time but now. He looked like a damn warrior of some sort. It molded to him as if it were a second skin, highlighting his toned muscles in all the places that would normally make my mouth go dry.

As I closed the distance between us, I could make out that his hands were covered in a mixture of dried blood and the same black ink that stained my skin. I wanted to be joyous that I had found Kade, and all on my own to boot, but I could feel the atmosphere of the room and it was heavy. The words I had heard thus far, loaded with contempt. Whatever scene I had just walked into, I had the suspicion that it was focused on Kade, as he was at the center of it all.

He remained silent but slipped his hand into mine and

squeezed as he returned his attention to the men before him. I followed his gaze, examining a large and empty throne that stood before us. Its red velvet cushions and black-rimmed exterior set it apart from the lesser chairs that the other men were sitting in.

To my left and right were two sets of three men, all clad in various shades of black. One wore a robe, others suits, and another wore more casual attire. I gathered that black was the choice of color around here, even though both ladies I'd met in the infirmary seemed ordinary in their appearance compared to these guys. The men before me seemed to vary in age, one maybe close to Kade's, all the way up to some with grayed hair.

Of course this council was made up of all men. I could see some similarities between the politics here and those back home, but at least they weren't all crypt keepers that needed to retire. As I scanned over them all briefly, each one of them was studying me with varying degrees of curiosity on their faces.

I might have fallen for Kade's black eyes quickly, but being around other demons was going to take some getting used to. It felt like starting over at square one again, trying to decipher all of the little expressions when you couldn't focus on the brightness of one's iris.

One of the middle-aged men—the one I'd determined was the friendliest-looking out of the lot of them—cleared his throat, vying for my attention. His hair was a deep brown and neatly styled, his face clean-shaven, and he wore a more casual type of suit. I couldn't even make out any buttons on the jacket.

"Welcome, Violet," he began as he leaned forward slightly, placing an elbow on his armrest. "Perhaps you can settle a matter for us so we may all go about our day. Kade's actions have caused quite the stir, and we only wish to get to the bottom of it."

I narrowed my eyes at him, unsure of what he was implying. Sure, my transition to demonhood was a big deal, but regarding anything else, I was afraid that I was in the dark on most matters at the moment. I nodded my head for him to continue.

"Prior to your arrival here, did you verbally accept the tethering?"

Shit, was Kade in some sort of trouble? Is that why he was with the council instead of by my side when I awoke? My thoughts were fleeting, but I couldn't dwell on them as I was on full display to six strangers, all with mixed expressions as they awaited an answer. I fought the urge to steal a glance at Kade, afraid that one wrong move might cause more conflict.

"I did," I said, quick but stern, making sure my voice was loud enough for all of them to hear. I could see in my periphery that some of the men seemed more at ease after my answer, while others remained unmoving. An unsettling feeling began to form in the pit of my stomach.

The gentleman who had asked the question then stood, a small grin on his face that I wanted to believe I could trust. I couldn't explain the sense of calm that sailed through me at that small kindness he offered. That tiny expression was a gesture that no one else had offered since I'd stepped foot in this room.

"Council," he began, "haven't they been through enough? We have our answer and a successful transition. Should we not be rejoicing that a life was not lost today?"

"A transition that was not approved by us or her," a man's voice boomed, and I wanted to shudder. My eyes shifted toward a man with a jaw and nose so slanted that I chose to believe it wasn't natural. His hair was cut like that of a military soldier, and the way in which he spoke made my stomach take a turn. He then stood, tearing the focus away from me and onto him. "How are you all so blinded to look past this?"

"Fine." The gentleman who was still standing opposite Mr. Military Man drew my attention again. "Violet, should you have been given the choice of death, or transitioning to a demon, which would you choose?"

"Demon," I answered, just as clearly as I'd answered before, but faster this time. I didn't want to give the man to my left any more ammunition than he apparently already had. The disdain he seemed to hold for Kade, and for myself, was evident and I wanted to side with the man on my right, who was coming off as more pleasant and considerate than all the rest.

"Thank you," he acknowledged before addressing the other men once again. "That being said, the only rule broken today was regarding the appropriate steps to be taken in a request for transition. I, for one, understand that this was an unusual circumstance, though I am not saying that this matter should be ignored. I think we should schedule another meeting in the near future so we can delve into this further."

"And its repercussions." The stern man all but spit in his retort.

The men around the room seemed to nod in agreement, but I became strangely fixated on the one who seemed intent on dragging Kade and me down. The feeling in the pit of my stomach was evolving, taking on a life of its own, and I could feel my nose turn up in disgust.

I swore I could hear a scream in the distance, and I glanced behind me but no one was there. Again, a shrill voice sounded, and I surveyed the room as the men began to commence light chatter.

"Welcome to Darthou, Violet. We look forward to getting

to know you," the gentleman spoke. He and the others all bowed their heads slightly in Kade's and my direction before they returned to converse amongst themselves.

Before I could even steal a peek at Kade, the scene before me vanished from view.

CHAPTER 2

Violet

The screaming stopped as soon as my eyes focused on my whereabouts, and I tried to shake it out of my head. Not even half an hour ago, I'd experienced those screams at such an intensity it had made my skin crawl and sent me to the floor. Rafina had quickly left, taking the screams with her, leaving me alone with Sarah who had instructed me to keep quiet. Luckily, this hadn't been as harsh of an attack. I was going to get to the bottom of this, one way or another.

In the blink of an eye, I'd been transported into an immense bedroom. My departure hadn't fazed me in the slightest—it felt much the same as when I'd passed through the mirror earlier on my own.

My hand left Kade's hold as I took a step away, examining the room and its contents. It too boasted high ceilings, and at this point, I wondered if everywhere I had been so far in

Darthou was all connected in some sort of castle-like structure. That was my only explanation for the concrete similarities. But this room had its own charm in the form of three arched stained glass windows that cast a beautiful array of orange, yellow, and red upon the wide-plank wooden floors. It seemed as if the sun was setting, given the angle of the blaze of colors.

A great four-poster bed caught my eye next, massive enough to fit a small family. The headboard was taller than me, its intricate carvings a fascinating maze that I wanted to run my fingers along. But it was the silken gray sheets and black bedspread that promised a comfort I wanted to enjoy. The bed was tucked away just far enough from the light of the windows, providing a comfort of darkness that could be illuminated by the great chandelier that hung above it. This one was different, using electricity instead of candles for light. Its glow was subtle right now, in no competition with the light from the windows.

This room alone put my tiny apartment to shame.

I turned to face Kade, and my heart sank. He was like a warrior who had returned from battle, but on the edge of tears. His hands were fisted so tight that his arms were shaking, and even though he was trying to be subtle, I knew he was holding back his emotions.

"Kade—" I took a step toward him, and before I could take another, he was around me. Encasing me in an embrace so tight I wasn't sure if I could breathe.

"I thought I lost you." His voice broke and I could feel tears prick my eyes at his confession. I tried to meet his arms with a grip so strong I could feel my muscles begin to ache. Whatever his suit was made of, it was hard and unforgiving as he pressed into me.

A series of rapid knocks on the door caused me to jump, and my head made contact with Kade's chin before he could release me. My heart was in my throat as my thoughts strayed to the last time I'd heard a similar sound. Brett had held Ms. Vanders at gunpoint, and against my better judgment, I had given him the chance to break down my door and hurt both her and me. I recoiled from the knocks that sounded again, frozen in fear.

"Fuck." Kade retreated through a narrow opening that led to a hall. He cleared his throat, agitated.

I peered around the corner, not knowing what to expect on the other side of the door. I knew Brett couldn't touch me here, but I couldn't shake the image of him knocking me down with his blow to my door, a crazed expression on his face. The ease with which he'd sent Ms. Vanders to the floor, as if she were nothing…the hate that had spewed out of his pores…it still affected me even here and now.

A man who seemed oddly familiar and dressed much like Kade, stood in the doorway. My line of sight zeroed in on the duffle bag he held within his grasp. I stepped into view and both Kade and the unnamed man glanced in my direction.

"I'll be damned. It did work." The man was stunned, looking me over from head to toe and back again as I inched closer. He was slightly smaller in build than Kade, with platinum blond hair that was buzzed on one side but had enough length on the other to tuck behind his ear. He appeared to be close to Kade's age, but I could be mistaken, considering that demons could shift and change their looks.

"Elias?" I spoke up, offering my best guess. He glanced at Kade as a small blush crossed his cheeks and he grinned.

"So he did mention me." He patted Kade on the back and welcomed himself inside, setting my bag down. He wore what I could only describe as samurai swords that were somehow secured on his back. "It's nice to finally meet you."

"Likewise." I nodded. "Thank you for my bag." I made the connection that he was the one in my apartment with Kade after my encounter with Brett. I hadn't been able to make him out very well, as my vision had been lacking, but the color of his hair gave it away.

"Of course." He paused as Kade approached us, leaving his door open. I couldn't shake the feeling that someone else might burst through it. As much as I tried to push away thoughts of the day's events, I was failing miserably.

"Any updates on Aleena? I've been…preoccupied." Kade swept a dirtied hand through his hair only to realize how filthy it was after it was too late.

I hadn't even had the chance to ask anybody about the Damian situation until this point, and I didn't know what had transpired on their end. But the fact that he was inquiring about his sister didn't sit well with me.

"What happened?" I asked, afraid that the absence of the third member of their Damian-seeking party might mean something bad. "Is she okay? Is Damian dead?"

Elias and Kade exchanged grave looks, and I knew that their mission had proved unsuccessful. I felt gutted, realizing that he was still out there. And to add to that, fucking Brett was probably running amok too.

"I just came from her place. Rafina has ordered her on bed rest until tomorrow to give her time to heal, so you can imagine how she's taking that." Elias blew out a breath as his eyes widened. I was looking forward to meeting this feisty badass of a sister that Kade trusted with his life.

"Was she badly hurt?" These guys weren't giving much information, and it was starting to get on my nerves. Elias and Aleena had joined Kade in the pursuit of finding and ending my ex-boss Damian who just so happened to be a saint. Judging by what little I knew so far, it hadn't gone according to plan.

I had no idea just how far their demons-and-saints rivalry dated back, but it was something I would have to familiarize myself with.

"Good, you're here." The gentleman who seemed to have sided with Kade and me at the council meeting brushed through the doorway, appearing out of thin air. He was taller than the other two by about a foot, I noted as he came to a stop before us. I hadn't expected him to be so tall, though he had been a short distance away during our brief encounter earlier.

"If you're here to drag me back into another meeting I'm not going quietly." Kade's face was etched with irritation as he spoke through gritted teeth.

"No, thankfully. I think I have calmed them enough to get through tomorrow's celebration before this subject gets brought up again. Staffan has it out for you."

"Believe me, I'm well aware." Kade crossed his arms and widened his stance.

Staffan must have been the man who gave me the uneasy feeling at their meeting. He seemed the total opposite of Rafina, and I couldn't fathom the two of them together. She was stunning and almost model-like with commercial-perfect hair. Staffan was stern and stuck-up to the point that, in all honesty, it made him seem like a dick.

But something was off with the both of them. Be it my heightened emotions at the time, or something else...I couldn't quite place my finger on it.

"I do bring a bit of good news. Since tensions are high with a certain council member, I requested that I be the one to complete your tethering." A small grin came across his face, but Kade's posture remained stiff beside me.

"And that's my cue." Elias bowed his head slightly before

he began to back away. "I look forward to getting to know you, Violet. I'll see everyone tomorrow."

The unknown man and Kade thanked Elias, and he vanished as he stepped through the doorway.

How did everybody come and go so quickly without a mirror? Was it some sort of demon power I wasn't aware of?

"How did you manage to pull that off?" Kade asked him, and I began twisting my fingers together.

The man shrugged and looked as if he was trying to choose the right words. "I may have ruffled a few feathers to get it approved, but that's not for you two to worry about right now."

He took another step toward me and I stilled at the attention, suddenly all too aware that I was only in a robe. It was all I wore when I appeared in the council room, a room full of unfamiliar men. I was frustrated that I'd met these people of power for the first time in nothing more. Not to mention the mess that still covered my skin. I probably looked like I had walked out of some sort of horror film.

Or who knows, maybe this was normal around here. How was I to know?

"Now, where are my manners? My name is Zan, I'm Kadriel's uncle. I believe you met my wife Sarah earlier. It's a pleasure to finally meet you, and I'm terribly sorry about the circumstances, but nevertheless, welcome." He tipped his head slightly and I instantly regretted how I'd left things with Sarah in the infirmary.

"It's nice to meet you too. And I'm sorry if I freaked out Sarah. I wasn't exactly in a good headspace when I…came to." I would have to offer an apology when I saw her again.

Zan offered a small laugh, amusement lighting up his perfectly sculpted face. "You definitely had her worried. She thought you were going to get lost crossing through for the first time. How did you manage to do it, exactly?"

I glanced at the two men who, come to think of it, had some small similarities between the two of them by their stature, complexion, and hair color. Even if Zan did have Kade beat in height.

"Do what?" I blinked at the men before me.

"Appear in the council chambers. What you accomplished takes quite some time to learn, even for a demon born of this world."

I opened my mouth to speak, unsure of how I did it, exactly. "I don't really know. I…was confused. Angry, even. I didn't understand why Kade wasn't there. All I could think about was him." I swallowed hard as I remembered reaching my hand through the glass without even trying. "Once my hand disappeared through the mirror, I just…" I didn't know how to describe it, and I could feel my cheeks heat from embarrassment at the attention I was getting. "It all happened so fast."

My gaze fell to the floor. I didn't have any explanation and I hated that my actions might have caused unneeded stress for others. Sarah, in particular.

"Well, regardless of how it happened, I think it worked out in your favor. And Kadriel's. Had you not done what you did, we would probably still be confined to that room battling things out."

I looked to Kade, who seemed fixated on my duffle bag on the bed and was seemingly zoning out of the conversation.

"Anyway, I know today has been challenging, and I am sure you both want to wind down before tomorrow's events. Would you like to complete the tethering now, or would you two like to get cleaned up first?" Zan looked between the two of us, but I wasn't sure where Kade's head was at as he remained silent.

"Kade?" I asked him, but he remained still, only letting his lips respond.

"It's up to Violet," was all he said, unable to acknowledge his uncle or me.

Zan turned his attention back to me and I rubbed my fingers together, reminding me of the black mess I was covered in.

"I would really like to get cleaned up first, if that's alright."

Slight crinkles formed around Zan's eyes and he bowed slightly. "Of course. Would an hour suffice?"

I nodded in agreement. I didn't even know what time it was currently, but surely an hour would be adequate to rid my body of whatever the hell this stuff was.

"Great, I shall see you both then."

"Wait," I stammered, afraid he would disappear just as quickly as the others seemed to be doing around here. Kade seemed to be walled off from this conversation, and I had so many other questions to ask that I figured I could use this moment to get some answers from his uncle. "Who all will be present for the tethering? I don't even know how to dress for this."

"Normally it is just Staffan and the two who are to be tethered. Sometimes, Rafina will be present, or others upon request. But it's a short and intimate affair that is all about the two souls joining. There is no special dress code. Had you entered our world under different circumstances, you would have been in your regular attire that you wore when crossing into our realm."

Direct and to the point. I was going to like him.

"Kade?" I waited patiently for his eyes to meet mine before

I continued. "Is there anyone you would like to invite?" It wasn't like I had anyone here anyway. For something that seemed like the equivalent of a marriage in his realm, I wanted to see if there was anyone else he wanted to share this moment with.

"Um…" His eyes searched mine as his words faltered. "Can't say that I've ever thought about that before."

Was the tethering ritual really so closed off from everyone else?

"I guess we'll see you in an hour." I offered a polite smile to Zan as he vanished just as rapidly as I suspected he would. I wanted to inquire about his disappearance, but Kade remained as still as a statue.

I waited for him to move, but he stayed motionless and emotionless. Warily, I passed him on the way to close the door. I was thrown by its weight as I shut it. What was it made out of, half a tree? I noted that there were no locks on it and eyed it curiously before turning back around.

The light from the stained glass windows was beginning to fade slightly as I drew nearer to Kade. I didn't know how to break the ice now that we were finally alone. I only hoped we wouldn't have any more interruptions for the next hour, so I could get up to speed on everything that had transpired today.

And take a freaking shower.

"Kade…" I gently took his hand and willed him to look at me, but instead, he looked in the opposite direction. I didn't understand why he was shutting me out, and that small action wounded me.

He left my grasp and began to walk away. "Let me show you the bathroom."

"Stop," I ordered, and he came to a halt. "Why…why does everyone seem so surprised by my presence? Why am I a demon?"

Becoming a demon hadn't been a part of the plan, and we hadn't even had the chance to discuss it, and yet here I stood, black eyes and all. The surprise Zan had shown at my ability to cross through a mirror already had me wondering if it was some sort of beginner's luck, or a lucky accident.

"Please, talk to me, Kade," I begged. I couldn't take another minute without answers, no matter how distant he was becoming. I didn't care how disgusting I felt—a shower could wait a while longer.

"You died, Violet," he replied softly, and I felt the air leave my lungs.

I couldn't have. Kade had gotten to me in time, I was sure of it. I couldn't have crossed over to Darthou had I been dead, so I refused to consider his words. There was no way.

"What? No. You were there, at my apartment. Y-you saved me," I stuttered.

He turned, and his face came into view, his whole body rigid. "I tried, but I couldn't save you. I might have bought you a few more minutes but...you died in the infirmary. We tried the tether, but you were too far gone and it failed. I didn't save you. You slipped away beneath my touch." He focused on his hands—just as I had suspected, I now knew the blood on him had to be mine. I concentrated on his pained words as I attempted to absorb the information.

I checked the hand that had experienced pain earlier when I was battling unconsciousness but saw no mark. I recalled the inability to breathe and the liquid that had seemed to consume me until everything ceased. I'd thought that maybe the pain and blood loss had caused me to pass out. I knew the treacherous agony to be real, as the memory was devastatingly vivid. Everything that had seemed to be a fleeting moment in time was really my body dying and Kade's attempt to save my life.

My heart had stopped for a third time in my life, and yet here I stood.

"But...how?"

"I didn't care about the consequences of my actions, or the hate that you might harbor for me due to my decisions, but I took you to Obsidian Falls anyway. My last resort was submitting you to its waters in the hope that they might save you. I had to try." His voice faltered on the last word. "And that was the last time I saw you until you showed up at the council meeting."

I still couldn't wrap my head around the fact that I had died. I should have felt something or suspected it at least. The aftermath of the car crash that had claimed my family, and my suicide attempt in high school, was proof of that, right? How was I walking about without any physical scars or any hindering side effects? How was my body moving without showing any signs of my supposed death?

I shook my head as I moved past those memories of my failing body, shoving them aside. The remembrance of choking on my own blood...

I paled as I recalled a brief moment prior to the chaos.

"What about Ms. Vanders?" I only hoped that if what Kade was saying were true, Brett hadn't taken two lives today.

That caused Kade to gawk at me. "What about her?"

Did he really have no idea how everything went down with Brett's arrival?

"Last I knew, Brett hit her with the end of his gun and she was on the ground just outside my door. I don't know if she was dead or unconscious."

His lips thinned. "There was nobody there when I arrived,

so I would assume she is alright. But I will have Elias look into it."

I only hoped that if her body was not still a crumpled mess, that she had managed to escape and was alive. The poor woman had been dragged into this shit show that she had nothing to do with. The incident was probably going to leave a permanent mark on her for the rest of her life. She didn't deserve this.

"And what of Damian?" I clenched my eyes for a moment, knowing in my bones and gut that he was still alive and out there.

"It was what we suspected, too convenient." A hand passed through his hair again, breaking up the rigidity of his posture momentarily. "He was ready and waiting for us, but with others. We killed a few of them, only to then find that they had us outnumbered."

He blinked away, only to then pinch the bridge of his nose. As if reliving some awful experience that was taking place inside of his head. I waited for him to continue, careful not to push.

"I was so fixated on getting to Damian that I…" He cleared his throat before his hand dropped to his side again. "Aleena swooped in to take a blow meant for me and she…"

"Got hurt," I finished, fearing the images in his mind from their earlier battle. I had no doubt he blamed himself for her getting hurt, but I couldn't help but feel responsible. I'd known there was a chance that someone could get hurt, but I didn't exactly stop them. I wanted the threat of Damian gone before I left just as much as Kade did.

The three of them against one saint was supposed to be enough. The tables had turned against them, a bitter pill to swallow.

"When I returned, I couldn't get to Eleander fast enough.

That's Elias's father. He was charged with watching you while I was away, and the moment I heard his voice, I knew. But when I got to your place, it was too late. Your body was already shutting down and you wouldn't last until the paramedics arrived."

"That's why you brought me here."

"I thought it was your best chance of survival, but not even Rafina could heal you." His tone revealed an anguish that gripped my chest, stalling my breath.

"So that's why you're in hot water with the council. Why they were asking if I had accepted the tethering or not. Or what I would choose between death or becoming a demon." It was beginning to become clear now. Kade's actions had been driven by desperation and love. But those same actions had broken the rules that seemed to be of utmost importance here in Darthou. Especially that of consent.

Kade nodded, but his face remained crestfallen. Not only had he failed in his mission with Damian, but he had lost me. Watched me die, and then tried by whatever means necessary to bring me back no matter the cost. No matter what consequences it may bring in his future.

"Had you answered any differently in that room, I would without a doubt not be standing here with you right now."

I didn't want to think about what Kade would be going through if I hadn't showed up when I did. I hadn't known what I was doing, and I certainly hadn't planned any course of action except to find Kade. Luckily for both of us, I'd proved successful in my efforts and put an end to the meeting that Kade had been the center of. For now, anyway.

"I only hope that you can, in time, forgive me."

I shook my head, confused. "Forgive you?"

I had never seen Kade more tortured than I did at present.

He looked as if he had aged by years, and for the first time since I met him, he looked exhausted to the point that he might collapse. There was even stubble forming around his jawline.

No doubt today and its events had proved stressful and challenging. The choices he'd had to make, the steps he took even while violating the very rules he had stressed were so important—it couldn't have been easy.

In a way, I felt as if I was seeing Kade for the first time, and in a human sort of way. He was usually a man so lighthearted and fun, sure in his ways and eager to answer any and all of my questions, but that was all put on pause. Had I not given away my presence at my apartment earlier, perhaps today's events would have taken a different turn.

Kade cleared the gathering thickness in his throat, then turned to walk away. "I'll show you to the bathroom."

Forgive him? For what, exactly? He fucking saved me.

I followed after him, my bare feet picking up speed to round the corner that was tucked away on the opposite side of his apparent home. At least, I assumed this was his home. Kade hadn't exactly come out to say that it was, but Elias and his uncle coming here in search of him made it likely.

I didn't want to end our conversation this way, and I knew this wasn't the end of it, but the clock was ticking until our tethering ritual. I held my hands out, examining them once more, realizing that the black matter was from my transition to becoming a demon.

Obsidian Falls, I wondered to myself. I would have to make a note to dive into the topic of that place when the time was right.

Once again, I was finding I had more questions than answers, and it bothered me. Like the question of how I wasn't dead, for starters.

It was obvious that my ability to pass through the mirror was already a perk, but I had so much to learn and discover. I didn't even know the full extent of Kade's abilities, so what would I be capable of? I didn't think I would take on any healing abilities, like Kade had inherited from his mother. And I already knew that by accepting the tethering as a human, I would have stopped aging, but did I even need the tethering to stop that process now? Oh! And what about Kade's masterful skill of changing his eyes with nothing more than a blink?

Dim lights illuminated a bathroom space that was about five times the size of mine. The shower looked to be the main focal point, lined with various natural stones of all sorts of sizes. No shower curtain or doors hid the beauty of the stones that would surround you once you stepped inside.

No privacy, I thought as I entered and peeked my head in.

To my right was a door that I assumed housed a toilet, but I didn't see the need to explore that right away. Further in were double golden sinks with a vast mirror above them that stretched up farther than I could reach even if I were to stand up next to it.

"There are towels in there." He directed my attention to a cabinet beneath the sinks and began to leave, but I caught his hand. I didn't want to deal with my thoughts on my own, and even if we were silent, his presence alone was a calm that I needed after all the information he had just revealed. If I tried to process it all right now, if I traveled down that rabbit hole, I would end up a pile of a mess on the floor.

"Stay," I said softly, willing him to do so.

This dark and tormented side of him made my heart ache, and I had the urge to soothe it by whatever means I could.

"Violet, I—"

"Please," I cut him off as I pulled him into the shower floor area. The difference in texture beneath my bare feet was a welcome surprise—the stones didn't seem slick but rather soft. Strange rocks that still had grip to them.

I untied my robe, tossing it from the shower and onto the bare floor as I waited for him. It landed with a hardened thunk, and I cringed thinking about how that piece of clothing would never truly be clean again.

Although hesitant, Kade began removing various weapons, some of which were concealed so well that they blended in with his suit thing he was wearing. I hadn't realized just how many weapons he had on his body. He left momentarily to set them on a bench near the entrance, and I used that time to find the source of the water and turn it on. It cascaded from the ceiling like a rainfall, several feet wide, and began to emit steam immediately without the need to warm up. I welcomed it. Black matter was soon circling down the drain by my feet, and instead of being disturbed by it and the direction my thoughts wanted to stray, I tore my gaze away.

I tried not to stare as Kade peeled himself out of his warrior-type armor that was flexible in some spots yet rigid in others. I didn't know if it was by design, or if the same black stuff that had seeped into the fibers of my robe had the same reaction with his apparel. It held some of its shape as he released it to the ground and he made his way toward me. If it made a sound hitting the floor, I couldn't hear it over the sound of the water surrounding me.

Wrapping my arms around him, I secured our bodies together in a hold beneath the falling water. Kade almost seemed uncertain at my embrace, but he relented, bringing his arms around me. My mind and body needed this just as I needed air to breathe. His presence alone was something to which nothing else could compare.

CHAPTER 3

Violet

Kade had washed away all the remnants of my apparent death and transition with such tenderness that I never wanted to leave the shower.

For the most part, I thought I knew the details of our tethering that we were now approaching, but I was still on edge about it. I sat upon Kade's bed as he disappeared into what looked to be his closet, waiting to see what he chose to wear so that I might try to use that to my advantage. I knew the contents of my duffle bag were slim, considering I'd been interrupted in my packing efforts, but for now I would have to make do with what I brought.

I had retrieved my blanket and sat with it in my lap, waiting for some comfort to come from it, playing with a loose purple string that I hadn't been aware of until now.

He returned to my view, wearing blue jeans and a black

shirt that was fit to perfection. It hugged him in all the right places without being so tight that it would look too small.

"Is this alright?" Kade must have caught my lingering stare at his abs.

I nodded and excused myself to the bathroom, taking my bag with me. Setting it on the bench next to Kade's armor outfit, I began rummaging through it. I settled upon a black blouse and my favorite pair of jeans. I had always had the tendency, ever since my goth phase in high school, to choose darker colors in the hopes that they would be slimming. And seeing as how most of the demons I'd met so far wore black, I was a tad grateful for that. But I would definitely have to take Kade up on his offer of more clothes. What I'd brought with me would only last a few days.

Catching my reflection at one of the sinks, I stopped in my tracks. I looked like me, but at the same time, I didn't. No longer was I covered in that yuck. My strawberry-blond hair was now free from that black stuff and my skin was wiped clean too.

But my eyes…my green eyes that my grandma said I had inherited from my mother, were gone.

I hadn't given much thought to becoming a demon, so now that I was one, what would happen next? I examined my eyes once more, pulling the surrounding skin to see just how far back the darkness went. It was like two big black marbles had replaced my eyes, but that seemed to be the only thing that had changed. That and my ability to pass through solid glass as if it were nothing. I looked forward to doing that again, but Zan's words and Sarah's worry about me disappearing came to the forefront of my mind.

What could have happened if I hadn't been successful in finding Kade? Would I have been trapped somewhere else entirely? Kade had made jumping through mirrors look like child's play when we were in the hall of mirrors. Granted, he was born a demon so he'd had plenty of time to conquer that feat, but still it begged the question—what could happen?

I imagined that it might be the equivalent of being trapped in a picture frame, and while the thought was intriguing, it was a bit alarming too.

I removed my towel and my eyes traveled over my now clean, bare, and unmarked skin. My fingers skimmed the surface in search of some sort of remnant that perhaps remained unseen to my new eyes in the wake of the bullets that had entered me. I shuddered as the shots ricocheted in my ears, a loud reminder of what my body had endured before I…died.

A part of me was beginning to believe it to be true, as I recalled gasping for air only to sputter blood from my mouth. I had chosen to believe that Kade had shown up in the nick of time, but even by his own admittance, his healing capabilities were minimal. My bruised wrists and injured foot were nothing compared to the bullets that had ravaged me. I pressed firmly into my skin at the places where there should have been holes, wounds that had apparently healed without a trace. It was strange that I couldn't sense any discomfort, as if nothing had even happened.

Was it the transition that healed me, or something else?

The sight of a slight movement over my shoulder in the reflection of the mirror before me had me retrieving my towel to cover myself. I wasn't sure why I was shy in front of Kade all of a sudden. The man had watched me for years, and had claimed every inch of my body within our short courtship, but I felt exposed nonetheless.

My face heated as he lurked in the doorway. His face harbored a pained expression that I wished I could replace with literally anything else.

"Is something wrong?" I asked when the silence became too loud.

He remained stiff, but his chin dipped down as his head dropped. "I…was thinking about our tethering."

I turned so that I could face him instead of his reflection, intent on drawing my focus toward him and away from me.

"Are you sure it's alright if I invite someone?"

His inquiry caught me off guard. I didn't know what I had expected him to say, but it wasn't this. "Of course."

"I would like to invite Sarah. I never would have thought that Zan would be given the chance to grant me my tethering, but seeing as they both raised me after the passing of my parents, I thought it might be…appropriate."

"You don't have to explain anything to me, although I do appreciate it." I swallowed, knowing that I owed Sarah an apology over our earlier encounter. Now I was going to get to do it sooner rather than later. "If you want her there, then she should be there."

"Thank you." He tilted his head slightly, possibly relieved that I was alright with his decision and request, but it was hard to tell for sure. "I'll invite her and give you some privacy."

Before I could say anything else, he pivoted and turned the corner. It was now that I realized he didn't even have a door to his bathroom, and I found that rather peculiar.

As much as I admired his home so far, from what I had seen, it lacked privacy. I could only assume that up until this point he hadn't had to worry about that too much. I didn't relish the fact that I would have to discuss this matter with Kade, but I would need to address it someday. Although I loved being in his presence, and the comfort he brought, I would need space of my own and occasional time to myself. Surely there was something we could work out, some sort of compromise.

I dressed rather hurriedly and ran my fingers through my hair, since I hadn't packed a comb or brush of any kind. There weren't that many places to search in the bathroom in the hopes of finding anything to detangle it with. And after getting to know Kade in the past few days, I knew he rarely ran anything through his hair but his hands.

I squeezed my hair in the towel with all my might, hoping to draw out as much moisture as possible, afraid that my shirt would be dampened in no time and it would cling to me. I couldn't locate a hairdryer, but figured our time before the ritual was running out. I sighed as I looked at the image I projected. It felt wrong that I had the same eyes as Kade. I didn't detest them, but the loss of my green ones was going to take some getting used to.

The loss of my *human* life was going to take some time to come to terms with.

I exited the bathroom area and found Kade sitting at the foot of his bed in the same spot I had sat. He joined me and I linked his hand to mine, almost unsure of the action but desperate to feel some sort of connection between us when everything else was strained.

"Are you ready?" His voice was low, an unsteadiness to it that read as nerves. Or perhaps I was merely projecting that onto him at this point. I couldn't tell for sure.

"As I'll ever be, I suppose." I could only believe that the butterflies in my stomach were the equivalent of what a bride felt on her wedding day. This tethering would bind us together and make us stronger. A united front with Kade was something that I was willing to accept as my future, even though there was still so much I had yet to learn about him and his world.

"Real quick—" I gushed, before Kade vanished like everyone else seemed to come and go. "Do you not need a mirror to disappear? Everybody around here seems to zap in and out faster than the speed of sound. And as far as I can tell, there's no mirror in your entryway, so how did Elias and your uncle just vanish like they did? How did you bring us here from the council room when the only mirror I recall seeing was the one that I passed through in the hallway?"

The corner of Kade's lips lifted slightly and I felt his spirits rise. It was the first glimpse of something other than dread or misery since we had reunited, and I was optimistic that I'd soon see more of it. I knew his actions and the events of today weighed heavily on him, but I took this small reaction as a win.

He reached into his pocket and produced the mirror that I had only seen once before, earlier today at the park. The small mirror, encased by a layer of black obsidian, glistened in a way that reminded me of the necklace I was missing. I didn't even know where to start in my search for it, but dammit, I had to stop misplacing that thing.

But maybe this time it wasn't necessarily my fault, considering I had no idea where my clothes had gone or why I was in nothing but a robe when I came to.

"We carry these with us at all times. Not only for communication purposes, but for traveling as well."

"When will I get one of those?" I questioned as I let my fingers graze the rim around the mirror, careful not to touch the glass.

"Someday. When we're positively sure you aren't going to get lost somewhere. I can train you, if you like."

Images of Kade in the hall of mirrors flitted through me, and I was a tad giddy with anticipation at the chance to be able to do what he did so flawlessly.

"I look forward to it."

I'd no sooner blinked and found myself in a new area. My eyes searched around me, taking it all in. I was now in a building of sorts that was vastly different from what I had seen so far.

Old, worn, red bricks surrounded us in a room that was longer than it was wide. The bricks beneath my feet were uneven, showing dead growth from grass and weeds that had tried and succeeded to break through the gaps.

On each side, there were maybe a half dozen crooked windows, letting in my first glimpse of the outside world. If I had to guess, I'd have said we were in the dead of winter. The trees nearby were covered in a layer of ice, and the skies were a heavy gray. I recalled the sunlight shining in through Kade's windows—the vast difference in lighting between here and there was puzzling.

There were no lights or chandeliers to be seen, the outside world our only source of illumination, and it seemed to be dimming fast.

It was more airy and open here. Perhaps the light coming in from the windows helped with that, even if it was a bit run-down, like a church long-forgotten in the country.

I wandered off toward the nearest window, taking in the gloomy beauty of the outdoors. It was the perfect weather for curling up with a blanket and a good book.

"Is there some kind of god I'm going to have to pray to now?" I offered a small hint of playfulness to my tone as I pivoted to meet Kade. I had half expected to see his features soften, but he remained stiff and distant, answering me with only a shake of his head.

"Ah, there they are," a now familiar man's voice broke through the silence.

At an altar on the far side stood Kade's aunt and uncle, and we began to approach. Zan and Sarah were still clad in their attire from the last times I'd seen them.

On a small, narrow wooden table that looked as old as the building lay a blade with a black handle, and a black cord that I assumed to be the one that would bind us. The thickness of the rope was smaller than my pinky.

"Kadriel, thank you for the invitation. I'm delighted I could be here for you." Sarah's genuine smile and human facial features were a comfort that made me miss home, and I felt a twinge of guilt. I knew she had only meant well earlier, and I'd run out on her the first chance I had. If only I could have reined in my panic long enough to talk to her and give her the benefit of the doubt.

"Actually, you can thank Violet." Kade finally spoke up, though quiet. "If it wasn't for her, I wouldn't have even questioned whether it was something I could do." I probably would have blushed, but my nerves were gathering as I came to a stop in front of the table and the blade that it housed.

This was really happening. I was here, in Darthou, now moments away from accepting an offer that I had initially laughed off as some sort of prank. Thoughts swirled around, emerging and telling me how crazy I was to be going through with this. It seemed like only yesterday that Kade had come into my life, and at the same time, it was like I'd known him forever.

Which was freaking insane considering I had only met him five nights ago.

"Well, thank you to the both of you then." Sarah beamed a smile so appreciative that it spoke volumes of the relationship that Kade seemed to have with them both. I wanted to get my apology out of the way but I didn't know if this was the right time. I nodded as a thought bubbled into my mind.

"Do I have to use the same hand?" I blurted before I had the chance to think it through.

That earned glances from everyone, and I shrunk beneath their combined stares.

"What do you mean?" Kade questioned, almost to the point of shock.

I held out my right palm, holding back a wince as I recalled the sensation I had felt when I was supposedly in the last moments of my human life. "Is this the one that was cut?"

Kade's mouth dropped open, almost horrified. "You…were awake for that?"

Honestly, I didn't even know the answer to that. My memory was foggy, flashes of it mixing with the substantial amounts of agony that my body had been capable of producing.

"I'm not sure. I just remember the pain." The alarm on Kade's face at my admittance was gut-wrenching. I instantly regretted that I'd even brought it up. It was just genuine curiosity, but I still felt regretful. I closed my hand and let it fall to my side.

"It doesn't have to be the same hand, no," Zan said. I could sense he was trying to calm Kade down with the softness of his voice. "Now, shall we get started?"

"Are you sure you want to go through with this?" Kade's interruption startled me and I whipped my head in his direction, my wet hair a heavy weight on my back.

"Kadriel," Zan said, as if in warning.

My lips parted as my jaw tried to recover from the notion of a possible betrayal. Why would he ask such a thing when he had spent the past several nights trying to win me over and get me to accept this very tethering that we were now mere moments away from? Was he having second thoughts? About me? About us?

"Violet." Kade spoke my name, but wouldn't look me in the eye. "You're a demon now. You're one of us, and you don't have to go through with the tethering if you're not ready." His face turned to stone as he focused on the materials separating us from his aunt and uncle, still not looking at me.

"Kadriel, the council and I heard Violet quite clearly accept the tethering and choose the path of a demon. If you two don't go through with this now, it will call into question everything—"

"I don't care!" Kade's voice rose and he clenched his eyes shut momentarily, as if to reel in his anger. Sarah visibly tensed in unison with me, recoiling from his sudden outburst. "I will take on whatever consequences come my way, but it is still her decision. She is innocent in all of this."

A small scream erupted in my mind and I flinched uncomfortably. That unsettling feeling returned and began to unfurl in my belly. This couldn't be happening, not again.

"I thought you two would be long gone by now." A man's voice echoed through the room and I stilled. I knew this voice from the council chambers, and I wanted to flee at the sound, but I looked over my shoulder anyway to confirm it.

Staffan was, at a leisurely pace, walking down the uneven bricks toward us with Rafina at his side. Her posture was different, now that we were no longer in the infirmary. She was quiet, reserved, and had her hands folded at her front with her eyes cast down. It showed who was the dominant one in their relationship. Not that I really had a doubt in the matter at this point.

By Kade's admission, she was a healer, and a damn good one at that. So what was it about Staffan that made her shrivel up next to him?

The smug look that Staffan wore as he crossed the length of the chapel made me want to punch him. I hadn't liked him in the council room earlier, and I certainly didn't have any better of an attitude regarding him now. This was only my second time in his presence, and it was already too much.

The scream grew louder as they drew nearer, and I could feel my eyes widen as I tried to suppress my facial reaction. It wasn't as bad as I had first experienced, but I feared that it could get to that point. My breathing became shallow, to the point that my chest began to ache as my gaze fell to the floor, willing the scream to stop. This was not the time to be sent into a fit of madness. I couldn't describe it as anything else.

I didn't want a repeat of earlier, not in front of everyone. I still had no explanation for it, and Sarah had warned me not to tell anyone. Something told me that what I was experiencing wasn't normal, and I feared that more than anything. In a strange new world where I had died and apparently been born again as a demon, I knew absolutely nothing. And the look on Sarah's face when I'd admitted what I had heard made me begin to fear the unknown.

I grabbed Kade's hand in the hopes it would provide a sense of unity before Staffan, and the scream lessened somewhat. Maybe that was what I needed. I just had to find something to focus on.

"We were just getting started." My grip tightened, and I only hoped it was subtle enough not to be noticed by those who surrounded us. "Zan has been kind enough to answer some questions that I had before beginning." I felt stiff as I stood before Staffan's scrutinizing gaze, still unable to meet it straight on.

"Well by all means, don't let me interrupt." He gestured for us to continue and I resisted the urge to turn my nose up at him and his slanted one.

The unwelcome interruption of Staffan's presence was a curveball I hadn't anticipated. Normally, he performed the tetherings, according to Kade. But I thought that Zan had been granted the opportunity to do ours, so why the hell was he even here? Was it really necessary?

And I noticed how he had only spoken for himself, so where did that leave Rafina? I didn't think she was tagging along just for the hell of it.

Not wanting to look at either of them a moment longer, I returned my attention to a wary Sarah and a stone-cold expression from Zan that resembled Kade's.

"I'm ready." My lips tightened as I tried to will away the scream that I still heard in the distance, hovering. So far it had only seemed to happen when I was in the company of Rafina and Staffan. They were the only common denominators. I didn't even know who to trust. The only people who seemed to be aware of my situation were Rafina and Sarah.

Due to Rafina's relationship with Staffan, I instantly ruled her out of any questioning. I knew Kade appeared to hold her in high regard, but given what I was experiencing, I had to go with my gut and treat both her and Staffan as the enemy until I knew more.

That left Sarah. Her earlier warning made me think she might know more than she let on. So now, not only did I have to apologize for running out on her, but I would have to find a way to get her alone so I could speak freely. Would she even help me? Surely if Kade meant as much to her as she did to him, she would, right? She had to.

And I didn't exactly want to leave Kade in the dark about this, but with the day he'd already had, did I really need to add to it?

Zan began to speak about our union and the tie before us. The cord that would link us together so we would share our eternity together. He picked up the tie and nodded to Kade, signaling for him to retrieve the blade.

The room was quickly dimming. The faint glow from the windows was fading fast, casting shadows upon the faces before me and the room. I didn't think we'd been here that long, but the sun seemed to be setting at an abnormal pace now.

Kade drew the blade against his hand, slicing into it in a diagonal from one side to the other. His crimson blood was evident as it began to pool in his palm.

Geesh. Just how far did I have to cut? It was then that I realized that the screaming had lessened. As much as I wanted to release a sigh of relief, I couldn't, as I was on full display and about to cut into my own hand like a damn cake.

I had half expected Kade to do the honors for me, but instead he held out the knife, handle at the ready for me to take it. I was beginning to think that he'd only cut my palm earlier because he believed I was unconscious and I was unable to do it myself, but that didn't help the anxiety consuming me. This type of self-harm was a hard pill to swallow—even if it was normal by demon standards, it still felt incredibly immoral.

Accepting the blade, I took a deep breath before mirroring Kade's exact gesture. With some hesitation, I drew it across my skin, watching as the red liquid began to emerge in its wake.

This time, the pain paled in comparison to the sensation I recalled from earlier. I wasn't sure if I was more in awe of the almost painless act, or the fact that I had cut into myself with such ease. Maybe it was because I had an audience, but I couldn't be certain. Kade had said that demons could still get injured, but I wondered what all my body could take now that I was no longer human.

I returned the blade to the table, my fingers skimming across the rough surface. Zan asked us to join hands and Kade took the lead on that without hesitation. Our wet palms met and we clasped our fingers together in a hold that sent a wave of electricity through me. I wondered if Kade felt it too, but his eyes were fixated on the tie that Zan was bringing toward our hands.

I watched intently as his uncle spoke in a language I had never heard before and began to wrap us from elbow to fingertips around our outstretched arms. I was mesmerized by his work, studying the cord that seemed to mold and form around our arms, though it had seemed like a limp piece of whatever it was when he'd first picked it up.

When Zan finished, he took a step back and my skin began to tingle. It was a warm sensation that the cord emitted as its heat began to grow. The blackened cord turned translucent as it began to fade away into our skin, burning as it did. My heart quickened as the small fire blazed into our skin, and I tightened my grip. Blood seeped from our joined hands and fell to the table as I tried to concentrate on my breathing. Slow and steady streams of air rushed through my flared nostrils.

I had a moment of relief as Kade returned my grasp with his muscles tensed. There was no doubt in me now that he was experiencing the same sensations. The world fell away as the cord settled into our skin and vanished, leaving a trail of sparkle-like flames before disappearing completely, as if nothing had ever happened.

When I returned my attention toward Kade's family, I found Sarah beaming once again with delight, and dare I say it—her eyes looked glassy. Zan's face was full of pride, in the most welcoming sense of the word. They both bowed their heads and Kade and I lowered our hands to our sides, dampened palms still attached. Mine didn't ache in the slightest, and I couldn't help but wonder briefly if he had healed it.

"Congratulations. We'll see you both tomorrow." Zan barely got the words out of his mouth and next thing I knew, I was in Kade's room once again.

He released my hand and I examined my own. The cut I had made for the ritual had vanished and all that remained was traces of blood beginning to dry.

"I went ahead and healed that for you," Kade said, but he seemed to be in a mood as he disappeared into the hallway.

These emotions of his were giving me whiplash, and I didn't know how to respond. One minute he was relieved that I had survived and was alive, if that's what I was. The next, it was like he was tormented to the point that he didn't know what to do with me. For someone who wanted me to be here and accept a life with him, he sure had an odd way of showing it.

He returned, cleaning his hand off with a rag as he approached, and then held out a hand for mine. He scrubbed lightly, taking away the remnants of the tethering ritual with it.

As soon as he was done, I removed my hand from his grasp and crossed my arms.

"What is going on with you?" I could feel my annoyance rising now that we were alone and away from prying eyes. "You court me, wanting me to accept the tethering. And the *moment* that we're ready to complete it, you try to change course? Do you not want to be tethered to me anymore?" The words spilled from my mouth in a heated moment, and I was afraid of the answer he might give. "You said that you would never lie to me, so talk, please."

Kade threw the rag across the room and out of sight as his face twisted. "I didn't want this life for you. The life of a demon." His voice was rising to meet the level of mine.

"It's because of you I even have a life! Demon or not."

"But you died because of me!" Kade's voice boomed at his admission. He blamed himself for everything that had transpired, but he was not the only one to blame. I was still trying to wrap my head around the very thought of my death, but his words—it pained me to hear them.

"Brett murdered you because of my failure to protect you." The exasperation in his voice as he spoke of my murder made me take a step back.

Murdered. Brett had done just that. It didn't feel as if he had, because here I was, standing and walking and talking in my new demon body. But hearing that word out loud somehow felt worse than the news of my death.

"Because of my choices, you can never return home. I have ruined any chance for a life you may have envisioned." His voice broke, thick with tortured emotions. "Damned you to a fate perhaps worse than death."

I shook my head as my voice quivered. "No."

What did he mean I could never return home? That wasn't part of the deal.

"Yes. You are currently missing, presumed dead due to the crime scene left behind." The manner in which he spoke twisted me in the most god-awful way.

"But…you said I could visit. That I could—"

"If you were still a human, yes," he cut me off. "But you're a demon now."

His words were opening new wounds as the realization began to sink in. Tears began to sting my eyes. Life as I knew it was gone. Could I really never return? Did my family really believe that I'd been murdered? God, did everyone think that?

I could only imagine the headlines, and people trampling through my apartment trying to figure out my disappearance. It wasn't supposed to happen this way. None of this was right. I couldn't wrap my head around how this was happening.

"All I have ever wanted for the past six years was to be tethered to you." I couldn't bring myself to look at Kade as he continued, desperation and exhaustion evident as he spoke. "And now, with my decisions, I have ruined the life you deserved. How could you ever even look at me again after I took your choice away? How could you ever return the love I have for you after this?"

I shook my head again as I put some distance between us, unbelieving. I kept telling myself that Kade did what he had to do to save me, but right now it didn't feel like enough. Memories of my family and my life prior to this day flooded through me, and my emotions were all over the place. I turned away as the tears began to stream down my face in a heavy flow.

I knew Kade blamed himself for everything, but he was not the only one at fault. If only I had listened. If only I hadn't opened the door. If only I had let Brett, or better yet, Ms. Vanders, believe I wasn't home, perhaps I wouldn't be here and in this predicament now.

The life I had hoped for with Kade, the one I had chosen with him, had been stripped away, all because of one action.

But I knew, with every fiber of my being, that Brett and Damian were at fault too. Brett might have pulled the trigger and ended my life, but Damian was certainly a part of it. There was no doubt in my mind that the timing was not a coincidence. Kade had been called off to deal with Damian, leaving me alone, vulnerable, and available for Brett to finish me off, thus ruining Kade's and my chance to be tethered.

I didn't blame my death on Kade. No, it was my fault.

Gunshots rang through my ears and my body reacted, jerking as if I had been shot all over again. Once. Twice. An anger began to spread through my body like a raging wildfire that could not be tamed. It spread through my body like I had opened a large oven door and I wanted to jump back.

"Ah!" A sound of pain erupted from behind me, and I looked over my shoulder at Kade. He was clutching his chest in the same locations where the bullets had struck me.

My tears ceased as his face contorted into one of pure shock and he pulled up his shirt to examine himself. His bare chest showed nothing, but the way he desperately tugged at his own skin in search of something that wasn't there made my blood run cold, cooling me down rapidly.

Kade panted as his muscles moved in exaggerated movements. With each sharp exhale, his body caved in on itself.

"We need to see Rafina," he wheezed as he lowered his shirt back down.

"No!" I shook my head, eyes widened in fear at the thought of seeing her, and worse, Staffan.

Kade's eyes narrowed at me as I turned the rest of my body to face him. "Something isn't right." His voice was frantic now, concern etched upon his face as he began to adjust and straighten himself out. "Your...tears."

The look on his face had me swiping the tears away. Was I not allowed to cry? Surely, I was entitled to be an emotional disaster after everything I'd been through leading up to this moment.

A darkness caught my attention and I examined my fingertips. I swiped at my face once more with the other hand, confused. My hands were wet, but with black tears. A moderate amount of curiosity overtook me, but it was soon replaced with panic. Given Kade's confusion on the matter, crying black tears might not be normal.

I stammered, offering the only alternative to his request for the healer he trusted. "Sarah. I need to see Sarah."

CHAPTER 4

Violet

I had no sense of time in this place, and I had yet to see a watch or a clock to help me figure out how long I'd even been here in Darthou. Kade had called Sarah, and both she and Zan showed up within moments. When Kade had said that everything would move quickly once I crossed over into Darthou, I highly doubted he could have predicted the extent of the problems we currently found ourselves in the middle of.

Kade had tried to plead with me to see Rafina, but I'd planted my foot down firmly. He couldn't fathom why, of all people, I would steer us in the direction of Sarah. As a human, it seemed she would be no help in explaining what was happening, but I assured him I would explain when I could.

To be honest, now I was scared not only for myself, but for the both of us. If Kade experienced some sort of phantom effects of my death, what if he could now hear the screams that plagued me when in the presence of Staffan and Rafina? I only hoped that Sarah could shed some light on the situation. She had been here longer than me, and maybe had an idea as to what was going on.

I refused to believe that Rafina was the only person we could go to for answers. I didn't care how high of a pedestal Kade placed her on, I didn't want to deal with her unless I absolutely had to. I knew Rafina had witnessed the debilitating state the screams had put me in when I first awoke, but I hoped she hadn't dwelled on it too much. And when I experienced them again at the tethering ritual, I had to believe that I'd covered up my reaction much better than the first time.

"Is everything alright?" Zan entered, leading his wife by the hand.

"Can I speak with Sarah in private?" I butted in before giving Kade the chance to speak. Everyone exchanged glances, but this wasn't something I was going to give up on. "Please?"

"Of course," she accepted, leaving Zan's side. "How about you take Kade to our place?"

"But—"

I cut Kade off before he could try to persuade me otherwise. "Please," I begged him with the most sincere face I could muster, without trying to cause him any more alarm.

Though hesitant, Zan placed his hand on Kade's shoulder and they were gone. I shut the door and returned my attention to Sarah. I wasn't sure if there was any way to sugarcoat this, but I felt backed into a corner and I had to trust that she would try to help me if possible.

"Something's wrong." I tried to remain calm, feeling as if a fit of hysteria was on the horizon. "I don't know who else to turn to." I didn't want to sound cheesy in my feeble hopes that I could trust only her at the moment, but I was scared because

I didn't know what was going on. Kade already thought there was a traitor amongst his people, and I was new to the game, so if he had to keep his circle tight, I would do the same.

"Is it the screams again?" Her voice was hushed.

"Yes. And no." I placed my fingertips at my temples, trying to focus. "There's more. Just since the tethering."

"Go on." I could tell that she was trying to guard her expression, but her hazel   eyes were a bit leery. I knew she had lived in a society of mostly demons for some time now, even having a couple of children along the way. I only hoped that she had learned enough in her time spent here thus far, to help me.

I would soon have to face Darthou's population myself, and that frightened me. But if I couldn't get an understanding of the screams, and the apparent pains that now plagued Kade, how could I ever leave the comforts of this room?

Kade's warrior-type armor came to mind. I knew he had some sort of position of power around here, and I hated the idea that his newly tethered partner might make him weak in some manner.

You couldn't tell me that outfit of his came with his watching gig.

"I heard a scream when I found Kade with the council. Then *again* when Staffan and Rafina showed up to the tethering, but neither were anything like what I experienced in the infirmary. It was quieter and not as intense, and it faded away once I cut my hand, but…" I hated to admit the next part, but I knew Kade might be sharing this exact information with his uncle even now. "I don't know if I have some sort of PTSD or what, but Kade…"

I was unsure of how to describe the way he had frantically tried to search his body for bullet wounds. I could see it so clearly playing out in my head, but it sounded absurd to say aloud.

"I felt as if I had been shot again. Like I was reliving it, and Kade seemed to experience the same thing." My voice shook as I recalled the feeling of those bullets entering my body. Quick and lethal, on their own path of destruction.

Her eyes widened at my admission before she blinked away, pondering that information for a moment. I feared in her silence that I had called her in for no reason, and that she wouldn't be able to help. I didn't want to believe that Rafina really was our only hope to find an answer as to why this was happening to me. To us.

"I know I'm new to the demon scene but this...this doesn't feel normal. And, to make matters worse, apparently when I cry, I cry black tears. So, there's that," I added, feeling overwhelmed.

Sarah moved past me, placing a hand on her hip and her other just below her chin, thinking. The silence stretched on and I was unsure where her mind was headed.

"It's not normal," she said, finally breaking the silence. "What happened to you and your transition to a demon has never been done before. The tears, even...that's concerning as well."

I took a step in her direction. "I know Kade said the transition was dangerous but—"

"Did he tell you why?"

My failure to respond told her that he hadn't, and she swallowed. Her tiny frame somehow became smaller as she contemplated how to begin.

"Let's use me as an example." I braced myself for whatever news she was about to deliver. I knew nothing about the transition that I had gone through, but I was sure as hell ready to find out.

"Say Zan and I came to an agreement that I wanted to become a demon. I would have to put in a request to the council, and once they accept, the process begins. Our tether would have to be separated, and from what I understand it is quite painful for both involved. They have to pry the very tie that binds us and remove it, taking my immortality as well. Only then can I enter the waters of Obsidian Falls."

"Kade mentioned that. Obsidian Falls," I butted in, to acknowledge that I had heard at least something regarding the matter.

Sarah nodded and continued. "This is the part that makes the transition so dangerous. No one knows why, but those waters decide your fate. As the water consumes you, your body either accepts or denies the change. No matter what, I would die in those waters. It is the unknown of whether or not I come back as a demon that persuades most to never attempt the transition. It's a gamble I would never dream of taking. I love Zan and the family we have, the life we have built, so I would never risk it."

Her face was saddened, and I could see the way this conversation must have gone with Zan. The chance of taking away a mother from her children—it was a choice not even I would make.

"But I was dead before I entered the waters."

"Exactly." She began to pace back and forth, and she seemed at war with her own words. I only wished I could hear what was going on inside of her head as she mumbled something to herself. I didn't want her to shield me from anything. She would open her mouth wider for a moment, as if ready to finally speak, only to snap it closed again.

I began to grow impatient. "Should I not have gone

through with the tethering?" I didn't want to believe that the ritual would hurt Kade, but I couldn't help but wonder if I should have held off on it, even though Zan had met that delay in protest.

"Do you regret it?'" Her query caught me off guard, but I quickly rebounded.

"If it hurts Kade, then yes." That was the last thing I wanted to be responsible for.

She nodded before she went on. "Look, Kadriel is stronger than you think. In fact, your tethering will make the both of you stronger, and connect you in ways you may not be able to comprehend yet. But that's something you two are going to have to explore yourselves. I haven't heard of this situation before, and believe me, I have spent my fair share of time combing through the history of demons and others alike, trying to make sense of this world I accepted.

"For what it's worth, I know that you mean the world to Kadriel. These past five days I have seen a whole new side of him that I never thought possible. And even though his actions today have proved troublesome, and seem ludicrous to others, there are some—like myself and Zan—who saw it as a desperate yet powerful act of defiance and love, that had to be done in the hopes of saving you by whatever means necessary."

"I think he regrets it to some extent, saving me." I swallowed hard, recalling the self-loathing Kade seemed to have toward himself. His tortured soul was a presence that loomed like a heavy and threatening cloud.

Sarah stepped in closer. "Would you have rather died?"

"Of course not. No." I was adamant that I would have chosen this life even if I'd known I was facing death and capable of making a decision.

"Then make sure he knows it." Her look was stern, almost

like a mother scolding her child. "Men like Zan and Kadriel carry a lot on their shoulders. You have to make them understand, tell them point-blank. Don't beat around the bush."

I tipped my head in understanding, momentarily stunned. "Okay."

"And as far as the screams and Kade's symptoms, I'll talk with Zan. We will figure this out, but in the meantime, try to keep your distance from Staffan and Rafina."

"Definitely." I agreed with her on that. Since they brought about the screams within my mind, I would stay as far away from them as I could.

"The tears, though…" She studied me as if looking for evidence. "Black?"

I nodded my head.

"Strange," she commented, and my spirits began to sink further.

Demonhood, unexplained screams, and black tears. If this didn't feel like a recipe for some kind of disaster, I didn't know what would. The fact that Sarah hadn't been able to provide me with any kind of explanations didn't help soothe my worries.

"Thank you, Sarah." I cleared my throat, trying to bite down my disappointment. "And, by the way, I'm sorry for how I reacted earlier. When I…vanished."

"Violet, you almost gave me a heart attack with that disappearing act." Sarah clutched the fabric of her sweater at her chest. "I didn't know where you had gone off to. Didn't even know where to tell others to start searching. For all I knew you were trapped in there."

"Wait, that can happen?" I blinked at her in surprise.

"More often than you think. Especially when you're new

to traveling that way. Even born demons can struggle when it comes time to learn that skill."

"Oh," was all I could mutter as I pondered that notion. I was reminded of how easily Kade popped in and out of mirrors, and wondered if he had ever fallen victim himself, lost in whatever the hell place was in between point A and point B.

I steered the conversation once more, unsure of how much time we would have together before it was brought to an end. "Can I ask you something? If just for argument's sake?"

"Hm?" Sarah seemed to have relaxed as our conversation took on a new direction, but she was intrigued at my ask. Just being able to talk freely with her had me climbing off of the ledge I'd been on just minutes ago.

"If I hadn't accepted the tethering, and Kade brought me here without me doing so, what would happen?"

Sarah shot me a look that went right through me, and I knew she was well aware that what I spoke of was true. I tried to backpedal in the hope of defusing the situation.

"When I was with Kade and the council, Zan asked me point-blank if I had verbally accepted the tethering prior to my arrival."

"As far as anyone is concerned, you did. The council would overthrow Kadriel if they were to learn otherwise." Her words struck a chord with me and I didn't like it. No wonder he was in such hot water standing in front of the council members.

"Overthrow? What is he, royalty?" A feeble attempt at a laugh left my chest, but as my eyes focused on Sarah, it gave me pause. "Sarah?"

"I think it's time we bring back the guys, don't you?" She began to head back toward the doorway and I followed.

"Wait, is that why everybody keeps bowing around here?"
Sarah opened the door and called Zan's name out loud,

then spun back to me. "Of course, Kadriel didn't tell you. I guess it's better you find out now rather than tomorrow."

"Tell me what?" I urged her to continue, but her other half and mine appeared in the empty doorway before she could divulge any more.

"Kade?" His grim look disappeared and was replaced with one of uncertainty as he realized I was in a much different mood than when he'd left me earlier.

"We'll see you two tomorrow." Sarah smiled as she looped her arm through Zan's, and with a double pat on his arm, they vanished.

Kade proceeded to cross the threshold and closed the door behind him, his movements too slow for my rising need for answers.

"Is there something you want to share with me?" I crossed my arms as I moved back into his room. The grand chandelier above the bed was the only source of light in our space now. The stained glass windows and corners of the large room were all dark.

"Regarding what, exactly?" He kept some distance between us as he skirted around me, assessing.

"You're more than just a watcher, aren't you?" In this world they had various jobs—watchers, seekers, and healers. But what else was he? "Are you some sort of king or something?"

One of the council members had mentioned something about not even Kade being above the law. I should have realized it then, with all the bowing, and with the delegation of tasks to others.

"I will be. In time." Kade leaned up against the wall, crossing his arms.

"So you're a prince," I said matter-of-factly. The thought

amused me, and I let out a small laugh. "You didn't think to share that piece of information with me? At least before this celebration thing tomorrow? Or was I going to be blindsided then?"

"I was going to tell you, but if you hadn't noticed, today hasn't exactly gone according to plan. In more ways than one."

I was angry that he was remaining so calm when my temper was increasing.

"You could have told me before today." My voice rose. I didn't want to pick a fight about this, but I couldn't help it. I had been on an emotional roller coaster, and this revelation wasn't helping one bit.

"I didn't want this piece of information to conflict with your decision."

"Do you think so little of me that I would base the tethering decision off of you being a prince? There's more to you than that, but it would have been nice to know. You said you would never lie to me—don't start now."

Kade pushed himself away from the wall, offended. "I never lied—"

"But you omitted the truth!" I shot back, heated. "You said yourself that being a watcher was your full-time job. You failed to mention how many jobs you have, and just how big a role you play here."

Kade's lips pressed into a firm line and he went rigid. I knew I was right, and it upset me that he hadn't shared this with me prior to today.

"I'm sorry." His quick apology caught me off guard. Kade's posture softened as he ran a hand through his hair and retreated toward his bed, sitting on the edge. "I thought I was doing the right thing. You had enough to worry about, with the possibility of starting a life here with me. I didn't want the title of queen in your future to scare you off. But now you're trapped here."

My thoughts came to a screeching halt as I gaped at him.

"Trapped?" I repeated. His use of the word *queen* didn't go unnoticed, but it was the mention of being trapped that threw me for a loop.

"Yes." His voice broke yet again. He looked exhausted as his head fell into his hands. "This isn't the future I imagined for us. And I know this isn't the one you would have agreed to."

I hated seeing Kade reduced to this. He put up a front when in the presence of others, and no doubt he had to, as a man of his—now known to me—reputation. But behind closed doors, reality set in. And while I could admire the fact that he was comfortable enough around me to let his guard down, I knew it was taking a toll on him mentally and physically. If I was going to be his queen someday, I had to be able to stand by his side and build him up, not be responsible for tearing him down lower than he already seemed to be.

Queen. Even the sound of it didn't feel real. But then again, becoming a demon hadn't really sunk in yet either.

One problem at a time, I thought. I blew out a slow and steady breath as I planned my next move.

I knelt before Kade and took his hands in mine, lifting his chin so he would have to face me. I tried to gain control of my erratic heartbeat, willing myself to meet him with the kindness and honesty that he deserved. I knew today had been trying in more ways than one. From the incident with his sister to my death, and all the decisions that weighed so heavily on him throughout it all.

"You did what you thought you had to do, and I will stand by your decisions."

"But you never accepted the tethering." He tried to lower his face, but I tipped it back up again, his stubble scratching against my fingertips.

"Let me finish." I had to soothe any doubts he might have if we were to move forward as united as the cord that tethered us. "Just so you know, I accepted the tethering this morning, but I selfishly wanted to enjoy what little time we had left before I had to leave. So if you ever have doubt that I want a life with you, just remember that. Remember that I stood with you before the council and didn't waver in my reply. Remember that I stood beside you and completed the tethering. I stand by those decisions that *both* you and I made."

His eyes bored into mine as I continued. "Maybe it's not the future either of us had pictured, but we'll navigate it and figure it out together. I know it isn't going to be easy, and I seem to be freaking out a lot, but—Darthou, this demon thing, and now *queen*? It's been a lot to take in so far, so please, *please* be patient with me. I can't seem to make sense of anything going on around me and I need some time to…adjust."

Kade remained still, and I wasn't sure if he was waiting to see if I was finished, or if he was just stunned into silence.

"I'm done," I clarified as I searched his eyes, desperate for him to say something. Anything.

"You were really going to accept?" The sincerity in his voice had me gushing an answer almost before he finished the question.

"Yes." I had to be direct so he would stop beating himself up over the actions and choices he had made today. I couldn't stand to see this side of him. I needed the Kade I'd been falling for. The one who answered my questions, teased me, and flattered me. "I promise you that I was going to say yes. I was packing a bag, wasn't I?"

Kade let out a slow breath of relief as a smile came across his face. The small act showed just how much meaning my words held, and I found myself beaming as his realization set in.

I cupped the side of his face in my hand and he leaned into it, kissing my palm. It was the very one that had been a part of our tethering ritual, and his touch sent a welcome shock wave through me that made me shiver.

Even though my reaction was small, it didn't go unnoticed by him. His expression morphed into one that I knew all too well. It begged for the connection that we so desperately sought in each other night after night. And with everything that had transpired today, I wanted nothing more than to get lost in him and let the world around us fade away.

"I suppose this is the time we should consummate our tethering." I looked at him through hooded eyes, knowing that the same thing was running through his mind.

"Only if you're ready."

Ready to push all of my problems aside and deal with them later? Sure. That's definitely healthy.

I stood from the floor and he stood from the bed, meeting me. I didn't know why my nerves were taking over, as this wasn't anything new. A trepidation overcame me, and I didn't know if it was because I feared things would be different now that we had tethered. Maybe it was the fact that Kade was some sort of demon version of royalty—it had me questioning why he'd chosen me out of literally anyone else. I couldn't explain it.

I nodded my head without breaking our eye contact. My voice was apparently out of service as I became speechless. My body began to thrum with anticipation as I lifted my blouse over my head and let it fall to the floor. Kade followed my lead, eyes never leaving mine as we undressed under the glow of his chandelier. It was almost like we both were apprehensive to make the first move.

Would this time be different? Would it *feel* different? My body was leading toward a *yes* with my quickening breath and temperature rising. I was beginning to feel warm, not just between my legs but across my entire body.

"This feels…" Kade reached for my tethered hand. I was met with a warmth equal to my own. I realized now that he had never felt cold to the touch since my arrival here. Our difference in body temperatures was always something I had noticed back home.

"Different," I stated as our fingers enclosed upon each other. I viewed our hands with a hazy intensity, wondering if this electric hum coursing through me was ever going to cease. My other hand floated up toward his chest, grazing his muscles as I lay my palm flat against his heart, curious whether it was beating as wildly as mine.

His head dipped down and my eyes fluttered closed. His mouth brushed lightly once, then twice, as if testing the waters. My lips tingled and I was eager to deepen the kiss, reveling in the tenderness.

Our hands roamed as we explored each other with a newfound lust, and I began to cave in to his touch as his erection pressed into the space between us. Every point where our bodies met, I felt as if tendrils of fire were igniting beneath my skin, and I selfishly wanted more. The need to feel every inch of him had me in a frenzy that I couldn't stop even if I wanted to.

Kade lifted me and rounded the bed, laying me down with ease. I parted my legs as his lips left mine and he began trailing kisses down my neck. His hips nestled between mine and I yearned for the act that promised a pleasure that would overcome us both.

His cock dipped into me as his face returned, and if my new set of black eyes had the capability of rolling back into my head, they were doing it. Kade entered me inch by inch and I squirmed against him, grasping at his back with my nails. I throbbed around his member, unable to stop moving as he took me.

Our jagged breaths mingled as he continued his slow and controlled movements, driving each time at a pace that was agonizingly slow and made me deliciously crave each reentrance. I fisted a hand into his hair and brought him to my lips, desperate to taste him again. The hum coming from my body was so loud it filled my ears, competing with the sounds of rasp-filled want from each of us.

My attention shifted toward my arm that had begun emitting a strange glow. I could clearly see where the cord had wrapped around me, almost like a flashlight beneath my skin was illuminating it. Kade stilled as he took in the sight I was witnessing and raised his own arm, examining the very same occurrence there.

He grinned from ear to ear as if this was a good sign, and then he lifted my back from the bed so I was sitting atop his lap. I adjusted myself to straddle him better in my seated position, and he took my tethered arm in his hold. He bent down and pressed kisses down the inside of my arm, from my fingertips to the crook of my elbow, and with each delicate touch, I involuntarily clenched around his member. It was like tiny fireworks were igniting beneath the surface and his lips were a welcome compress that ricocheted those fiery cracks throughout the entirety of my body.

When he finished, I lifted his arm to my lips. His head

rolled back, and I took joy in knowing that the feeling was mutual. His cock pulsated and I ground my hips against him with each new kiss I planted. Who would have thought that this binding would be capable of bringing such immense pleasure?

When I reached his elbow, he tipped my head up and kissed me hard, with a desperation for my mouth that spoke of our need for each other. My bare chest met his, nipples hardened to the point that they ached, and he began to move again, withdrawing slowly only to buck into me.

Our lips broke apart but we held each other's gaze. I could barely focus on him as everything around me seemed to fade away in a blur. Each thrust made my jaw drop farther, and with each exhale of his I took in a sharpened breath.

We continued on in our passionate bliss until we fell apart, loud and hard. I had the fleeting worry that if there was anyone in the hall or if Kade had any neighbors, they were getting quite the earful, but I would do it all over again with no regrets. It was an explosion so intense that I thought I might pass out as it rocked through and claimed us.

The glow from our arms faded as we came down from our combined highs and our sweat-soaked skin began to cool. We stilled, unmoving, as our heart rates began to stabilize and our bodies relaxed into one another.

"Thank you," Kade said, and I lifted my heavy head from his shoulder to meet his gaze, attempting to raise an eyebrow in confusion at his thanks.

"For saying yes. To the tethering." My chest swelled at his words, a warmth beginning to blossom again. "I love you, Violet."

I wanted to thank him for saving me. I wanted to tell him that while I may not be able to say those last words back to him yet, I did care for him, and deeply. In a way that I had never felt before with anyone else.

But when my words failed me, I let my lips press to his once more, hoping that I could show him just how much he meant to me.

CHAPTER 5

Kade

She's actually here.
Violet was cuddled up beside me, and alive.
But as a demon.

I still had difficulty wrapping my head around it. I had never entertained the thought of a life with Violet as a demon, fearful that the transition would take her life and I would live out the rest of my existence without her. I would have rather had her reject the tethering altogether and lose her, than risk her life to become like me.

Yesterday's actions flooded through my mind at rapid speed and I retraced my steps, trying to figure out what could have happened to her.

She quit breathing. Her heartbeat stopped. She was dead as I carried her limp and lifeless body to the one place I could think to use as a last resort.

How *did* Obsidian Falls bring Violet back from death? Its waters were the greatest mystery in Darthou, and it had produced some kind of miracle in bringing her back.

Or did it?

I knew in my gut that something was wrong the moment I saw her, but I'd been too afraid to admit that out loud because then it might become true. I couldn't put my finger on exactly what it was, but her presence had changed. And it wasn't just because she'd lost those bright eyes that used to bore into mine with such an intense curiosity—her very essence was…different.

Perhaps it was just that up until this point, I had only known Violet, the human. Now, that part of her had died.

My breath stalled as I recalled the moment I'd first laid eyes on her walking into the council chambers in nothing but a robe. Her skin, covered in black matter from the waters that took her under. Her brutal death, a vivid memory that would forever haunt me. Even as she timidly stood before us, I still had trouble believing what my eyes were seeing, fearful that it was a trick. Scared that the woman I had longed for, for years, was really upright and standing beside me.

And wearing her very own set of demon eyes to match my own.

There had to be a catch. When was the other shoe going to drop? Would Obsidian Falls truly grant me this kind of victory? The waters had saved and resurrected the woman I loved, but at what price?

Even now, after completing our tethering, part of me was still in shock—even though she was finally mine in every sense of the word.

Mine.

Violet's breaths were soft and even, her plush lips parted slightly as her air came and went. Her naked body was slack against mine. Her breasts pressed into my side, one leg hiked up and above my knee. This luscious frame of hers had my cock stirring to life as I focused on each point of contact between our skin, and I swallowed hard as I clenched my eyes to suppress the urge to wake her. To claim every inch of her and solidify the fact that she was real. Touch every spot that would make her cave to my every whim and desire.

There was a calmness radiating off of her that I wanted to submit to as well, but I couldn't shut my mind off. I was tired, sure, but I couldn't surrender to the luxury of sleep, or bury myself deep inside Violet. As much as it pained me, I had to check in on my sister and find out if Elias had been able to track down either Damian or Brett.

My blood began to boil at the mere thought of those two bastards.

Careful not to wake Violet, I carefully slid her off my chest and onto the bed. I tucked the blanket around her and stood.

The room would be pitch-black to a human's eyes, but Violet would soon find out how well her new eyes could see in complete darkness. I was quick to retrieve my boxers and pants, making sure my pocket mirror hadn't fallen from its hold on the right side. I cast a long glance back at Violet before I took off down the hall and into my watching quarters.

I flipped a light on at my desk and spoke Aleena's name as I began tapping a mirror on my wall in the hopes of getting her attention. I hadn't yet had the chance to visit her, let alone talk to her, since she had been injured. The shit show that had followed our return to Darthou was beginning to give me a headache.

When her response took too long, I tapped the glass again

and this time, harder. I made my way toward the shelves by my couch that housed my liquor bottles and poured myself a double of whatever drink was closest to me. Just as I was about to bring the amber liquid to my lips, Aleena finally answered.

"The fuck do you want?" She was agitated, and rightfully so considering she'd had a chunk taken out of her side during our battle against the saints. It was a blow meant for me, and she had put herself in harm's way to take it. I was both grateful and fucking furious at her for doing that.

"Nice to see you too." I began crossing back over to the mirror where she had appeared. When my eyes finally landed on hers, I tried to cover up my concern. Her brown hair was a mess, gathered on top of her head, and her face was pinched in pain but she was trying to hide it with her anger. I knew her heated greeting was brought on by her wound, the healing of which was not a simple fix.

"You're crazy, you know that?"

"One could say that you are as well for taking that hit. Guess it runs in the family." My eyes narrowed at her as she bit her tongue. I knew why she did it. Big sister looking out for little brother who was inching closer to his possible tethering and reign. Hell, I would have done the same for her in a heartbeat and without thinking.

What was that saying humans always said? *Everything happens for a reason.*

Had I been injured, I wouldn't have been able to retrieve Violet. She would have been dead before I could even get to her. My mood sank lower, thinking about the possibility that had been so close to being a reality. It was gutting, and I downed my drink to chase that thought down.

Aleena winced as she tried to readjust herself. She was propped up against bright pillows on her bed, and the view I had was only of her face and neck. I only hoped that she was through the worst of her healing at this point. Trying to close a wound of that magnitude took serious concentration and skill. I had no doubt she could do it, but it did take time to heal the inside as well as the outside.

"I hear congratulations are in order." The words left her lips as a sore hiss followed. She took a beat before gathering a slow and controlled breath. "How is she, by the way?"

"Alive," was all I could think to say, then followed up with another one-word reply. "Sleeping."

She narrowed her eyes at me, as if my lack of a response was a bit underwhelming. Instead of confronting me about it, her next question went in another direction.

"Is he dead yet?"

As much as it pained me to see Aleena struggling to recover, it helped me to talk to her now. I knew she would be able to recover from her injury, but the remembrance of her cries and the horrid sight of her injury after that saint had slashed through her side still gnawed at me.

"The fucking asshole who shot her," she seethed, her face reddening.

"I was going to get an update from Elias after I checked in with you."

"Kadriel," she scolded, but then retreated as her pain got the best of her and her outburst. She paused for a moment, nostrils flaring as she attempted to reel herself back in. "I'll be fine. I *am* fine. Rafina helped as best she could, the rest is up to me now."

Rafina.

One problem at a time, I had to remind myself.

"I'll help Violet get ready for the celebration tomorrow."

"What? No, you're in no condition to—"

"Shut up." She rolled her eyes as she drew out the words to silence me. "I'll be expecting her at my place at nine."

I shot her a disbelieving look. I wasn't sure I was ready to unleash my sister on Violet just yet, but I knew the two would want to meet each other. All the nagging and pestering from Aleena over the years of my pining—it was all leading to this point. Now that Violet was finally here, in whatever capacity, Aleena would be persistent in getting to know her.

"I'll get her ready for the big day, get to know her a little bit. It'll be fine. A bit of girl bonding is all." Her voice was becoming too light, like she had an ulterior motive, and I stiffened, toying with the idea.

I knew the belongings Violet had brought with her were limited, judging by the size of her bag. Hell, she hadn't even put any makeup on before we went to our tethering ritual, so it made me wonder if she'd even brought anything besides clothes and her childhood blanket.

Aleena had also had a hand in helping put a dress together for Violet for the celebration, should she accept the tethering. The night Violet had first summoned me, I had alerted Aleena, Elias, and Zan. And luckily, my uncle had taken it upon himself to notify the council members.

Thank fuck, because one less visit with them was a blessing in itself.

Time had been ticking since then, and Darthou had been abuzz about their future king's possible mate coming into the picture. And nothing got them talking more than the probability of a future queen who was supposed to be human.

"Don't make me pull the 'you owe me' card." Aleena's face set into a firm expression, one now void of pain but full of sisterly annoyance.

"One could say you were doing your duty to protect your

future king." I raised a brow, fully intent on getting a rise out of her.

"Fuck you. Nine o'clock. And tell Elias to stop smothering me. I can't stand those freaking puppy dog eyes."

"I'm not your—" She ended the connection before I could finish. "—messenger."

I let out a prolonged sigh as I was met with my reflection in my wall of mirrors.

Five nights ago I had been a panicked mess. Probably staring at myself in this exact spot, trying to figure out if the man reflected before me was a man that Violet would accept. I had toyed with my eye and hair color, skin tone…hell, I had even tried beefing myself up and slimming myself down, but it had all felt wrong. I had attempted to compare myself to the men in her life, the ones she had taken interest in, men she had dated and others she had wished to. Social media pictures she had practically drooled over, thinking she never even had a chance, her lingering gazes on abs and pants hung too low.

But in the end, none of them looked like me.

Perhaps I was a bit full of myself in thinking so, but I wanted her to accept me as the man I had come to be. I knew she would look for more than just my appearance, but she had accepted me that first night, just as I was. I grinned as I recalled our first night together.

Violet was finally mine, and I had to see to it that the ones responsible for her pain would pay for their crimes.

Starting with that damn ex-boyfriend of hers.

I tapped the glass, summoning Elias who answered far faster than my recovering sibling.

He looked nervous, apprehension quick to cross his hardened face.

"What is it?" I asked, suddenly overwhelmed with

whatever bad news he was going to bring me.

"You're not going to like it," he started, and my stomach dropped. I had half a mind to go to his place to hear it in person, and the fact that Elias wasn't inviting himself over now that we had our connection wasn't sitting well either.

Even so, I didn't want to leave Violet. The last thing I needed was for her to awake and find me missing.

"Elias." I urged him to proceed, already on edge.

"I can't locate either Brett or Damian."

"Neither of them?" My voice strained as it rose. I began swiping at mirrors, bringing up every place I knew either of them to frequent. Homes, workplaces, vehicles, and everything in between. I had about a dozen images springing to life before I felt Elias at my back.

"I've been scouring all of them, and nothing."

I shook my head, frustrated, as I kept bringing up more images until my wall was full. "When was the last time we had eyes on them?"

I took a few steps back, taking in the various views. Some were so still it was as if they were merely pictures hanging on the wall. Others showed people who were of no interest to me right now. Except that fucker drinking on Maple St.—that guy was up to something shady, and I'd make it a point to find out what later. *Just pile that onto my damn list while we're at it.*

"That's the thing. My dad and I haven't spotted Damian since the factory. It's like he just vanished. And the same goes for Brett."

"How?" I questioned him further, suddenly doubting my best friend and his ability to find the two men responsible for making my life a living hell.

"I can't find a single feed, image, or anything of Brett leaving Violet's apartment building. Nothing." Elias was almost panicked by his failure to provide me with any information.

"Humans and saints don't just vanish," I stated the obvious, only for my best friend to shoot me a look.

"You think I was born yesterday?"

My jaw was clenching. Rage was pumping through my veins and the need to fucking kill someone was growing by the second. Saints couldn't travel by mirror as we could. They could travel through portals of their own making, but that was something that was rare to come by anymore.

Was Damian older than we had initially thought? His mind games already aged him by at least one hundred years, but now traveling by portal? That was the only explanation as to why we had never seen them entering that abandoned factory.

And now Brett had disappeared?

Well fuck me seven times to Sunday.

My expression grew grim, and I knew I needed to retrace the steps myself. I wouldn't be able to concentrate until I did. And that started with Violet's death. I swallowed hard, lifting my arm to bring up her apartment and focusing on using the reflection on her dark television screen.

I used to watch her through her standing mirror, its long surface the perfect view of her and her home. She had a knack for positioning it with the perfect view for me, both here and at her grandmother's home. She almost made it too easy for me to watch her.

But now, that mirror had shattered. The broken shards could barely be seen from my new point of view as I began rewinding the footage like humans used to do on a damn VCR tape.

"Kadriel—" Elias held his tongue as I shot him a look of

warning. I knew he was trying to spare me from seeing it, but I had already held Violet's dying and dead body in my arms, so I knew what awaited me. Now, I just needed to watch it play out, and figure out how in the hell Brett had managed to escape.

From the television, I could see the upper halves of Elias and me disappearing, appearing, and soon Brett and Violet came into view. My back stiffened straight as a board as I prepared myself for Violet's last few minutes alive in the only world she had ever known. It gripped me, constricting around my heart, that she would never be able to return to the life she once had.

"Shut the door," I ordered Elias before I could bring myself to play the footage. I didn't want to take the chance that Violet might wake up and find us here. And worse, witness her own murder before our very eyes.

Once I heard the click of the door, he joined me at my side as I let the events unfold before me.

It was like an out-of-body experience. Watching it as if I were there, but I wasn't. Violet had made me aware of Ms. Vanders' role in this, and her voice on the other side of the door chilled me. The ruse that was used to get Violet to open her door was clever, and I saw red as Brett kicked open the door, sending her flying to the floor with such force that I had little doubt she had damaged her arm on impact.

Violet had backed herself into a corner. Her small home provided nowhere for her to hide. She begged, pleaded, and I could see the wheels turning in her head as she weighed her options while Brett's rage filled to the brim and ran over.

Two shots. Two fucking bullets flew through the air and Violet didn't even have time to react to them. I didn't even flinch as I took in the sight before me, my blood pumping furiously fast and rushing to my ears.

Just hours ago, I had experienced the same damn thing. Zan had no explanation for it, and I wasn't exactly in the mindset to try to explain it to Elias. Now, I wanted to seek out revenge. To fucking annihilate this guy and reduce him to ash by whatever means necessary.

I rubbed at my chest, a soreness forming as I recalled that memory. It deepened, sending my nerves on a roller coaster as they ricocheted around like a pinball in a machine.

Until an overwhelming panic began to set in, replacing it. I blinked, confused. The panic came from my arm and swept through my body, spreading like wind taking your breath with it. I staggered back, realizing what it was.

Violet. It was her, and the connection from our tethering.

I might have had my doubts about Violet being a demon, but this—this was a good sign, even if it was puzzling to experience it. The connection was stronger when demons tethered. The ability to feel your mate's emotions and feelings was a perk to some demons, while others saw it as a curse. I would imagine you would only have a problem with it if you had something to hide.

Luckily, I had nothing of the sort when it came to Violet. I would recite my day-to-day life like an audiobook to bring her up to speed if that was what she wanted.

The realization hit me like a brick—the calmness I had felt with her asleep at my side had been our connection taking root, and now something was off.

Was she sensing my anger and desire to end a life?

"Keep looking," I ordered Elias as I began swiping away all of the images before us. "I have to go."

Knowing he would see himself out, I rushed from the room and down the hall. My chest was tight with unease as I found Violet curled up into a ball on the bed, whimpering. Though naked beneath the sheet, she was sweating profusely. Her hair clung to her face, eyes screwed shut as she tried to grab at the mattress beneath her.

Whatever was going on inside that head of hers, it had its nails dug deep.

Instead of trying to wake her, for fear of her lashing out, I fixed myself to her backside and drew her into my frame.

"No, no, no..." she repeated over and over, her voice breaking on each utterance of the word. She was weak against me, unable to push me off as I brought her close, hugging her tight and secure. Her heart was clamoring around her chest, beating like it was in a boxing match with her ribs.

"Shhh..." I attempted to soothe as I kissed the top of her head. I bit down the panic that was burning in me like a wildfire, mustering up any kind of calm I could find in my hopes to combat it.

Slowly, her body began to relax, her movements becoming minimal. Her heaving chest began to ease and her heartbeat started to level out. I breathed in through my nose and out through my mouth, trying to focus on calming myself and her.

Whatever was going on in her head, it didn't wake her, but instead kept her hostage while she slept. I hadn't been witness to Violet having any kind of nightmares before. Tossing and turning, sure. Occasional snoring, even. But this...this was new.

I hugged her as tight as I could without bruising or suffocating her, willing her to have a peaceful sleep and nothing else.

CHAPTER 6

Violet

I couldn't be certain of the time, but judging by the soft light coming in from the stained glass windows it had to be early. I'd been lying in bed wide-awake for a while, in a tangled heap with Kade, afraid to move and wake him. His steady breathing and relaxed features made him quite the sight, one I hadn't had a chance to fully appreciate yet. I knew he said that he didn't require as much sleep as humans, but either yesterday's stresses, our consummating activities, or both seemed to have worn him out. I couldn't bring myself to disturb him.

Last night had been, for lack of a better term, intense. I had no other word for it. The connection we had shared, and the intensity of our frenzied lovemaking, was one for the books, and I hoped it wasn't just a one-time thing.

Everything about it felt different. Dare I say it, even *I* felt different. My body felt alive and ready to conquer all. I had an energy that made me want to sprint and a mood that couldn't be dampened.

Or so I thought.

My mind swayed toward thoughts of my family. Of the scene that must have been left behind. I assumed the police would be the ones to find my grandma and break the news. That was heartbreaking in itself. And I knew after that, once she gathered herself, her next call would be to Aunt Cindy.

I didn't know what was worse—the fact that I might be considered dead to my family, or the fact that Brett and Damian were still out there.

And who would've thought that Brett was capable of murder? Would he try to harm anybody else? He hadn't even blinked an eye when he struck Ms. Vanders with the base of his gun. I still didn't know the details of Brett's "tendencies" that Kade had mentioned, but his calls to my work and threatening texts came to the forefront of my mind. And I couldn't forget him showing up at my apartment in the middle of the night, drunk and pissed off to high heaven that I had been in a photo with another man.

And then there was Damian.

Kade fully believed that Damian was involved in this whole situation. The thought that he was still alive and moving about his life as normal today at work shot so much anger through me that I found myself wiggling out from beneath Kade's arm.

I knew that Brett had been the one to pull the trigger, but not knowing the extent to which Damian was undoubtedly involved was unnerving. I had to get my mind off of these guys, and fast.

Kade and I hadn't even had the chance to discuss our meetings with Sarah and Zan last night, so I couldn't let myself spiral to the point of hurting him again. I had no idea just how much the tethering connected us, and if I kept dwelling on Brett and Damian, I was afraid of what might happen to Kade.

Nobody should have to feel those damn bullets but me.

Retrieving Kade's shirt from the floor, I slipped it on. The soft material was a welcome feeling against my skin as it hugged me, and I inhaled his citrus scent. I glanced back to make sure I hadn't disturbed him, and when he didn't budge, I tiptoed out of view toward the bathroom. This place was unbelievably quiet, and I was afraid if I made any noise it would wake him, so I thought I would explore a bit.

Upon passing the bathroom, I found a darkened hallway that split off into two directions. I'd seen it when Kade had shown me the bathroom yesterday but hadn't given it another thought until now. I continued on and to the right, letting my hand trace along the stone wall until I came to a door and I opened it. A large wooden desk came into view with a computer, tablet, and lamp. In my opinion, it was too clean to have been used very much. No papers, folders, or pens could be seen as I drew closer.

The room was large in width but it was missing the high ceilings that had been everywhere else until now. It was clean and tidy and divided into sections that reminded me of people who wouldn't let their food touch on their plate. Just past his desk was a set of bookshelves and a lounge chair that I could see myself curling up on. I wanted to scan the books to see if there was anything of interest but carried on toward the workout equipment—a treadmill, some machine that I knew was for arms, and shelves with various weights and items that looked familiar, but I couldn't name them.

The farthest corner of the room housed what looked to be a music station, and I came to a stop. There was a keyboard and a cello out and on full display, but there were others that were cased, a mixture of woodwind and brass instruments. There were stacks of lesson books and tattered pages strewn about that showed me he spent time here, maybe more so than the rest of the room. I grinned as I imagined him seated on the bench, pouring himself into the music that he had talked of so fondly, jealous that he apparently had a knack for the art of it all. As much as I wanted to pluck away at a few strings and let my fingers dance along the ivories, I resisted.

Dragging my attention away from Kade's music corner, which seemed to be the only place so far that wasn't arranged in an orderly fashion, I stopped dead in my tracks. How I'd missed this up until now was mind-boggling.

Taking up almost the entirety of the opposite wall of the room was a wall of mirrors. They were assorted sizes, varying in height and width but no higher than what Kade could probably reach. There were no frames separating them, only different variations of glass thickness, each one butted up against the other.

The way all of these mirrors fit together on the wall was astounding and impressive.

I knew without a shadow of a doubt that this was what he called his watching quarters. This was probably where he'd watched me, for the past six years. But with this many surfaces, how on earth did he keep track of twenty-something people? Did he have each of them tuned in to different people at the same time, or did the wall display itself to him like a giant flat-screen tv?

Before I even realized what I was doing, raising my hand toward the glass, I caught movement in my periphery and I jumped.

"Curious, are we?" Sleep clung to Kade as he offered a small smile, pleased that he had caught me off guard.

My heart leapt into my throat as I took a step back from the wall.

"Always." I spoke softly as I took in the sight of him in his boxers leaning against the doorframe. This sexy view of him was a welcome sight in the morning, even if I had about jumped out of my skin at his sudden appearance. I had hoped I would have more time to explore alone, but maybe leaving the confines of the bed had woken him after all. I wondered how long he had been standing there.

"This is a lot of mirrors, Kade." I dragged my gaze away from him and took another step back from the wall. I couldn't even let my eyes settle on my reflection as I kept scanning over the dozens and dozens of mirrors.

He shrugged as he made his way over to me. I noticed the absence of the stubble that had been forming around his jawline, despite never having seen him shave once.

"Come." He took my hand and led me away, passing a decent-sized couch that was nestled in front of the wall. My lingering gaze on the mirrors didn't go unnoticed, and he let out a slight chuckle. "I promise, I will show them to you in time."

"Why not now?" I glanced one last time about the room as he escorted me toward the door where we'd both entered.

"Because we have a big day ahead of us and breakfast is here."

"Oh?" I felt my stomach, confused that I hadn't even had the slightest urge to eat since I'd arrived. I hadn't eaten since the outing with Kade yesterday, and that had been a late breakfast—how had I not been hungry at all?

We reentered the bedroom area and a small tray was sat upon the foot of the bed. There were glass bottles of water and a beautiful array of colored fruit, arranged so pristine it looked as if it belonged in a magazine, too perfect to possibly be edible.

"I totally forgot to ask about pancakes. I'm sorry. If you want some I can—"

"No, this is fine. This looks amazing." I reached out and plucked a slice of strawberry and popped it into my mouth. It was extraordinarily sweet and I welcomed the explosion it set off on my tongue. I moaned in appreciation. "You have room service here?"

That earned a lighthearted chuckle from Kade. "I guess you could say that we do, yes."

My eyes bulged, knowing that I could get into some serious trouble knowing that. But a fruit platter such as this had to have a hefty price tag on it. Guess there were worse things I could be eating right now.

"So, I know we have this celebration thing today but…" I grabbed a blueberry and popped it into my mouth before continuing. "We should probably talk about last night."

Kade raised a dark brow as he hesitantly picked up a slice of kiwi. I wondered if it was his favorite, since he was digging into that first. "Which part?"

I sat on the side of the bed, which he must have made already, apprehensive about telling him about everything that had transpired with me since awakening as a demon. Despite Sarah's warning, he deserved to know, if he didn't already. I wasn't aware yet of what he and his uncle had discussed last night, but I knew he needed to hear it from me. The longer I waited, the worse it would look to hide it.

"Well…last night when you experienced those pains, that wasn't the first strange thing to happen since I've come here."

His chin dipped down and his face remained guarded, not giving anything away.

I explained about the screams I'd been hearing—the bloodcurdling screams when I first awoke in Rafina's presence, and Sarah's warning. I heard them when in audience with the council, but not at such an extreme volume. And then again when Rafina and Staffan had arrived to our tethering ritual last night.

But even with the unexplained screams when those two were around, that wasn't what frightened me the most. The worst thing was the fact that Kade seemed to feel what I had felt at the impact of those bullets.

I was scared for him, afraid that our tethering would weaken him. I didn't want him to experience these things that I had no explanation for. I only hoped that Zan had some sort of explanation for what was happening, since Sarah hadn't exactly been forthcoming with any information.

I hadn't even been a demon for twenty-four hours yet, but I knew in my gut that this wasn't normal.

"Zan did tell me about the screams." Kade spoke quietly and my shoulders caved forward. "I'm grateful to hear about it coming from you though."

"I should have said something sooner." I felt guilty omitting that information before now. Zan and his wife had been nothing but kind since I'd arrived, and I didn't want to be the cause of any strife between Kade and his family. Even though the time I had gone without telling him was minimal, I hated the idea that I might have created any trouble or divide.

"The tethering connects us in many ways now that you're a demon. One being that we should always be able to find each other. Not that you seemed to have any problems with doing so yesterday even before the tethering. And, we should even be able to feel, to an extent, each other's emotions."

Interesting. I wasn't sure if I should be alarmed by that or not. However, I couldn't deny that I was intrigued.

Kade fell silent for a moment, perhaps lost in thought about something, before he continued. "But Zan and I have never heard of what I experienced yesterday. I have been shot before, and that felt damn near identical to it." He shook his head as if trying to dispose of a memory he would rather not recall. The image of Kade being shot again was something I didn't even want to bring to mind, but my head had other plans.

"What? Why? Who the hell shot you?" My words stumbled out of my mouth as I stood. Devouring the fruit that had been delivered to us was now the furthest thing from my mind.

"Relax, it's a part of training." He was nonchalant, as if it were no big deal, further fueling me.

"Training?" My eyes shot up in terror. "What kind of training is that?"

"How to take a hit. How to recover and heal."

I snorted the most unflattering half laugh of my life, shaking my head at how crazy that sounded. "Who would voluntarily get shot for that? That sounds like some sort of fucked-up punishment!"

"Don't police officers get tased?" he probed, but it only infuriated me more.

"Tasers don't fucking blow your brains out. They don't…" My words fell as my head went back *there* again.

At home, in my bedroom, nowhere to run and nowhere to hide as I faced Brett and his gun. My body grew hot, uncomfortably hot, as I could feel my eyes sting with the knowledge that he pulled the trigger not once, but twice. Before I could hear the shots, Kade was flush against my front and embracing me.

I choked back the sob threatening to rip from my throat as I peeled away the memories of Brett in my old home. I hugged Kade back, gripping him tight as I willed myself to be present. I tucked my cheek against his smooth chest and inhaled, letting everything go quiet as I calmed down.

"The screams…" Kade's voice vibrated beneath me. "If you hear them again. You'll tell me?"

I nodded slightly. "Yes."

Kade let out a measured breath through his nose. "If it's somehow connected to Staffan and Rafina, there's a good chance you're going to hear them today."

"Why? The celebration?" I was panicked at the possibility and broke out of our hold.

He tipped his head in confirmation, jaw set. My fingers knotted, knowing that I could at some point be in close proximity to them today. The screams were a vivid memory that I didn't want to relive under any circumstance. Especially if there was a chance they could hit me as hard as the first time I'd experienced them. It had sent me into a crippling state of worthlessness.

"Hey—" Kade separated my hands and took them in his. "Everything will be okay. We just need to get through today, and we'll get to the bottom of this. But Sarah is right—we handle this at our own discretion for now. Nobody else needs to know."

"Even Rafina?" I questioned.

"For now, yes. Even Rafina." He pulled me into him again, but gentler this time, and I let my hands link behind him, seeking his comfort.

"I have to take care of a few things this morning before the celebration begins, but I will make sure that once we meet again, I will stay by your side no matter what. And if something happens, if you feel or hear anything, let me know. Promise?"

"Yes, but what am I supposed to do in the meantime?" I looked up into his eyes, uncertain of his plans for me. But he seemed to already have my morning mapped out.

"Get ready with my sister."

CHAPTER 7

Violet

Kade and I appeared outside of another door, in a hallway that made me certain I would get lost in this place if I were to walk around by myself. I had no idea just how big Darthou was, though Kade had promised to give me a tour once our day of celebration was over.

Perhaps even the chance to go outside, because apparently, most of the locations I'd been so far were all inside this giant concrete fortress. I was itching to see the sun that could only be seen through stained glass windows. I found myself missing its rays of light.

My grip on Kade's hand tightened as he knocked on the door.

"Are you sure you have to leave?" I asked as I hugged onto his arm.

"You'll be perfectly safe with Aleena. She can be intimidating to some, but she has a big heart so don't let her fool you."

Safe, I thought. I needed to worry about being safe? Did I need to be worried about anyone else in particular besides Rafina and Staffan? I'd just add that to the growing list of worries that occupied my head.

The door swung open and a gorgeous, sleek-yet-toned woman appeared, wearing a white robe with black polka dots. Her hair was a vibrant pink, styled like that of a rock star. On one side it was braided toward the back, and the volume on the other side made me wonder how on earth she got it to stay like that without making it look plastered.

"Pink? Really?" Kade shook his head as I looked between the two of them. Her eyes narrowed at him, and before I could even react, she hauled off and hit him in the arm.

"Asshole," she huffed as she pivoted and retreated into the room. Her robe was so short I was afraid if she raised her arms too high, we would catch a glance of her behind.

I gaped at Kade and he rolled his eyes, entering behind her while pulling me in until he could close the door. "Happy to see you too."

Aleena's room came into view and it was the most colorful thing I had seen since I'd arrived. Her windows gleamed purples, pinks, and blues in the same patterns as those in Kade's room. She had furs, and enough furniture to complete the place without looking too crowded.

She even had some sort of art hanging from the walls in staggered positions that I found myself fascinated by. This place was the most interesting I had seen by far, and I wanted to inquire about multiple things. Aleena's taste in decor gave me an insight into her that Kade lacked in his living space, minus the music corner.

"I almost died, you know." She crossed her arms as she whipped around to meet us.

"She's exaggerating," Kade said near my ear, then returned his attention to his sister. "We both know we can't be rid of you that easily."

She stuck her tongue out and popped her hip to the side.

"And you do know today isn't about you, right?"

She scoffed at him. "Don't you forget, every day is about me." She flipped him off and I couldn't hide my amusement at their banter. Even if the injuries she'd sustained yesterday were really that life threatening, they both seemed to be hiding it well.

"But you—" Her attention turned toward me and I froze beneath her scrutinizing gaze. Kade definitely had the intimidating part right. The way she zeroed in on me had me holding my breath. "You have been the topic of great debate around here, causing a divide like oil and water."

"Aleena—" Kade cleared his throat. "This is Violet. Violet, this is my sister."

"Hi," I managed. She cocked her head to the side, not returning a greeting as she eyed Kade again. I was pretty sure she could throw me around like a rag doll. The muscles in her arms and legs were evident in each move her body made. She wasn't even bulky by any means, just femininely strong, if that were a thing.

"You're fucking mad, Kadriel." She took a step closer to me, examining me from head to toe. I wasn't sure what she was trying to look for. "I can't believe it worked."

"You're not the only one," Kade agreed as he gently squeezed my hand. It was then that I realized I was still clinging to him like a koala to a branch, and I loosened.

"You guys seem to think of me as some sort of demonic miracle," I remarked, trying to shrug off the awkwardness of our first meeting.

Aleena cracked a half smile and finally met my stare once she was done looking me over like some shiny new toy. There was a moment of softness to her face, her flawless complexion giving away an ounce of kindness before she snapped back to business.

"I like it. I like you. Come, we have much to do." She pulled me away from Kade and we vanished before I could react. I was transported to a space that resembled a mix between a bridal boutique and a department store.

Tall mirrors took up one side, and in front of each one there were raised platforms. There were racks upon racks of clothing that appeared to be sorted by color. It reminded me of how some people arranged their books by the same rule.

There was a hint of cinnamon in the air, a comforting smell that made me think of all things fall. Even though it looked like a store of some sort, it had a homey feel to it. The warmth that this shop exuded, with its cream-colored walls and white crown molding, made it feel like a place back home.

A strange twinge of longing and heartache reared its head as I tried to swallow down that word.

Home.

"Welcome, welcome." Aleena released my hand and backed away, allowing room for a woman who looked to be in her forties to come strolling to my side. A tape measure was hanging around her neck and it swayed a bit before she stopped. She was somewhat heavyset, but her strides were quick. I noticed her light brown eyes right off the bat. A friendly human face had me smiling at the interaction already. It was kind of funny, realizing how hung up I was on the whites of people's eyes now.

"Rebecca, meet the demonic miracle and queen-to-be, Violet." I shot Aleena a look of disbelief that she would introduce me as such, but she displayed a playful grin as she made herself comfy in a plush navy-blue chair. She was definitely a character I looked forward to getting to know. Not that I had much choice in the matter—she was Kade's sister and I wanted us to get along, after all.

"The pleasure is all mine, Violet." Rebecca bowed to me, and to Aleena, before returning her attention to me. Well, at least now I knew why everyone kept bowing. I thought it had just been for Kade, but now it was apparent that it was for me too. This was going to be weird to get used to. Or, would it be terribly rude of me to ask them *not* to do it?

"Now, I understand you might be in need of some clothes." She began ushering me around the shop while Aleena sipped on some pink drink that appeared out of nowhere. It matched her hair way too well to be an accident.

Rebecca asked me all sorts of questions about colors, style, and what I was most comfortable in. We roamed the racks and she became my very own personal shopper, never letting me carry a thing for myself even though I tried. She had a notepad that she would scribble in periodically when I spoke, and she busied herself moving to and from what I assumed to be a fitting room behind one of the mirrors that turned out to be a door.

The ease with which we conversed and strutted around the rows of apparel was a nice change of pace. I felt a comfort with Rebecca that I hadn't known I needed.

She had been into clothes and fashion all throughout her life, even before she had come to Darthou. Entirely self-taught, she had taken it upon herself to learn the ins and outs of what the latest trends were and weren't. Rebecca prided herself on never finding a body that she couldn't cater to, and it was clear from our brief time together that she absolutely loved what she did.

This seamstress had a passion that had followed her from her old life to her new one. It only further begged the question of what I was going to do now that I was here, and it was a loaded one.

Kade wasn't kidding when he said the whole clothing debacle would be taken care of. I was thrown off when Rebecca said she would have everything delivered by the end of the day tomorrow and taken aback that I wouldn't need to try anything on. She only took two measurements before leading me back out to Aleena, who was still firmly planted, swirling around what remained of her drink. Aleena's resting bitch face made it impossible to tell if she was pissed, bored, or just relaxing.

Plopping down beside her in a chair that matched hers, I sighed. "There are a lot more clothes here than it looks." I blinked at the racks, thinking that we had to have rummaged through them all at this point. "And she's human."

I wasn't sure why I'd let those last words leave my mouth, and I snapped it shut as I skimmed the room to make sure Rebecca was out of earshot.

That seemed to amuse Aleena and she sat forward. "That she is. And it's okay to ask her about it."

I nodded slightly. I was definitely going to do that. So far I had met Sarah and Rebecca, both who had successfully tethered and were still human. I felt at odds with myself not knowing where I really fit into the mix.

I was now, no thanks to me, going to be labeled as a demonic miracle, so I didn't feel as if I fit into the tethered-human category, but I didn't feel like I belonged to the demons either. Where *did* I fit in this puzzle? I wasn't sure, but I was eager to ask Rebecca about her tethering process and was hopeful that I might meet other humans today.

Ugh…the celebration. Just how big of a shindig was this, anyway? Not knowing the number of people who would be in attendance was beginning to eat away at my nerves.

"I know she's got you covered with your day-to-day wear—" Aleena leaned in. "But if you need anything else, just let me know."

I raised an eyebrow at her and her look flattened. "Anything else?" It was unclear where she was going with this. "I'm not following."

She raised a brow, her arch was something to strive for. "If you need anything…underneath."

"Oh, I think we've got the essentials. I should be good." I offered a polite smile. One of the few measurements taken had been around my bust but not my rib cage. I still found that odd.

Aleena adjusted herself in her seat, a sly and mischievous smile crossing her lips. "If you need anything more *tempting*, just let me know."

My cheeks heated as I realized what she was referring to. I was screwing her brother, for crying out loud. This was awkward, right? It felt awkward.

"Or just keep it easy and be naked. What do I care? Just letting you know you have options." She downed the rest of her pink drink, obviously delighted by herself and the silent stupor she had put me in.

"Now—" She clapped her hands together. "What are we going to do with your hair?"

"Oh, um…" I grasped at the ends of it. "I'm not sure. I don't really know what to expect for today. I just know we're celebrating Kade's and my tethering."

"You call him Kade?" she asked as she set her glass down on the small gold-brushed table in front of us. Her facial features softened.

"I do." My voice wavered.

She nodded her head slightly, acknowledging the fact. Aleena leaned back into her chair, crossing one leg atop the other, revealing even more leg.

"I guess I've noticed everyone else here refers to him as Kadriel. He said it was alright though. Is it not?"

"No, no it's fine." She waved her hand, trying to dismiss the situation.

"What is it?" I pushed, wanting to know why she'd even brought it up in the first place. I didn't remember Kade hesitating when I'd asked if I could call him that. The sound of *Kade* on my tongue just sounded more natural than *Kadriel*.

"I just haven't heard anyone call him that since…well, no one has really called him Kade besides our mom." She picked at the hem of her robe, unable to look at me.

To say that the air left my lungs was a mild understatement. "I'm sorry. I had no idea. He never told me that."

Now that she'd mentioned this news, I would have to have a conversation with him about it. Did it bother him? Surely he would have told me if it did. He hadn't told me much about their parents, just that they had died by the hands of saints, and I didn't want to push him on the subject as I knew the wound of losing family all too well.

"He probably wouldn't." She smoothed the fabric over her toned leg and shook her head. "Never mind that. Let's start getting you ready."

She stood and I followed after without her needing to

beckon me, heading past the racks toward a door in the back that housed a room full of beauty products that were so orderly it looked like a high-end cosmetics store, enhanced by lighting that showed off all that was available and ripe for the picking. It didn't look like anything had ever been used here, unlike those cosmetic stores at the mall. Those samples out on display gave me the major ick factor.

Aleena put on some music while I took a seat on a hair-salon-type chair, and then she got to work. She ran her fingers through my hair, assessing it before breaking out a brush and curling iron.

I caught her mouthing the words to a song that was unfamiliar, but its beat had me tapping my toe as the melody moved into the chorus. It was a catchy tune that I found myself asking about, which then spiraled into an easy flowing conversation about music. The excitement she spewed about the subject made me realize for the first time that she and Kade really were brother and sister.

I was starting to see a familial resemblance, but I half wondered what her natural hair color was. I had to admit, the pink was a bold but awesome choice that really worked with her skin tone. I guess her complexion did kind of match Kade's, only hers was slightly darker.

"Are you tethered?" I asked her when our conversation fell flat, and she froze a moment before moving on to another strand of my hair.

She pursed her lips before shaking her head no. "Not tied down. I've got too many obligations."

And yet she was here doing my hair and helping me get ready for the day. I was grateful for the chance to get to know Kade's sister, even though she was giving mixed vibes. Given how much Kade had on his plate, I didn't know if I fully believed her. Not wanting to rustle any feathers, I diverted the conversation a bit.

"You're a seeker, right?"

"Oh, he really *has* mentioned me," she mused as she released a curl. "All bad things?"

"No, I promise." A small laugh left my throat.

"Oh, come on, do tell. What has my little brother spilled on me?"

"Not much. Just that you're an intimidating badass who he trusts with his life." I watched her reflection in the mirror as she smiled. I chose this moment as my chance to sway the conversation where I needed it to go. "In fact, it seems like you and Elias might be the only ones he trusts with his life."

Her face faltered for a fraction of a second before she recovered, and I knew I had struck a chord. "We three are close, I'll admit."

I decided to push a bit further and test the waters by bringing up yesterday's events. I didn't know in great detail what all had occurred, but I knew it wasn't good. Especially where Aleena was concerned. "I'm sorry about yesterday. I—I heard you were hurt."

Her perfectly pouty lips formed a thin line and she ran her fingers through my bouncy hair. "It was nothing Rafina and I couldn't fix."

At the mention of that name, my stomach began to turn. Kade had held Rafina in such high esteem before my transition, and I wondered if Aleena did as well. As much as I knew Kade could trust his sister, I didn't think she was aware of the full extent of the details from yesterday. At least, as far as my story was concerned.

"She seems to be really good at her job then." I crossed my legs and shifted in my seat. As of right now, the two people I didn't trust seemed to be in positions of power, and that worried me. Staffan appeared to be an annoyance to others, but Rafina was on a much higher pedestal. I had to tread carefully if I were to discuss either of them. "How long has she been a healer?"

A faint smile crossed Aleena's features and her whole body softened.

"A couple of centuries, at least." She began playing with the back of my hair, figuring out what she was going to do next. "I don't keep track."

My eyes almost bulged out of my skull. "You say that as if it's nothing. A couple of centuries?"

Aleena was entertained by my reaction. "Age isn't really an issue here."

My gaze fell to the floor. "That's what Kade said." Granted, when we were discussing it I had been disgusted by the fact that Damian was well over one hundred years old. But now that this was my world, the long life expectancy of demons was a concept I would have to learn to accept. They had immortality and shifting abilities on their side, after all. It was strange to think that this was my world now too.

Aleena began pinning up the top portion of my hair, giving volume but still maintaining the waves she had worked with ease. When she finished, she moved toward the assortment of makeup and began to peruse it, picking out a few items before returning to me.

She swiveled my chair away from the mirror and I came face-to-face with her. Her striking beauty hit me once again, and I wondered if she was self-made or if this was her real appearance, sans the hair. Kade had seemed put off by her choice in hair color today, which made me wonder just how often she switched things up.

"So if demons can shift at any time and change their appearance whenever they want, how can you keep track of who they are?"

"It's hard to explain, but it's a feeling you get when you're in their presence. The more you get to know someone and the more time you spend with them, you'll be able to pick up on it quicker." She began priming my face and retrieved a powder-blue sponge that she wet before squeezing it, making it plump up and double in size. "It's in the energy they give off."

My thoughts strayed to the day that Damian had showed up unannounced at my grandma's place, and the close proximity between him and Kade, which had me recalling his words regarding the situation.

"Kade said that something about Damian was familiar, so he could have met him before?"

Aleena nodded. "It's possible, but we don't exactly make it a habit to be in the presence of saints. So trying to pinpoint them is a whole other level of confusion. It doesn't help that they know, for the most part, how to avoid us and our ways of watching."

"Yet Kade knew I was working with one." The thought still angered me. Thinking that I knew someone, only for him to turn out to be somebody else entirely, with an agenda still unknown to us. I felt like my life had been a lie ever since he'd offered me a job opportunity. Was I just a pig being led to the slaughter the moment I accepted it?

Aleena scoffed. "When Kadriel figured that out, I thought he was going to go mad."

I cocked an eyebrow, silently urging her to go on.

"You don't know this, but four months ago he almost crossed over. He couldn't stand the fact that he couldn't keep tabs on you at work. What tipped him over the edge was when that saint gave you a ride home one day."

I knew the exact day she was referring to. I could clearly see myself in the passenger seat of Damian's massive truck, tint on the windows so dark that I didn't know how he avoided getting ticketed for it. The truck had smelled brand-new, as if it had just rolled out of a factory, and yet it was the only vehicle I had ever seen him drive.

My car had failed to start that day, and I found out later it just needed a new battery, but Damian had kindly offered to take me home so I didn't have to wait out in the cold for a ride from someone else. My other coworkers had already left by the time I'd made it out to my car, so Damian's offer was even more appealing at that point in time.

"But didn't he need my blood to release him?" My injured foot had brought him into my world and into my bedroom. While I knew he'd been in my world before, it was never with me.

"Yes. He can't interfere with your life until then. But he was willing to risk it all. He thought Damian might make a play on your life since you two were alone."

I had never feared the presence of my boss until Kade showed up. But knowing what I did now, I could only imagine the turmoil Kade had been through in the years spent watching me. Each innocent conversation, each outing when we casually ran into each other—was it all orchestrated for Damian's benefit? I could feel my skin heating with fury at his betrayal and secret agenda, but I couldn't let myself dwell on it.

"What stopped him?" I attempted to take deep and calming breaths, trying to focus on Aleena's pampering of my face.

"Me." She took a step back, almost defensive as she crossed her arms. I wasn't sure if she was expecting me to be mad at her admission or what.

"Oh?" I was curious about her reasoning for butting into that situation. Had Kade sought her opinion on the matter, or did she insert herself into it? If Kade was the only one who was allowed to watch me, how did she find herself involved at all?

"Just because I renounced my chance at the throne, it didn't mean I was about to let him throw it away."

"For some human?" I added before I could change my mind.

"It's not that." She dipped a brush into some rose-colored blush and swirled it a few times before returning to my face. "If Kadriel had crossed over and intervened, violating our rules, our family's ties to the throne would be gone."

All of this new information was interesting, and I wondered why this strong and beautiful woman before me would renounce the throne when it could have been hers. If she was the badass that Kade said she was, why wouldn't she want to rule? Why had that all fallen onto Kade's shoulders?

"So who would rule if Kade was unable to? Zan?" Surely he or his children were in line if Kade and Aleena were out of the equation.

"Uncle Zan filled in temporarily after the death of our parents, but he abdicated once Sarah was with child. He thought I might change my mind since I was older and able to tether. But once the decision was finally mine to make, he was less than thrilled when I said no to tethering and gaining the throne." There was a trace of annoyance in her voice as she spoke. Perhaps this was still a sore subject.

"You have to be tethered or request one in order to put yourself in line for the throne. And since my nephews are not of age and I have no plans of tethering, Staffan would be next in line." Her posture went rigid momentarily before pressing the blush to my cheeks.

I stilled as I let that sink in. I wanted to turn my nose up in repulsion that Staffan was even a consideration to lead Darthou. Regardless of who led, even though I didn't know the extent of their duties or reach here, I refused to believe that Staffan would be a better choice. Screams aside, there was something off about him, something unsettling. And even though Aleena seemed to speak fondly of Rafina, I believed both she and Kade were on the same side in their distaste for her other half.

"Knock, knock!" a voice called from the other room, grabbing our attention. Aleena rolled her eyes and backed away, placing the blush and brush down on the counter.

She strode out of the room at a brisk pace as the voice called for Rebecca, in a tone that sounded as if she were calling a servant. I rose from my chair to find who the voice belonged to, only to pause before entering the doorway as I heard Aleena's harsh voice cut through the music still floating through the air.

"She's busy."

"Of course. I'm just here to pick up my dress and then I'll be on my way." Even I could tell by her voice that she was a fake, from her delivery of words. It was blatantly obvious that Aleena had a disdain for her, and so far she was doing nothing to prove herself unworthy of it.

"You know where it's at, get it yourself," Aleena practically spat at the unknown woman. "Rebecca doesn't have to wait on you hand and foot."

"But what if she enjoys it?" I began to roll my eyes, just as Aleena had at her arrival. Was this chick for real? "Come on, I'm sure you loved it just as much when you were her apprentice."

"Fuck off."

Coming into view, I joined Aleena at her side, copying her stance with feet firmly planted and arms crossed. She exuded a strong presence in her stance even if she only wore a robe, and I wanted to help her in any way I could. That, and I wanted to put a face to the person that I already had problems with.

"Oh, you must be the lady of the day." Her caramel-colored skin had a bronze to it that was by no means natural, and the arrogance she wore was a strike against her that I could taste on her words. She wore a black winged eyeliner that made her eyes appear wider than I knew they were. It was an odd optical illusion.

Her dark brown hair was cut bluntly just above her shoulders, and her gold outfit made me think she might be part Egyptian or something. She looked like a damn model, and between her and Aleena, I felt like an ugly toad.

"Violet is your queen-to-be and you will address her as such." Aleena took a step forward, arms at her sides.

"Aw, that's cute."

I noted her defiance and joined Aleena, inserting myself into the conversation. "And who are you?" I stood my ground, well aware of my half-painted face as my eyes bored into hers.

"A throne chaser," Aleena interrupted. "She's had her sights set on Kadriel and me since we were kids. All she wants is power, and to make others think that she *is* power."

"Dimitra, I have your dress over here." Rebecca hurried in and retrieved a garment bag from a wall filled with them. I wasn't sure how she could decipher which belonged to who, as I didn't see a name on it and couldn't make out what kind of dress was inside the silver bag.

Dimitra held her arm up and to the side, waiting for Rebecca to place the hanger into her waiting hand. The fact that she wouldn't even look Rebecca in the eye or thank her for the garment didn't go unnoticed by me, and even though I didn't hear any screams to sway me in the direction of disliking her, her actions and words thus far spoke volumes. I knew she couldn't be trusted. Her lack of respect was something I wouldn't tolerate.

"I believe you were looking to thank her." I tried to remain cool, yet I was boiling beneath the surface as I spoke. Apparently, my words amused her.

"Was I?" She gleamed boastfully, as if she was better than everyone else in the room. "See you all later." She then left, just as quick as she had arrived, vanishing from view.

I turned to Aleena, shocked at how someone could be so unpleasant, insensitive, and downright rude. "Who the hell does she think she is?"

"She's a snake, and never let yourself be swayed otherwise."

"Now, Aleena, it's fine. I'm fine." Rebecca tried to defuse the room but I could see right through it. Deep down, I knew that it bothered her, but she clearly didn't want to cause a fuss.

"No, it's not. She walks all over you, and others. She has no right." Aleena was silenced as Rebecca approached her.

"Please, I'm fine. Don't give it another thought. Now, go finish with Violet. I'm almost done with her dress." She attempted to shoo us off before she turned to leave herself, disappearing into a doorway on the opposite side of the room.

I could tell Aleena was frustrated as she all but stomped her foot before taking off back toward the makeup room. I hurried after her, wanting to delve into this Dimitra bitch further. But once I saw Aleena's face, I could tell she was in a mood, so I pivoted, scrambling to find something else to talk about.

"Apprentice?" I stammered as I returned to my chair. "Have you worked with Rebecca?"

"Yeah, sort of. I guess." She busied herself with more makeup, probably more than she could possibly need. But I wasn't exactly a makeup guru myself, so how was I to know what all she intended to use? She had already applied more things to me than I used on a normal day.

When I could tell she was still hung up on our encounter with Dimitra, I took a beat to figure out my next line of questioning. I didn't really want to talk about myself. I felt boring compared to the world I'd been thrown into. For crying out loud—they had room service, could travel by mirrors, and could shift and change their appearance. What could I possibly have to offer that would measure up to that?

"I could tell by your room that you have a flair for design. Kade's bedroom is honestly kind of bland compared to yours."

That earned a small laugh from her, and her shoulders caved inward a bit. It was a nice break in the thick tension that had grown in the space we occupied. "Maybe you can get him to change things up in there. It is rather dull."

"And maybe you could help me," I followed. "So spill. Where did you come up with your taste and style? Any of that come from Rebecca?"

A fondness came over Aleena as she pursed her lips, contemplating how to begin. I remained still as she continued to work on my face, paying no mind to what colors or tools she was using. I brought all of my focus onto her and her words and the way she gushed about her love of fashion and design combined.

When she had met Rebecca as a child, she was stunned to learn that she'd been a seamstress in her life before her tethering. Aleena had latched onto her and together they kept up on the latest trends and styles, even creating their own parties to watch fashion shows and such that took place in my world. Rebecca taught her everything she knew about sewing and creating masterpieces from a single material, and it had blossomed into so much more.

Aleena eventually found herself creating lingerie in her spare time and found that avenue of interest to be what she most desired. It was from there that she took off on her own, and now she worked on her own pieces in her spare time, which it seemed she had too little of. Her love of creating and crafting was evident, and I found myself thrilled for her to have found joy in these things. I sensed a little entrepreneurial spirit in her.

"Well, should you ever have a spare moment for me, I would love to see your collection. Maybe even take you up on your earlier offer."

"You don't have to do that." She shook her head.

"No, I want to. I love that you have something you're so passionate about. Maybe I can even find something for myself." I beamed. I really was serious about seeing her collection and what she was up to now. In her time spent with Rebecca, I could see that their bond meant a lot to her. She really did have a softer side underneath her hardened exterior.

"Violet, I have about a dozen pieces in mind for you already. Your curves are just…" She imitated a chef's kiss and I could feel myself blushing.

Although I was damn proud of my body and its curves at times, there were other times when I still felt as if I wasn't enough. Wishing I was just a bit smaller around the waist, or my breasts were just down a cup size or my arms a little more toned. I could never rid myself of the negative thoughts for long before they came creeping back in. Self-doubt and the cruelty of others growing up had definitely taken a toll on me, and to this day I still struggled with it all.

"And I'm sure Kade was more than happy to get his hands on you. I have no idea how he resisted sex for as long as he did. Demon boys are just as horny as human boys, but for whatever reason he stayed the course. Waiting."

"Did he ever date anyone while he watched me?"

Aleena's head snapped up, her gaze meeting mine as her hand paused before the new brush could meet my face. "Definitely not."

It was nice hearing that he hadn't, but then there was that guilt again. Guilt about all the guys I had dated over the span of those six years.

"It's weird to think about it. Him waiting," I began, unsure of just how much I should be confiding in his sister. "Obviously, I didn't know about Kade yet, but knowing that he held out for me while I fumbled and failed in relationship after relationship is just…well, it makes me feel like shit."

Aleena grinned. "I could always tell when you had a boyfriend. Damn brother of mine went from sulking to douchebag, real quick."

That, I could imagine. Kade had admitted that seeing me with other men was difficult, and I knew if the roles had been reversed, I wouldn't have been in a good mood about it either.

"No dates or anything?" I wasn't sure why I was still pushing for clarification. I already felt crappy enough.

She toyed with a thought in her head and I half wondered if she was going to try and sugarcoat anything for him. "He hung out with a few people. Dimitra even, once—but it was never anything serious. The moment they tried to make a move, he dropped them so fast it was like their heads spun with the speed of it all.

"I can't tell you how many have practically thrown themselves at him, but he has a steady will that I've never seen before. Probably why he was so damn grumpy all of the time. Hard to figure out who just wants to be friends and who wants you for your throne."

That statement made Kade's life seem even more lonely. Perhaps that was why he kept Aleena and Elias so close, because they were the only ones who didn't try to get anything else out of him. It was kind of sad, but I supposed anyone with any kind of line to royalty might have troubles like that.

"Were you surprised that he found a human? That he requested me?"

She shook her head. "No. That never bothered me. Felt kind of premature, sure. But once he sets his sights on something, he can be a beast to deal with. He wasn't going to take a no from the council or anybody else regarding you. And there was definitely pushback."

"Seems like this council is more problematic than it's worth." The council had yet to be in my good graces. Zan was the only one I even cared about at this point.

"Ha! You have no idea."

She clapped her perfectly manicured hands together as she took a step back. Seeming pleased by her finished work, she turned my chair so I could take a look in the lighted mirror. I felt as if I'd been airbrushed to perfection and photoshopped into a magazine. I was speechless, to say the least. And when I found her eyes searching mine for a reaction of some sort, I stood.

"Thank you," was all I could mutter. I didn't know if I had ever felt more beautiful. And I looked like me, but at the same time I didn't. It was a strange sensation, as I had never been this dolled up before. All I could think to do was hug her, and she stiffened. I had the sense that Aleena might not be the affectionate type, so I slowly backed away, offering an apology for my response.

"It's fine. I'm glad you like it." She waved it off and ushered me from the room and through the door where Rebecca had disappeared earlier.

She came into view along with numerous mannequins, but the one she was currently stationed at took my breath away. Not only was the mannequin shaped like my body type, but the dress itself was a sight that I didn't know I needed to see. Never had I worn—let alone seen—an article of clothing that was specifically made for me and my figure, and I was stunned in the best way.

"I'll be back shortly." Aleena disappeared before I could say anything, vanishing at my side as I gaped at the dress before me.

It was a floor-length gown with a dangerously low V-neck that stopped a few inches below the breasts. The straps were narrow and almost see-through. Black appliqués were placed strategically across the upper half of the dress, with a red backing. The black bled down into the A-line of the skirt, just barely skimming the floor.

When she turned the mannequin, the dress shimmered beneath the lightning, almost like minuscule diamonds were embedded into the fabric, remaining invisible until they were illuminated. I hadn't known what I would be wearing to the celebration, but I certainly hadn't expected anything like this.

"Is it to your liking?" Rebecca asked as she closed the door behind me.

"It's absolutely beautiful." The piece looked like it would have taken months to make, but yet here it stood before me.

I heard a nagging voice in my head, terrified that it

wouldn't work out. That she had gone through all of this work for me, for nothing. Up until today, nobody from Darthou had ever dressed me or taken any measurements. There was a reason I never bought clothes online. I needed to try them on before buying, because of my body shape. I hated having to return things when they didn't work out.

"What if it doesn't fit?" I asked timidly, barely able to meet her eyes. If this dress didn't fit, I might cry.

Rebecca's face crinkled slightly as a smile crossed her features. "My dear, I've been doing this for quite some time. It will fit."

CHAPTER 8

Kade

My mood soured the moment Aleena vanished with Violet. Knowing our shared connection was taking root and growing, I had been careful to guard my emotions, fielding them off in fear that they might transfer onto or literally into her.

Violet hadn't mentioned anything about any nightmares that might have plagued her last night, the gripping panic that had held her in a sweaty and frightened state. I didn't want to bring anything up in case she didn't remember any of it. No sense in stirring up any more problems than we already had.

I had an inkling that she truly didn't remember any of it, judging by the mood she had been in since she had awoken. I myself had woken up shortly after she decided to start down the hallway. I let her indulge in her exploration while I ordered some breakfast and dressed.

After all, this was her home now too. Although, this wasn't supposed to be her only one.

Fists balling, I took off for Elias's apartment where instead of any pleasantries, I was soon banging on his door and demanding his attention. My composure was slipping and I could feel my face cracking.

It wasn't supposed to be this way. The life Violet wanted had been torn away. Her fucking *life* had been ripped from her, and someone had yet to pay for it.

I beat on the door again, not bothering with our little code of a rhythm we used for one another. When I reached for a fourth strike against the wood, the door swung open to reveal my best friend, and I brushed past him before he could get a word out. I barely had time to catch a glance of his "what the fuck" face as I made a beeline for his watching quarters.

"Take it you haven't found him yet, since I haven't heard from you." My voice sounded far more bitter than I meant for it to, and I knew he shouldn't get the brunt of my anger, but I was too close to blowing off my top at this point to care.

Elias was on my heels, but ready to take on my mood anyhow. The man had seen me at my best and worst moments. The fact that he had stuck by me through it all, and never wavered or backed down, was a true testament to the bond we shared.

He was like a brother I'd never had. We'll just choose to ignore that he occasionally fucked my sister.

"It's not like I'm not trying, Kadriel."

Hands on my hips, I came to a stop in front of his mirrored wall. It was much like my own, only the glass surfaces here were in a bit more pristine condition. Granted, his apartment and mirrors were newer, so that was a lot of it.

I rolled my neck, trying to release the tension building, but it wasn't working. There was an unsettling ball of rage forming in my gut and radiating outward. If I didn't get this under control, it was going to pass onto Violet and that was *not* okay.

There was so much that we still needed to discuss, but I was being pulled in a million different directions. I wanted nothing more than to be focused on my future queen, but I had a council breathing down my neck, a saint stirring shit up, and an unknown and troublesome issue between Violet, Rafina, and Staffan. And on top of all of that, Violet's murderer had apparently vanished into thin air. No wonder I was fucking losing it.

"Have you petitioned the council on that guy in Dubuque yet?" I turned to him and crossed my arms, fists clenching again.

Elias zeroed in on me, an unease crossing over his pale features. "Why do you ask?"

"Where is he now?" I questioned further, keeping my poker face in place.

"No." He saw right through me, and I fought to keep my composure. "I know what you're thinking, and no."

"You haven't talked to them yet, good." I turned away, swiping at the closest mirror, a large one that was almost the size of me. Recalling the vehicle I had last seen that murderer in, I brought it up, only to find it empty.

My nostrils flared, not knowing where to look next. I was well aware that Elias was going to attempt to talk me down, so I wasn't going to give him the opportunity.

I placed my palm to the mirror and changed my appearance as quickly as I passed through and into a muggy, humid, and sunny Iowa day. Turning my head to the left and right, I scanned across the parking lot to make sure no one had seen a six-foot-two man just pop out of thin air.

Donning a pair of brown eyes, sandy blond hair, and a darker complexion, I looked into the vehicle that had been used in the kidnappings of several young women, all of whom had met their demise shortly after coming in contact with their rapist and executioner.

I should have done my surveillance beforehand, and I was well aware that this was a rash decision. But here I was, going after a human this time, not a saint.

"Kadriel," Elias hissed as he appeared before me. "Are you fucking mad?"

I stared at him for a beat before cocking my head to the side. "Yep."

Brushing past him again, I began to make my way up to a worn and tattered apartment building that looked more like a drug house. Broken shutters, chipping red paint, and the cracked and broken stairs leading up to the door were clear indicators of the wreck that awaited us inside. I already knew the filth I was walking into was going to require another shower, and as soon as I stepped foot past the beaten white door, I was met with a smell that caused my nose to scrunch.

Cat pee, mold, and garbage. Fucking nasty. This place was uninhabitable and should be marked for demolition.

I eyed the mail slots to my right, hoping there might be some names attached to the numbered slots, but when those failed me, my head whipped in Elias's direction. He'd only bothered to turn his hair a darker blond and brought out the whites of his eyes.

"Which one?" I kept my voice low as a man's raised voice echoed down the hall. He was yelling at someone and his words were slurred. I knew he wasn't the one I was looking for, but judging by his tone, I deduced that he was a piece of shit.

So help me if he was getting ready to attack someone, I might be inclined to pay him a visit too.

"Think about this." Elias's frustration was evident as he tried to get me to change my mind.

"Which. One," I repeated, trying to make my breaths shallow. I didn't know what would be worse, inhaling these disgusting fumes through my nose or allowing them to enter in through my mouth. Did it even matter at this point?

"Three B," he mouthed, growing more and more pissed by the second.

"Thank you," I said. But before I took off down the hall, I swiveled back to meet him. "Now, are you going to seek, or do you want plausible deniability?"

His lips tightened, and I swore I could see the wheels turning in his head.

This. This was what we talked about so often. Ridding this world of evil before too many lives were lost. This murderer was just one of many who had lived for far too long. Too many lives had already been taken by his hands, and we had to fucking ask for permission to snuff him out before he took any more. He was beyond any kind of redemption at this point. Causing more and more harm, the longer he lived.

"Fucking fuck," Elias muttered, losing out on the war he was fighting. He took off down the hall and I couldn't help the crazed grin that swept over my face. I knew I looked like a madman at this point, and I couldn't care less.

Following him, I realized we had entered the decrepit apartment building from the back side. The B rooms were to my right and descending in number, and just as we passed the halfway point we arrived at the door of the lucky man of the hour. I was disgusted by how accustomed I was growing to the repulsive smells and stained carpet lining the hall. There were spills on the walls and a light flickering at the end from a bulb that was getting ready to go out. I noted that the yelling man had ceased his tangent, and zeroed in on the door before us.

Pity, I thought. We could have had a bit more fun with another poor sap to take.

With a snap of the doorknob, Elias broke in and didn't even hesitate to cross through the threshold. There was a visible layer of scum on the linoleum, and replacing the cat piss was the smell of rotten food.

As I closed the door behind me, Elias waited for me to join him. The dated kitchen looked like it was from the seventies. The barely visible yellow countertops housed boxes and cartons of to-go food containers and bags, flies swarming about them. I eyed the peeling wallpaper of green and orange tomatoes on the vine. Mold spores were evident, their growing splotches enough to get this place condemned.

People actually paid money to live in this filth?

Elias began to move through the kitchen, not even flinching as a fly zipped by him, taking a left through a narrow hall. The floors barely groaned as we moved almost silently into a bedroom that had dirty clothes strewn about and a mattress with only a sheet beneath a man who was passed out cold. There was a steady stream of drool seeping out of his mouth and onto the mattress that belonged in a dump. Better yet, this whole building just deserved to be torched.

Letting myself shift back into my normal form, I stared at the man. Adrenaline was beginning to surge through my veins. I needed to punish *someone* for everything that was out of control and going wrong with my life since my failures yesterday.

I sneered as I took a step forward, joining Elias at his side as we watched the man sleep. Blissfully unaware of our presence and the end he was about to meet. Trying to decide just what kind of punishment to inflict on him—now, that was half the fun.

But we didn't have time on our side. Not with the tethering celebration drawing so close.

Fuck.

"I can't do it." The words flew out of my mouth before I could stop them. My teeth came down on my tongue until I could taste my own blood.

Elias gawked at me, voice hushed so as to not wake the man before us. "What the hell do you mean?"

My head swayed in disappointment with the realization that hit like a swift strike to the jaw.

"Violet," I muttered as I stole a glance at the arm that had tied us together. *Tethered* our lives and entwined our futures around one another. "I can't risk her sensing it."

His brows rose in understanding. "You can feel her?"

I nodded slowly. "At times, yes. I haven't even had a chance to talk to her in detail yet about what being a demon tethered to a demon entails. And to make matters worse, she's getting ready with Aleena right now. Last thing I need is Violet alerting her." As much as I wanted to actively participate in this man's demise, I couldn't risk Violet and what she might encounter if I did.

Elias nodded slowly, letting that information sink in before a sinister grin began to form as he relaxed into his normal chosen appearance. I soon matched him, knowing full well what was running through his mind and appreciating the fact that we were finally on the same page.

"Seems a waste to come this far and not see things through," he muttered as he turned away to face the sad excuse of a man before us.

I took a step back, delighting in the fact that Elias was stepping up when I couldn't. It might not be the death I wanted to truly witness, but for now, it would have to make do.

"Then by all means, don't let me ruin a good time."

I emerged from the shower now clean of the grime from that crummy apartment building. Now if only I could rid my memory of the smell of that place, I would be a lot better off.

I had taken way too much joy in watching Elias end him. His death was a bit quicker than I would have liked, considering his crimes against women, but we didn't exactly have time on our side.

Elias had taken off to get himself cleaned up, and then he and his father were going to take on the task of finding out what the hell had happened to Brett.

First him…then Damian.

Sauntering out from the bathroom, I ran my towel over my head a bit too rough in the hopes of catching any more streams and drips. I fished a few items out of my closet, not concerning myself with what I picked out, since I was just going to have to change into the garments Rebecca had chosen for the big day. She was going to have my clothes delivered to my uncle's place, and I was going to get ready there.

I wasn't the type of guy to get all dressed up. Hell, I remembered Zan and Sarah's tethering celebration, when I'd thrown a fit in the suit that had been tailored to fit my small frame at the time. It was too restricting and too proper.

I also recalled losing my temper when told that Elias

wasn't able to sit with us at the head table. When I had tried to sneak away to join him and his family, my mother took me to the side of the room, and while she didn't scold me, she pretty much laid down the law as gently as she could.

Funny how that little encounter with my mom was one of the few memories of her I had left. Her long hair had been piled atop her head in an updo that had to have taken hours to complete. I remembered the long gown she'd worn that my dad complimented as soon as he laid eyes on her, and her shy reaction to his words. I had never known a time when my mom and dad weren't in love. I couldn't even recall them ever having a fight. Sure, they exchanged words at times, but they always seemed to work things out.

It was the same for Zan and Sarah. Although they didn't always agree, you could see that their affection for each other never wavered. Their bonds were as strong as the cords that bound them together.

And now I hoped to have that same thing with Violet.

Staring down at my arm, I imagined the blackened cord that had dissolved into my skin. A link between us and growing. It was exciting and overwhelming all at the same time. There was so much I wanted to show her, to teach her, to experience with her. Now, we would have nothing but time.

Collecting my pocket mirror from the bed, I summoned Zan to make sure he was ready for my arrival. The moment his face filled the glass, I left for his home before I could even return his greeting.

Already clad in his attire, he gave me a look that stalled me for a moment. Not only because of his demeanor, but because of his resemblance to my departed father. He was classed up in formal wear with his hair fixed neat, and I suspected there was some gel coming into play.

"You're late," he announced, as if I didn't already know.

Zan's watching quarters were much like my own in size, but not decked out in sports memorabilia like Elias's. His area was more relaxed and lived-in, never shying away from letting Sarah or the kids come and go as they pleased as long as he was present. There was a section in the corner with bean bag chairs and a couple chests full of toys for their sons, and even a little reading nook for Sarah beside them.

Zan really needed to get with the program and go digital, though. He was one of a few who still preferred paper over electronics. The heaps of paper on his desk made their way across his table. There were various books thrown into the mix here and there, possibly research related.

While my uncle used to be a watcher, his talents seemed to get him pulled in various different directions now that he was on the council. Because of that, he didn't have very many humans to look after. Which was a good thing, considering you never knew when the kids were going to come flying in here with their latest creations or gadgets.

Laying eyes on the garment bag that was slung over one of the chairs at the table, I began slipping my feet from my shoes and removing the shirt I had literally just put on. I hadn't wanted to chance appearing half-naked in front of my aunt or cousins, not knowing what I was popping into.

"Kadriel," he implored, trying to gather my attention as I removed my sweats and began shrugging on the dress pants that were creased so sharp I swore they could stand on their own.

I waited until they were fastened around my waist before I met his gaze.

"Uncle." I crossed my arms as if a few more seconds without this over-the-top ensemble could save my sanity.

"Is everything alright with Violet? With the both of you?" He took a step forward, concern etched across his features. His suit jacket had some similarities to my own, only his was more refined and subtle with its mix of grays and blacks.

"Yes." I nodded, a small lift coming to the corner of my lips. "I can feel her, Zan."

"Already?" He took another step forward. I knew he would never be able to share this kind of connection with Sarah. It wasn't possible through their demon-to-human tethering.

I looked down at my arm, still just as amazed at my bare arm as I was just moments ago.

Bobbing my head once more, I lowered my arm. "It was so subtle at first, I didn't even realize it was happening."

Zan studied me for a moment, but didn't convey whatever was going on inside his head. He cleared his throat before offering me a pat on my shoulder.

"You don't realize how lucky you are, Kadriel."

"Doesn't feel like it most days," I offered, reflecting on my losses as of late. Violet shouldn't have died in the first place. That, I would never be able to forgive myself for.

"Violet is persistent. A strong-willed woman who will find her place amongst us. I still can't fathom how Obsidian Falls brought her back, but there must be a reason."

What Violet didn't know, what I had yet to tell her, was that Zan had been watching Violet long before I was. Shortly after the accident that had claimed her parents and brother, Zan had found her. Escaping death in that horrible car crash had already put her on our radar, and undoubtedly, that of the saints as well. Then, in her teen years, I had the privilege of laying eyes on her for the first time.

I had been dipping my toes into the waters of watching, taking on my first few humans to watch, and Zan had been an integral part of my learning.

I could see her so clearly, curled up into a ball at the back of a bus with tears streaming down her face. Her gaze out the window, a blank stare with unblinking eyes. The oversized charcoal hoodie she wore was pulled up over her head and her hair was cascading down her chest, longer than it was now.

A part of me recognized that look. Empathized with her. Like the world was falling onto your shoulders while your life was crumbling at the same time. Not knowing why you kept on living, and wondering what was the point of it all when you just couldn't find it in yourself to be happy. To *find* happiness in anything. Just going through the motions of everyday life to make others think you had your shit together.

When you didn't, and you were far from it.

It was strange, how a single look from her drew me in. At first, I visited Zan more often, hoping for glimpses of her. Then, I began planning my schedule around hers. Knowing that she was still in school provided a new sense of structure to my day. My uncle was quick to catch on, noting how attached I was becoming.

And once I found out that she had tried to take her own life, I asked him if I could take her on as one of my charges.

There was pushback, of course. But when I told him of my intent to put in a request for a tethering, Zan knew just how serious I was. And instead of brushing it off as some sort of infatuation, some phase I would grow out of, both he and Sarah eventually came to support me.

I ate lunch with Violet when she was all alone at a table in her high school cafeteria. I read with her as she stayed up way too late, lost in a book and unable to close its pages. I took notes, obsessing over those who lied and toyed with her. My hit list grew quickly, faster than the doodles in her notebook over men she dreamed about. If I hadn't had my uncle looming over my shoulder and constantly checking in, I knew I would have done something stupid to come to her defense.

When Violet thought she had no other friends around, I had been there for her, whether she knew it or not. I cared for her long before I had ever imagined a life *with* her.

My obsession with her was an unhealthy one, that I knew. I had recognized it long ago.

"Kadriel."

I shook my head, blinking away my abrupt trip down memory lane.

"Sorry, what?" I removed the tank that I would wear beneath my vest and slipped it on over my head before Zan repeated the words that were lost somewhere in the air.

"I asked if she had heard the screams at all since yesterday?"

I shook my head as I tucked the fabric into the waist of my pants before gathering the vest and undoing its buttons at the front. It was sleek and structured, some kind of boning in the lining of it. Just great. I thought I had asked Rebecca to downplay my outfit and try to keep it as comfortable as possible.

"No, thankfully. But I suspect she might experience them again today." I was soon closing the vest and groaning as I had to stiffen my back. That jacket wasn't going to be any better than this. I rolled my eyes just thinking about shoving my arms into the black sleeves with intricate red swirls spiraling out.

"Has she given you any more information about them? Was it one? More than?"

My head shook again in denial. "She said screams, as in plural."

"Hm…" He thought to himself, his jacket barely creasing as he shifted his position. "Any chance it was her own screams?"

I blinked up at him, considering his words for a moment.

"Violet went through something traumatic."

"No shit," I shot back, both in annoyance at his statement and at this damn costume I was going to have to wear all day. It probably belonged in some sort of period drama. I knew Rebecca had poured her heart into dressing us all, it was a task she took to heart and enjoyed. Hell, the woman had been dressing me my entire life, but it still irked me that I had to get all dressed up for this.

Just because our bloodline was pure demon, that didn't make me weigh myself above the rest of the demons—and humans—of Darthou. King-to-be was merely a new title I would wear. And I would do that in a fucking T-shirt and jeans from now on. Now, if only I could convince everyone to let me wear that for the coronation.

"Kadriel," Zan scolded. He never did like it when I used language around him. Mainly because he was afraid his children would pick up unneeded words. But last I checked, the door was closed, and I knew he muttered a few curses from time to time as well.

"If and when Violet experiences them again we can try to ascertain the facts from there."

"But the longer we wait—"

"I know!" My voice boomed through the enclosed space and I struggled to keep my head up and level with him. He, Sarah, and I had every right to be concerned. This situation, Violet's situation, was uncharted territory. Zan had told me point-blank last night about how worried and uneasy Sarah had been after witnessing Violet shrink to the ground with screams that no one else could hear.

The very fact that Rafina had left, removing herself from

the infirmary before figuring out what in the hell was wrong, was unusual in itself. I had never known her to back down or fucking disappear without figuring out what the hell was going on.

Unless, she already knew.

The very thought threatened any chance I had left of a good mood. I closed my eyes for a beat, trying to settle the bubbling anger threatening to surface.

My uncle and I were silent as I poorly attempted to put on my shoes. Their leather was as unforgiving as the rest of this getup. I stood and gave my head a shake, feeling the strands of my wavy hair drying and becoming lighter atop my head.

"I'll meet you there," I said as I grabbed the jacket and threw it over my arm. "I have something I have to take care of real quick."

Zan eyed me warily, then took a deep breath before he closed in and set his hand on my shoulder once more. His face softened, a warmth to his eyes that I rarely saw.

"I know things haven't turned out exactly as we had anticipated, especially as of late, but…" His eyes swept the floor before meeting mine. "Remember that you're not in this alone. Your parents would be proud of this moment, and of you."

I wanted to shrink away from him, pained by all of the things in my life my parents had missed in the past, present, and future.

"Thank you," I mumbled, before leaving his watching quarters and appearing in the infirmary. The ghost of his hand on my shoulder was a heavy touch that lingered on in the moments that followed.

Taking a moment to collect and rein in my emotions, I glanced about the room, making sure it was empty. Practically everything could be seen from my position at the front, right next to the very slab that Violet had passed away on. I bit down the emotion that took hold in my throat, trying to prepare myself for company.

As if I had beckoned her by my thoughts alone, Rafina appeared in my periphery. A lengthy gown dragged slightly behind her and hugged her body while being modest at the same time. Her hair was down and swayed slightly as she approached, a look of apprehension on her face.

"Everything alright, Kadriel? Is it Violet?"

I kept my face calm and void of any expression, choosing to not acknowledge that I knew what had transpired in this very room when she was in Violet's presence.

"Well, I'm hoping you might be able to help me locate her necklace. She can't seem to find it, and I was pretty sure she was wearing it when I brought her in."

I knew she had been wearing it when I had last seen her, pulling her body down into the black waters of Obsidian Falls. But the necklace, along with the clothes she had been wearing, was missing. Undoubtedly her clothes had met their end, but her necklace should have survived it all.

"Ah, yes." She held up a finger as she bent at the knees, pulling out a drawer beneath the slab. I could hear the chain as she fetched the item from its spot out of my sight. She held out her hand, nails painted in a pale pink as she turned her wrist and released the black bar into my hand. I tucked the necklace into my pocket, noticing the absence of blood on it, as if it had already been cleaned thoroughly.

Offering her my thanks, I began to back away, but Rafina was quick to come around the slab and draw me to a halt before I could vanish.

"Did everything go alright with your tethering and consummation?"

Prior to yesterday, I wouldn't have thought much of her question. Now, I was second-guessing her and wondering if there was an underlying meaning to her words.

"Everything went well. Thank you."

"I'd like to see her again, once the celebration is over. Our time was cut short, and I didn't get to welcome her as I would have liked to."

"Well, we will be at the celebration. I'm sure you won't be able to miss us." I offered a small grin. Fat chance I was going to let Violet be alone with Rafina anytime soon. I was already apprehensive about what would happen to Violet when in attendance at the party. The thought had already occurred that Rafina and Staffan might not be the only ones who brought out the screams in her mind.

"I know." She smiled shyly, brushing some hair back behind her ear. "But I'm sure you can understand that Violet has had a remarkable return from death. I would like the chance to check in with her. Make sure she's doing alright."

Rafina was coming off as genuine as they come, and if she was hiding anything, she was damn good at it.

"Let's just get through today. Then, maybe we can work something out."

"Alright." She bowed her head, her tucked hair falling forward once more as she disappeared.

My eyes squinted at the spot on the wall where she had once stood, my mind going a million different directions. Concocting multiple scenarios, possible betrayals, and hidden agendas that could be at play here.

Of all the demons, Rafina would be the one who I would least suspect of doing such a thing. But perhaps that was what made it so much easier for her to slide under the radar, undetected.

CHAPTER 9

Violet

Aleena soon returned, dressed to kill. She wore stilettos that didn't seem humanly possible to walk in, sleek black pants tailored and pressed to the hills, and a fitted jacket that revealed a lace corset of some sort beneath. Everything she wore was different shades of black, her hair the only vibrant accent to her ensemble. But what really caught my eye was what she wore upon her hands—metal fingertips, each one with a nail about an inch long, connected by chains that disappeared into the sleeves of her jacket. She caught my gaze and grinned.

"How do I look?" She spun around, letting me bask in the glory that she was, and I could tell she was loving the attention.

"Lethal. And sexy as hell." I blinked at her.

"And you…" She circled around me and poked the center

of my back with a metal fingertip, causing me to straighten. "Keep your head held high."

I inhaled as much as the dress would allow as she came back into view again.

"You look fucking amazing." If she was going to be my hype woman for today, she was doing it well, even though my nerves were beginning to gather and rise, making themselves known.

"Language, Aleena," Rebecca scolded as she returned from changing herself. I couldn't help but notice that we were all clad in shades of black. For a day of celebration, it seemed as if we were dressed more for a glorified funeral. "I'm glad we went with the appliqués. You were right."

That little crumb of information didn't go unnoticed. "You both worked on this?" I asked as I turned to look at myself in the mirror again. My palms gently smoothed down the material on my hips, and the movement revealed a slit that went about thigh high, but soon hid itself again amidst the fabric.

Aleena shrugged it off but Rebecca spoke up. "We did. And I must say, we make a good team." She beamed proudly up at Aleena who was practically towering over her now. Both Sarah and Rebecca, the only humans I had met so far, seemed short compared to the demons I had found myself in the presence of. Was there something in demon genes that made them taller, or was it a choice that was made by shifting? Perhaps it was only a coincidence.

"Well, thank you to the both of you then. I don't know how I can ever pay you for this masterpiece, it belongs in some fashion show or on a red carpet."

The two exchanged a glance and I got the feeling I was missing something. I raised an eyebrow, wanting to be clued in on their amusement.

"Oh my dear, you don't owe us anything," Rebecca responded.

"But—"

"Nope." Aleena held her hand up to silence me. "Come. I'm sure Kadriel is getting stir-crazy with you being out of his sight for so long."

I managed a quick goodbye and thanks to Rebecca before I found myself in a small and cozy room. There were candles lit about the place, a few chairs, and no windows. It was more like a closet in size. Maybe a walk-in closet, but still. I thought a California king bed would take up the entire space.

"Just sit tight, he'll be here shortly." And she left before I could object.

Was I ever going to get used to people popping in and out in the blink of an eye? Did I need to ask them to do me the courtesy of letting me know before they zapped me into another setting? And how did everyone stay in shape around here when they could just teleport to any place they wanted to go? Did they even have to work for it, or did their shifting abilities take care of it all for them? The questions nagged at me, and now that I was alone with my thoughts, I was getting anxious about what the rest of the day might hold.

Just how many would be present for this celebration? What was my role to play besides being introduced to countless faces I had never met, both demon and human? I began biting the tip of my thumb, drowning in my own worries as they rose to abnormal levels along with my heartbeat.

"Are you alright?"

I whipped around at the sound of Kade's voice as I grabbed at my chest. "Christ, you guys should wear bells or something when you do that." Even though I was annoyed by his sudden appearance, it did help with the nerves just having him near. I shook out my hands as if I could shake it all away, and Kade stepped in closer, retrieving them in his.

"You're worried," he stated, and not as a question.

Anybody and their dog would be able to deduce that. I was freaked, and on the verge of becoming terrified before he popped in.

"I can feel it." He kissed the back of my hand as my eyes searched his.

"How?" Maybe he was just reading my body language, because I felt like a trainwreck, even though my face was painted to perfection and I was wearing this gorgeous dress that I never could have imagined myself in.

His eyes searched mine as if he was studying me. "As soon as I showed up, it felt as if it was washing over me. Like waves coming off of you."

"The…tethering?" I asked as I released his hands and crossed my arms beneath my breasts. It made them bulge forward against their fabric confines. I caught Kade's glance at them and found a bit of amusement in his temporary lust.

Kade only offered a slight nod of his head in confirmation.

"Great." I shook my head. "Not only can you experience my strange phantom pains, but you're an empath now." If he could feel this, what else could he feel? Was I no longer allowed the privacy of my own inner turmoil?

"Wait, just…relax."

I shot him an exasperated look. There was no way to relax, especially when I wished to flee right about now. Why couldn't I meet the people of Darthou one at a time?

"Just close your eyes and let your mind go blank." His voice was pleading and soft as I let out an irritated puff of laughter, shaking my head.

Reluctantly, I did as he said, freezing in my stance and closing my eyes.

"Now…take a deep breath. Focus on what's surrounding you."

I did as he said and could sense peace flooding through me as I exhaled slowly. I could feel my body sag, my lips parting as I let it course through me, consuming me.

"What do you feel?" he asked, and I knew this was the very sensation he was just referring to. It came off from his direction in droves, over and over again, radiating through the air.

"Calm," I said with my next exhale. My worries were melting away as I let the feeling take over. It amazed me that this seemed to work both ways. We could feel each other, but to what extent?

"Keep them closed." He could have been inches from my face now, as I noted the faint breeze of his breath.

What I hadn't expected was for the waves to shift, starting to come from behind me to my right. I turned in that direction, eager to feel the comfort he provided. But there was something else thickening the air. A change that was taking root, and I found myself heating up. A warmth spread over my skin like I was standing in front of a small fire. It soon converted into a minimal blaze that had my heart picking up its pace, and I clenched my thighs to suppress the need that was blooming.

"Kade." I was breathless as I spoke his name, overcome with a desire that only he could satisfy. My knees buckled and he was there, steadying me. I met his eyes with an equal intensity as our breaths mingled in our closeness. My hands smoothed over his regal attire, a black suit ensemble that was trimmed with a red to match the color infused into my dress. I wanted to fist the fabric of the lapels in my hands and bring his lips to mine, but the fabric hardly caved to my touch. It broadened his shoulders and his overall stature, making him appear larger than I knew him to be.

"You look deliciously mouthwatering." He grazed my lips as his body pressed into mine.

"You sound like you're going to eat me," I teased, trying to push him away for fear of him ruining my makeup that Aleena had worked so hard on.

His head dipped down into the crook of my neck, softly planting a kiss before I felt his words against my skin. "Maybe I will later."

I held my breath as images of him between my legs made my temperature rise and soar through the roof. My back bent, curving my spine as I pressed away from him enough to look him in the face.

Vibrations surged between us, mingling until they clashed, and I swore to whatever holy entity I was supposed to be praying to now that I wouldn't pass out from the intensity of it. His hand found the opening of my dress, skimming my bare thigh in taunting strokes as my lips parted. I was so turned on, body on high alert at every point where our bodies touched, that I might detonate the moment his fingers found their way to my center.

Our eyes never left one another, searching and waiting. It was almost a test to see who would look away first, but neither of us were willing to budge. The vulnerability that came from Kade watching me watch him, almost—

"You had better not be messing up my masterpiece," Aleena's voice chimed, right as a fist met the door.

I jumped away from Kade, separating us. I felt as if I needed to walk into a giant freezer to put out the fire that was running rampant in me, although that was quickly replaced with the remembrance of those damn knocks. The horror that had come into my life just moments after experiencing them. My heart was in my throat, threatening to cut off my air supply.

I struggled to breathe, my body shuddering as shots began to riddle my body again. I backed into the wall, tears springing to my eyes as I jerked two times as if I could avoid them, but I failed. I fought against the impact, trying to focus on the present. I wasn't in my apartment anymore. I wasn't staring at a madman who had his gun fixated on me. For now I was safe, and far, far away from Brett.

Bracing myself on the wall with my palms, I saw Kade hunched over and gasping for air just as Aleena came barging in. The click of her heels sounded more distant than she truly was. I gripped at my chest, trying to still my heart that was trying to jump ship and kill me.

"You two can fuck all you want later, they're ready." The look of annoyance melted from her face as she began to examine the states we were in. "Are you guys alright? What the hell happened?"

Kade groaned as he stood, his affliction still evident on his face as he inhaled, shakily. "They can wait."

"What the—"

"Not now, Aleena. Just give us a damn minute." Kade's agitation was quick to cut her off. I figured she had another curse word on the tip of her tongue, but that didn't stop her from shooting daggers with her eyes.

God, Aleena could look really fucking scary. As beautiful as she was, she had a deadly air about her that chilled my bones with a single look.

When Aleena's lethal stare met mine, my mouth was spilling an explanation before I even had a chance to think it through.

"Kade can feel what I can feel."

Her eyes narrowed, but other than that, she remained unmoving.

"It's like I'm being shot, all over again," I wheezed. The air rushing through caused more pain to my chest but I pressed on. "Kade can feel it too."

She nodded as if in understanding, but it was subtle. "What triggered it?"

"The knocking." Kade stood, straightening his back and smoothing out his jacket even though there wasn't a crinkle or crease in sight. He was in front of me within two steps, taking my hands in his and rubbing the backs with his thumbs. The tranquility that came from his touch had me peeling myself from the wall. I closed my eyes, focusing on that small act and concentrating on the rise and fall of my chest.

"Was that it?" he questioned me, and all I could do was offer a small bob of my head.

"No knocking from here on out, got it." Aleena's voice was faint, conveying an emotion that I had yet to witness from her.

Don't mind the late human who apparently has PTSD. Let's just tiptoe around her and never knock on doors again or else she's going to experience those gunshots while taking Kade down with her.

I felt pathetic. Weak, even. Every knock I had heard on a damn door since arriving here had sent me into a panic. Though, this was the first time it was accompanied by the gunshots.

Aleena fixed her pink hair that fell over her right shoulder, making sure it was in place just right. "I hate to skim over this as if nothing has happened, but Zan and his family have probably already been seated by now. I'm supposed to be next, so you two need to get a move on."

She waved a little goodbye with her metal-clad fingertips and was out of sight before either of us could speak.

Kade reached inside his jacket, retrieving something from his pocket.

"I paid Rafina a visit."

I froze in place at the mere mention of her, waiting for him to continue. I had specifically asked him not to involve her, and he had already seen her in the short time we'd been apart?

"Not for that, I promise." I half wondered if he could sense my alarmed thoughts. His hand unfolded and my black obsidian necklace came into view. "She had removed all your belongings after retrieving you from Obsidian Falls. I'm sure your clothes were beyond repair, but she did manage to save this."

It glistened in the candlelight as if it were brand new, a shine to it that reminded me of the first time he presented it to me only nights ago. I turned and moved my hair, allowing him to secure it around my neck, and it fell between my breasts, no longer cold against my skin.

"Thank you." I smiled in all earnestness as I rolled the stone between my fingers. Kade took hold of my loose hand and kissed the top of it, but what I really wanted was for him to continue and kiss me everywhere else. I wanted to sequester myself in this room with him and reclaim the heat that had overtaken the both of us just minutes ago, before everything had gone south. If it meant not having to move on with this day of unknown celebration, I would choose this. I would choose us.

"Violet, we should go."

Kade was leading me out of the small room and down a hallway. My grip on him tightened with each step. I was beyond grateful that neither Aleena nor Rebecca had tried to put high heels on me. When I had seen the extravagance of this dress, that was where my mind went immediately—painful shoes that I would be stuck in for hours on end. I never understood the intrigue of them, thinking they were more of a hassle than they were worth.

Hell, I didn't even go to either of my proms, so the last time I would have worn that type of shoe would have been at my Uncle Steven's wedding, and that was almost a decade ago now.

I had been given the choice between two pairs of flats, and one shoe that had a bit of a wedge heel to it. Deciding that no one would be any the wiser to what I was wearing beneath the dress, I opted for the muted black flats that looked the most comfortable. From the moment they slipped onto my feet, I was sold.

The nerves began to take over once again and I squeezed his hand, eliciting another wave of calm as he tried to soothe me.

I was unsure what kind of day lay before us, but grateful that he was finally by my side once again.

CHAPTER 10

Violet

My introduction to the masses took place in the same manner as a bride and groom being announced together for the first time.

Great wooden doors opened just as a loud voice boomed, welcoming us into a vast room that put palace ballrooms to shame. Cheers erupted as an unknown man announced Prince Kadriel and Queen-to-be Violet into the massive area.

Sensory overload swept over me as I tried to take in the sea of people dressed in black, the stained glass windows, the gothic cathedral ceilings and numerous crystal chandeliers that formed a line and cast a beautiful glow over the space. There was so much beauty to gush over that I wanted to stop to appreciate it all, but Kade kept hold of my arm, moving at a steady pace down the aisle that was created for us to pass through.

As expected, the number of black eyes outnumbered those of humans, but I was pleased to see a variety of ages amongst them all. From babies to the elderly, they were scattered about. I kept holding out hope to see Rebecca in the throng of attendees, but it was like searching for a needle in a haystack.

Their welcome was a roar to my ears that didn't cease until we reached the end of the room, which felt like the size of a football field.

Kade's family stood at a rather long table, beautifully set with silver and gold furnishings that looked as if they should belong in a museum. An ivory cloth was draped across its entirety, with a gold shimmer that became evident as we drew closer.

This was my first glimpse at Zan and Sarah's family. Their two boys were between them, peeking their heads around the chairs that were in front of them. As their blackened eyes found me, I offered a smile at them, delighted that we would finally get to meet. Aleena stood on the opposite end of the table just three spaces away from Zan, and I assumed those two chairs were reserved for Kade and me.

We turned to face the crowd and a silence fell over the room, making the quiet ring loudly in my ears at the abrupt change in volume. I held my breath as everyone's eyes were on us, even though it felt like all were on *me*. I wanted to cast my gaze down, but I remembered Aleena's metal nail to my back and stood tall, choosing to look over the tops of their heads instead of directly at them. I never chose to be the center of attention in any situation, so this was certainly overwhelming. But Kade's calming presence at my side was slowly gnawing away at my plight.

"Welcome, everyone," Kade began, and I tried to squash

my urge to flee from the spotlight. Now knowing that Kade could feel what I could, I couldn't let it be a distraction. Even though I didn't think I would be able to help it much.

"It's certainly been a while since we have gathered like this, and it gives me great pride to see you all here to celebrate Violet's and my tethering."

I scanned the crowd, finding pops of color here and there to separate the sea of black. I inadvertently met curious eyes that seemed fixated on me and others that seemed to cling to the words that Kade spoke.

"We look forward to the next Blood Moon, when we can unite as king and queen, but for now let us feast and enjoy the company of others, celebrate, and welcome Violet to her new home." He placed his other hand on my arm that was hooked into his and grinned down at me. That gloriously immaculate and tender smile that made my heart skip. It trumped the anxiety that tried to surface at the mention of *blood* again, and all I could do was grin at him in return.

The roars erupted once again as we left our mark, and he escorted me around the table. A pang of sorrow lanced through me as I reflected on his use of the word *home*. I wasn't sure how long it was going to take to get used to that.

This was my home now, but the thought of never being able to visit the place I used to call one was still a tough pill to swallow. Kade must have sensed my war with myself and squeezed my hand, releasing waves that acted like a type of sedative. I took in a deep breath when it caught me off guard.

I mouthed a *thank you* as he pulled out my chair for me. The back of it was so high that it went above my head, and Kade's too as he sat.

Aleena was to my left, another pink drink in hand as she leaned back casually. "Any chance I can get one of those?" I asked as I crossed my hands in my lap. I tried to remain straight-backed, afraid that if she caught me slouching, she would make it her mission to remind me to sit up, even though she seemed to be making herself comfortable. "Please tell me there's alcohol in it."

"Not a fan of crowds?" she asked, brow rising.

"That obvious?" I kept my sights either on her or the table before us as Kade and Zan began conversing beside me. I had looked up long enough to notice that there were more tables that had been hidden from view when we entered. But now that people were beginning to sit, they could be seen. Chatter began as waiters began to flood in, balancing trays of food, from an arched doorway on my right.

A young man who looked about the age of my cousins Troy and Torrance began to place his trays at our table and he bowed. He was rather thin and shaky, and I wondered if he was as nervous as I was. His chestnut hair was trying to fall into his face, but with a quick shake of his head, it moved back into place.

Aleena asked him to retrieve a drink for me, and before he could leave, I thanked him. His look of astonishment as I spoke didn't go unnoticed.

"Of course." He bowed again before exiting and I returned to Aleena.

"Is he even old enough to be doing this? He looks just as freaked as I am."

"Remember how you said demonic miracle? Darthou has been abuzz since your arrival. They don't know whether to fear you, worship you, or both."

I couldn't hide my surprise at that revelation, and Aleena was eating it up.

"If they didn't find out yesterday that you transitioned to

a demon, they know now. You're a mystery, and by far the most interesting thing to happen around here in well…probably forever."

That was definitely not the kind of attention I wanted to attract. I just wanted to fade into the background, but now here I was front and center, and being introduced to the masses as their queen-to-be. This wasn't what I signed up for, and it was no wonder Kade was agonizing over the decisions he'd made leading up to today.

If he had been able to tell me of his royal status in his own time, would I have been more comfortable about easing into this new life and position I was thrust into? I knew the answer was no. I was a hermit, wanting to hide at this very moment, and I didn't think there was anything that could sway me otherwise.

Except maybe alcohol.

The young man returned with another tray of food, placing it at Sarah's end of the table and bowing before coming down the line to me. He bowed again as he set my drink down, an exact replica of Aleena's only filled to the brim.

"I'm sorry, I didn't get your name earlier."

The young man froze just as he had before. "Jacobi, your highness."

I was stunned at his reply. I wasn't going to have any of that.

"Please, call me Violet. It's nice to meet you, Jacobi."

Kade must have caught on to the conversation, and I saw Jacobi shoot a worried glance at him before returning his attention to me.

"Yes, ma'am. I mean…V-Violet."

"How is your mother, Jacobi?" Kade asked politely, and the boy dragged his gaze back toward him.

"She's fine. She's working in…in the kitchen." His stutter made me want to reach out and comfort him, but I didn't know if that would help matters. He seemed intimidated by us and the situation he was in. I knew he was uncomfortable, and I wished I could take that away from him.

Kade dipped his head in acknowledgement. "Well, make sure to tell her hello for us. I hope to see you both out here to enjoy the festivities after a while."

Without another word, Jacobi bowed again and left, retreating toward the doors he came from quicker than he had arrived. The way in which Kade and Aleena spoke to him gave me hope. They didn't treat him like a servant, like Dimitra had treated Rebecca earlier, and I was relieved. Not that I had expected them to, but just the same I appreciated it.

"He seems sweet." I took a sip of my drink and was grateful that I could taste a hint of the alcohol on my tongue along with a strong cherry flavor.

"He is. A little late to grow into his own, but he's had a tough go of things." Aleena set her drink back down and her face faltered for a fraction of a second. She seemed to favor her perfectly stoic face that acted like a mask. Another thing she had in common with her brother.

"How so?" I inquired, but found Kade answering instead.

"His mother tethered to a human decades ago. And when Jacobi was born, his father petitioned the council several times to become a demon." Kade's voice lowered, and I began to lean in his direction as much as my dress would allow. "But when the request was finally granted…"

When Kade's words came to a pause, I finished for him. "He didn't make it."

My gut dropped as I recalled Sarah's words last night. How transitioning to a demon had basically a fifty-fifty chance of surviving it and coming out on the other side of it a demon. I mourned for the boy I had just met, and took a big swig of my drink to chase down the thought of Jacobi's and his mother's loss.

The trays before us had collections of cheeses, meats, fruits, and vegetables. We helped ourselves, dishing the food onto the pristine plates before us. I hadn't known what to expect, but the simplicity of it all had me appreciating the arrangement. No wonder Kade had never had a corn dog before if this was how they ate. Between the fruit this morning for breakfast and this, it seemed as if demons were all about fueling their bodies rather than indulging in countless other offerings. Family get-togethers and buffets back home in Iowa had always boasted grilled foods and mixed salads, both nowhere to be seen here. I missed the cheesy potato casserole that my grandma could whip together on a whim, no recipe needed. But there was no such thing here.

"Everything alright?" Kade leaned in and I noticed he had doubled down on kiwi once again. "I'm sure they can make you something else if you like."

I shook my head. "Nonsense, this is fine. There's a lot of people to feed." I popped a cubed piece of cheese into my mouth and found it was a sharp one that I enjoyed.

"Desserts will come later. It's kind of an all-day affair."

"Will there be cotton candy?" I blinked up at him and tried to fight the urge to bite my bottom lip so I didn't ruin my lipstick. I knew he would remember the last time we had consumed the fluffy treat.

He tipped his head closer to me, his voice a low warmth that had me on the edge of my seat. "I think that could be arranged."

My stomach dropped from beneath me and the air left my

lungs as a scream ignited in my head. Even in a room full of others, it became prominent and pushed to the forefront of my mind. I felt my face pale, stricken with fear in a room full of so many.

Kade's jaw tensed as the realization set in. He placed his hand over mine, and I took it and began to squeeze as if that would abate the voice in my head.

In unison, our heads turned to find Staffan and Rafina making their way toward our table. My nails were digging into the back of Kade's hand and I knew, at the very least, they were going to create little crescents from the pressure. Sadly, I wouldn't be surprised if I drew blood.

They bowed before us, and I noticed how their black attire had a silver sheen to it up close. Rafina's dress was simple, classy, and showed little skin other than her forearms and neck. I thought it strange that Staffan's suit revealed his bare chest underneath, the outline of his pecs on display. He was showing off more chest than Kade was.

I tried to focus on what they were wearing and suppress the scream erupting inside of me, but I was failing. This was worse than when they had decided to show up yesterday at our tethering ritual, and I wanted nothing more than to flee. As if I didn't have enough to worry about with one shrill voice, another soon joined in, and it took every ounce of strength I had to remain still and emotionless.

"We just wanted to wish you both congratulations. A mighty fine day this has turned out to be." My stomach did a flip at Staffan's words. I could taste the fake sincerity on my tongue.

Kade thanked them, and just when I thought they were about to depart, Rafina left Staffan's side and drew closer to me. If it hadn't been for the wails in my head, the vast difference in her presence compared to his should have put me at ease. Her demeanor was friendly and inviting unlike that of her other half, but I couldn't find my voice to speak a single word.

"Violet dear, when you find the time, I request your presence in the infirmary. I just want to make sure you are acclimating alright. I know your transition has been unusual, for lack of better terms." A part of me wanted to believe that she was coming from a good place in her invitation, but I couldn't shake the queasy feeling that was overcoming me. Like the one piece of cheese I had eaten was going to try to come back up and shoot her in the face.

I nodded my head slightly as Kade answered for me. "We shall see what time allows. Thank you, Rafina." His dismissal was evident. She returned to Staffan and they made their way back into the crowds, disappearing and taking their screams with them. But even so, the echo of them lingered.

"Violet, may I escort you to the bathroom?" Sarah's voice sounded distant, but I knew she was standing behind Kade's chair and mine.

"I can take her," Kade interjected.

"No, you stay." Sarah's voice was one that warned she was not to be argued with.

"It's…fine." I scooted my chair out slightly and stood. Perspiration was beginning to form along my hairline and I felt faint, weak even.

"I just need a minute." I had to get out of here and compose myself. Get my head on straight. If my encounter had affected Kade at all, he didn't show any signs of it, but it rendered me useless when face-to-face with the only two people who seemed to bring on the bouts of screams.

Though my legs were wobbly, I was relieved to exit and

follow Sarah out of the grand room and into a quietness that was welcoming. I held my chest with one hand, my heart beating ferociously as I tried to come off of the ledge I'd been on.

Were Staffan and Rafina going to be present the whole time? Was it just their closeness that brought on the screams at that level, and why was this worse than our encounter at the ritual? I thought I was losing my mind.

Sarah led me down a hallway that was worn down enough to make me think we were heading in the direction of some kind of tomb. It was eerily silent and void of any other life from what I could tell. Its stones were old and worn, nothing but the sounds of our feet and shuffling of our dresses filling my ears.

It spilled into a split hallway that ran to my left and right, but Sarah opened the first rugged door that we approached. She flipped on a light and I did a double take at the switch, surprised that there was even working electricity in here. There was a pleasant fragrance of flowers, yet none could be seen. It appeared more like a storage room than anything else, and I wondered what type of furniture was hidden beneath each cloth that was draped over the numerous pieces. Once she closed the door behind us, I shook my head.

"I don't know if I can go back out there." I could finally hear my own thoughts forming, but I was beside myself. "Not if they're there. I don't know how."

"The screams?" Sarah was quick to catch on.

I nodded fast, tears forming in my eyes, and I panicked as I began to fan them. I couldn't leak black tears, especially not now. I was afraid of making a scene on a day that was held in such high importance by everyone. I was to be their queen, and I was excusing myself at the beginning of the meal. The day of celebration had barely kicked off and I was already running for the hills because of something that had no explanation.

"I don't know what to do. I don't know how to get them to stop. It's like I can't function properly when they're around."

"Just breathe," Sarah tried to soothe, but it was no use. And I was getting tired of being told to do just that. Breathing didn't help, nothing did.

"I can't. Not when I don't even understand what's happening. The only constant is it happens when Staffan and Rafina are around, and they seem like pretty important demons here so it's not like we can just ask them to leave."

"No, but does distance help?"

I toyed with her question, not certain myself. "Have they been here since we arrived?"

"I believe so. I was a little surprised they came forward when they did. Not sure why they couldn't have held off on their approach until after the first course. Rather rude, if you ask me." Her eyes widened a bit, the copper color on her eyelids popping even more.

"Do you think they know something? Rafina was there when I had the first attack." Referring to it as such was the closest thing I could relate it to.

"Zan and I did discuss the possibility. The way Rafina excused herself when it happened was odd. She didn't even try to assess you when it was happening. It was very unlike her." Concern was etched on Sarah's face, and I felt as if we were on the same page.

"So she knows something." I began to pace back and forth. I wanted to rub my temples to soothe the tension, but I was afraid I would leave marks in the makeup that Aleena had tried so hard to perfect. What if Rafina wasn't who everyone thought she was? What if my so-called unexplained rebirth was all her doing? But if that was the case, why did I have these screams when in the presence of Staffan as well?

"That may be so, but it's not a matter we are able to tackle today. Zan and I will try to keep them at bay as best we can. But if for some reason it gets out of hand again, just come here to calm yourself. I'll be sure to let Kadriel know which room we went to in case the two of you should be separated."

I nodded in agreement. "Isn't this just a storage room?"

"Of sorts." Her face fell with a sadness I hadn't seen her wear before. "When Kadriel's parents passed, their thrones and decorations for the great hall were moved in here. When you two take over, they will be brought out once again."

"Oh." That was a heavy subject I hadn't been anticipating. Now that I looked at the covered chairs with that knowledge in mind, they did look rather large, and their shapes were that of thrones.

Sarah crossed back to the door and hesitated on the handle, glancing back at me. "Do you need a few more minutes, or are you ready?"

Trying to steady my breath, I nodded, following her out before she shut the door behind me. We walked at a casual pace this time, back through the corridor she had led me through, and I began to overhear the commotion from the great hall. Only now, a musical melody began to form as we drew nearer.

"Kind of refreshing being able to actually walk somewhere. Everybody just seems to pop in and out. They don't even give me a heads-up when they're about to do it."

That earned a soft chuckle from Sarah. "You get used to it. But then again, you're a demon now so in time you'll learn how to do it yourself."

Something about the way she spoke and referred to me as a demon caused me to wonder about something. "Can you do it? Or other humans for that matter?"

"Afraid not. Zan and our children will possess that ability, but I never will. I guess it's one of the perks of being a demon. Part of the allure, if you will." I could tell that it bothered her, and I didn't like that their world would deal her a shitty card like that. Sure, you could live forever here with your tethered partner, but you would never be able to cross through mirrors like they could or change your appearance.

Out of the countless questions I had plagued Kade with, I had never inquired about crossing through mirrors myself. I had been wrong to assume that I would be able to do it if I accepted the tethering. But I guess now that I was a demon, I would get to experience the perks of being one.

"So yesterday, when I left the infirmary, were you just stuck there?" I stopped in my tracks. That place didn't have any doors that I could find, just the mirror that I myself passed through.

"Kade requested I be by your side in his absence, so Zan knew where to find me. But I do have my own pocket mirror so that I may communicate when needed. I can write and speak to him, but I can never pass through on my own."

We stopped just outside a doorway that would lead us back into the celebration, and I checked my reflection in an oval mirror on the wall that was encompassed in gold. I was trying to hype myself up, remembering to keep my chin up and back straight. I knew there would be countless sets of eyes upon us, upon *me*, once I reentered.

"Well, when I'm around, I am happy to walk wherever we need to go. I would like to learn to navigate around Darthou just as you have."

"When you get the hang of transporting, you might think differently." I could tell she meant well with her light laughter, but the action didn't reach her eyes.

I hated that our demon and human bodies were separating us in a way I hadn't known they could until now.

"Then promise me you will give me a reality check and remind me of my human roots. Demon is not all that I am, and I don't want it to be." Granted, I didn't know what all being a demon meant yet, but I didn't want to lose the person I had become up until this point. That woman had been through a lot, and I never wanted to forget that she had shaped the person I was today.

"I can do that." Her warm smile made it to her eyes this time, and they crinkled at the edges.

"By the way, Sarah, you look beautiful today." Her black dress was refined and elegant. The empire waist was flattering around her bust and elongated her figure. Small and intricate swirling designs could be seen imprinted on the silk, and while subtle, it provided a layer of detail that was appealing to look at.

"Thank you, but I pale in comparison to you. You are quite the vision. Very befitting of a queen-to-be."

I knew she meant well, but my eyes bulged at the end of her statement.

"Now, on with the show?" She stuck her arm out and I looped mine through it. Ready to face the crowd once more.

CHAPTER 11

Violet

The day of celebration was pretty much an extended version of a wedding reception. There was a band of demons—and one human might I add—and when they took a break, music that was even known to me began to fill the air in their absence.

Kade remained by my side, always keeping attached to me in one way or another, be it by hand or with an arm around my waist. Sarah did as she said—she and Zan would split off occasionally and I would lose track of them, but I knew they were on patrol, so to speak. Aleena skirted around the room, her hair an easy target to find in the sea of others.

I was introduced to countless people as they approached us, and sometimes Kade even initiated the encounters. There was no possible way I was going to remember the names flying through the air, and I found myself getting overwhelmed with it all. For the most part, everyone we met seemed excited or pleased that Kade and I had tethered and they looked forward to our rule. I didn't know what all that involved yet, but I was going to find out those responsibilities soon enough. I didn't know what was expected of me, and I had to find out. My worries would never cease until I could gather that information.

Even then, I was still probably going to freak out over every little detail. Was I supposed to be leading organizations and kissing babies? Would I be tasked with forming alliances or signing documents? What the hell was the queen of Darthou supposed to do?

One thing was for sure, however—Kade was being put through the wringer when it came to me and my chaotic mind. Before the day was over, he might start to question just who the hell he had tethered to. I had lost count of the calm waves coming off of Kade each time I began to get worked up.

Servers began bringing out more trays and Kade returned us to our table, weaving in between those standing and dancing. Gone were the meats and cheeses, and they were replaced with breads, jams, and pastries galore. All finger foods again, and I wondered how many times we were going to be served. I had mainly picked at the sharp cheese earlier, so the comfort of breads was a welcome sight.

"Where's Elias?" I asked, as I hadn't been able to find him yet. I scooped up a red-filled pastry and popped it into my mouth. Its sweetness was such a divine treat that I deposited a few more on my plate in fear that if I left, I might never see them again.

"Working, I'm afraid." Kade retrieved his goblet of a clear liquid that I assumed was water. I hadn't noticed him drink anything else but that, and yet I kept downing my pink drink. I didn't know what was in it, but I drank it as if I was parched. I wasn't sure if Jacobi was keeping it filled for me or what, but it was appreciated.

"Why? Shouldn't he be here? I figured everyone was." I glanced around the room until I couldn't even make out faces anymore, just blurs. Just how many were not in attendance? There had to be hundreds in here alone. "He's your friend, he should be here. Like your best man or something."

That earned a grin from him and he set his drink back down. "Unfortunately, there are some matters that can't stop because of a celebration. He said he might try to stop by, but I'm not sure."

"Well, do we need to take him some food or something?" I took another pastry from the tray, leaving my stash on the plate alone.

Kade pulled out his mirror from his pocket and gave it a weird sequence of taps. I expected it to get foggy, but it didn't, and Elias's face popped into view.

"Oh my gosh, I can see you!" I took the small mirror from Kade's grasp and smiled at Elias. Both men, both present and not, chuckled.

"Elias, you should be here!" I exclaimed. I knew he meant a great deal to Kade, and I wasn't going to take no for an answer.

"I would, but—"

"No excuses. You need a break."

There was a glow to the side of his face, and it drew his attention away momentarily before he returned his focus back to me. I pleaded with him once more, unashamed of how pathetic I might sound to this guy who I didn't even know and had only met once so far.

"Please don't make your future queen beg," Kade butted in, and I playfully elbowed him in the ribs.

"Alright, alright." Elias held his free hand up in surrender. "I suppose I could make an appearance."

"Good! We'll see you soon." I handed the mirror back to Kade, unsure if I had to do anything special to hang up, but he returned it to his pocket without a second glance.

I downed the rest of my drink and set it on the table, earning a raised eyebrow from Kade. I needed a break from meeting people and if I stayed here, I knew I would overindulge myself with the food before us. I dragged Kade into the throng of people who were beginning to dance to a slow tune that the band had returned to play. The stringed instruments were a comforting sound as a melody began to form between the gaps of voices chattering.

We began to sway, and I gazed up into Kade's eyes. I knew others around us were trying to give us some space, but it was in limited supply given how many were in attendance. A warm feeling began to settle in my chest, a longing I hadn't felt before. I half wondered if it had something to do with our tethering, if I was feeling something that he was. But it didn't hit me in the same way as the waves of peace or seduction I had felt earlier in that small candlelit room. This was different. It was more than a fondness and comfort, and I knew that even though we had only known each other a short while, something was blossoming.

Barely a week, to be exact.

"You really do look amazing," he dipped his head to whisper in my ear, his dark hair skating lightly across my face.

"Do I not look amazing any other time?" I teased, crinkling my nose. The air between us became thicker and a simmer began to take place in my veins.

His lips brushed the tip of my ear and I inhaled his scent, closing my eyes. There wasn't a citrus-smelling soap of any kind in his shower, so I still had no idea where that glorious smell came from.

"You don't need a stitch of clothing to get my attention." His words sent a shiver down my spine and my mind soared with the possibility of taking Aleena up on her lingerie offer just to have some fun.

"Nor do you," I agreed, feeling a flow of energy between us as the song shifted keys and morphed into another song entirely. "But I will admit, you look mighty handsome right now."

A pink flame in my periphery caught my attention and I witnessed Aleena making a beeline toward something. Her face was rather intent, as if on a mission, her features harsh and pissed off. I would hate to be on the receiving end of that.

"What's wrong with your sister?" I paused as Kade followed my observation, locking in on her.

"Elias."

"Elias?" I repeated, confused. I looked ahead of her to find his blond hair. Sure enough, Elias was straightening his jacket as if he had just popped in. He seemed unaware of storm Aleena approaching.

I followed behind Kade, still connected by our fingers as we made our way over. We passed others, narrowly grazing bodies or dresses and I apologized as we continued on. Some glanced curiously while others remained unbothered by us as we reached our destination. Elias seemed to shrink in size as I caught a bit of their conversation. Or, her side, at least.

"I didn't need it. I would have been fine!" She was obviously worked up about something and some attendees were glaring over at the scene beginning to unfold.

"Perhaps you two can take this discussion elsewhere," Kade cut in, but it sounded more like a command with his set jaw.

"Glad you could make it, Elias," I chimed in, hoping to defuse whatever was going on here.

He offered a partial smile but I could tell by his posture that he wanted to become one with the wall behind him. He wasn't able to hide his expressions as well as Kade and Aleena, and I could relate to him on that level. He seemed vulnerable at the moment, and I felt at fault because I had invited him. Well, I practically demanded he come.

"Let's get you something to eat." I gestured for him to follow me and returned to our table, leaving the siblings behind. I knew there was more than enough room for him at our table, yet there were no extra place settings or even a chair for him. "I guess we need an extra plate." I peered through the doorway the servers kept going in and out of.

"You don't have to do that. I don't need anything."

"Nonsense, I can find one for you. I'll be right back." Just because I had an important status around here due to my tethering and the demon I was involved with, it didn't mean I was incapable of getting a plate. I didn't need people waiting on me hand and foot and I had no desire for it.

I followed a server through an arched doorway and down a narrow corridor, grasping at the slit in my dress to keep my leg out of view as it kept appearing due to my hurried pace. I could hear some clanging of dishes and utensils the farther I walked. The temperature around me began to rise and I knew the kitchen was close by. No doubt the ovens were working overtime pumping out those delicious pastries. I would have to find out what those little, red-filled things were.

The hallway curved and my sights set on a figure that was

huddled up on the floor outside what I assumed to be the doorway to the kitchen. He looked like the server who had frequented our table, and my heart sank. He sat still with his arms wrapped around his legs, his only visible hand almost white with strain.

"Jacobi?"

My voice must have startled him, and he scurried up to stand as if he were in trouble. He swiped at his eyes, wet with tears. I again remembered that my black tears were not normal after observing his clear ones.

"I'm sorry. Do you need something?" He stood up straight and smoothed out his vest but was unable to look me in the eye.

I hated that he worried about doing his job when all I could think about was what was causing his troubles.

"I was just searching for an extra plate, but don't worry about that. What's wrong?" I leaned up against the wall beside me, trying to get out of the way of another server coming out with a tray full of varying drinks. She eyed us momentarily, then hesitantly bowed her head before leaving us.

"It's nothing, really. I should get back to work." He tried to dismiss himself, but I couldn't let it go. He was obviously upset and I couldn't leave him like this.

"Where's your mom?" I asked, and his head snapped to mine. I couldn't tell if he was afraid that I'd asked about her or if he was just shocked into silence. I was grasping at straws to try and get him to talk, and I couldn't be certain if this was the right direction to move in or not. "Can I meet her?"

He blinked at me and I noticed his middle finger began tapping at his leg. Another server exited the kitchen, and Jacobi didn't miss a beat as he led me into the kitchen without protest. We made our way through the biggest industrial-sized kitchen

I'd ever seen before. It was about the size of my high school cafeteria but looked state-of-the-art with its shiny appliances and countertops. It was so clean it was hard to believe they were whipping food and drinks together and sending them out.

We passed by several others, busy at their stations, and my presence garnered a few stares and mouths falling open. I smiled politely as we arrived at the backside of a woman who had the same chestnut hair as Jacobi. She was tall and slender, working at a counter that was covered in flour. She was definitely hard at work and while I hated to interrupt, I wanted to get to know the two of them. I felt strangely protective of Jacobi. Especially now knowing that he had a human father who had died trying to transition, I felt a need to form some sort of connection with them.

Jacobi cleared his throat as we came to a stop. "Mom?"

"Yes?" She continued moving her arms as she kneaded the dough before her.

When she didn't turn around, he repeated her name, and she turned. Her eyes widened as she caught sight of me and she patted her hands on her apron as she bowed. I half wondered how she knew who I was, when I was certain I would have remembered her face had I seen her before this moment. Her dark skin was quite the contrast from her son's.

"You don't have to do that." I shook my head, nervous about how to proceed.

"Mom, this is Violet, Kadriel's tethered mate. Violet, this is my mom Jaxana." I tried to repeat her name quickly in my head in the hopes I would commit it to memory, but I was a bit hung up on the use of the word *mate*.

"Pleasure to meet you, Violet. What brings you back here, is there something wrong?" The concern on her face made me worry that she might think her son did something to warrant my arrival, and I had to make it clear that it was nothing of the sort.

"Not at all. In fact, everything has been amazing so far. I just wanted to meet the mother of the young man who has been taking care of our table."

She seemed stunned at my admission, and I wanted to try and put her at ease some more while I was at it. A hush fell over the kitchen behind me and I worried that my being here might be cause for concern for the lot of them, which was not my intention. I hadn't meant to throw a wrench in their well-oiled machine of an operation back here.

"I appreciate that, thank you. We look forward to serving you."

I tried not to scowl at the word *serve*. I didn't think I would ever get used to the so-called title I was going to wear someday. I didn't want others placing me on this pedestal that honestly, I didn't really sign up for.

"While I'm here, I do have to ask. What are those little ball-like things with the red filling? They are by far my favorite thing I think I have ever tasted in my life. It's like a donut and a croissant had a baby or something. It's amazing." I let myself gush over the pastry in the hope of putting everyone at ease, but when I felt an arm around my side, I realized that the hush that had fallen over the kitchen might not have been about me, but about my other half.

Jaxana and Jacobi both bowed as Kade joined us. For a brief moment, I wished I could have had this time to myself. But then again, I'd just run off on my own and deserted the party without telling anyone but Elias. I was sure Kade was just concerned when I didn't return right away, possibly even fearing that I was hearing those screams again.

"You might as well have just brought her a tray of those

for herself the way she's hoarding them." He poked fun at me, but I couldn't be mad because it was the truth. They really were that good.

Jaxana beamed and took us over to the pastry chef who had helped make them. We took a moment exchanging pleasantries, but I could tell that our being here in the kitchen changed the atmosphere around us. I noticed prying eyes and lingering looks from all corners of the room, and I was soon ready to depart so they could carry on about their business. I felt out of place amongst them all, and I didn't like it. They were all dressed for their respective jobs, and Kade and I didn't fit in.

"Well, everything is wonderful, as always. I do hope you all can excuse yourselves long enough to join in on the fun for a bit." Kade was earnest in the delivery of his words and I knew his kindness toward them was not an act.

"Actually," I began as I observed Jacobi standing in the corner with his head hanging low, staring at his feet. "Perhaps Jacobi could use a break? If it's not too much trouble."

Jaxana looked between me and her son, whose head had popped up at the mention of his name. He opened his mouth as if to protest but closed it quickly.

"Could we grab a couple of extra chairs? For Elias and Jacobi?" I asked Kade, and he was prompt in his response.

"Of course, join us."

Jacobi reluctantly left his corner and followed us out. I thanked his mother again and said a few more greetings and thanks as we exited. The smell of baking bread was so aromatic that I found myself wanting to stay and hide away in here, but I knew that wouldn't do well for those who were hard at work. I really would just be a fly on the wall. Perhaps eating while at it, but I would stay out of their way.

Upon returning to our table, Kade and Elias retrieved some extra chairs. I gestured for Jacobi to take Aleena's place for now, seeing as she was nowhere to be found, and her place was cleared so I figured it wouldn't hurt. Even after the men returned with chairs, they stood conversing as Elias ate from the plate in his hand. As much as I wanted to eavesdrop on that conversation, especially since their faces had turned a tad serious, I turned toward Jacobi who was as stiff as a statue beside me.

"Feel free to eat something if you're hungry."

"Why are you being nice to me?" His question was a curveball that I should have anticipated. I hadn't asked any other servers to join me at the head table, just him. I could understand his confusion.

"Should I have a reason *not* to be nice to you?" I countered.

We fell into an awkward silence. I didn't want to keep him against his will if he didn't want to be here. But letting him sulk outside of the kitchen didn't seem like a better option.

"Look, I don't mean to cause a fuss, and I apologize if I did." I sat back in my seat, well aware of the stares in our direction. I wasn't sure if it was just because of me, the server I had sat beside me, or both.

"I'm sure it's obvious. I am very new here and I don't know what the hell I'm doing. But when I saw you upset outside the kitchen…" I didn't mean to call unnecessary attention to it, but he deserved the truth. "Look, I wasn't exactly popular growing up. I was the odd kid that lost her parents and never really found a place where I fit in."

Jacobi's head fell a bit when I mentioned the loss of my parents, and I wondered if he knew that I already had knowledge about his dad. A part of me regretted even bringing it up, not knowing how long it had been since he'd lost his father.

"And now here I am, only finding out last night that I am apparently supposed to become some queen of a world I never knew existed until only days ago." I swallowed hard, not sure why I was confiding in a young boy I had just met. Maybe I saw a bit of myself in him, or maybe I was misplacing it. Either way, I couldn't stop myself from continuing. "I think I would rather sequester myself away in the kitchen than be front and center out here."

I tapped my fingers once on the table, waiting for him to say something. Anything really. He had no reason to trust or confide in me about anything, but I knew a troubled soul when I saw one. I just wanted him to know that he wasn't alone. That was a feeling I knew all too well.

"You don't have to stay if you don't want to, and you don't have to tell me why you're upset. I know I'm a total stranger to you, but believe it or not, I do care."

He sniffled, the sound barely audible to my ears. I fully expected him to flee at the chance I'd given him, but he remained at my side. I refrained from talking and let my mind enjoy the music filling the air. I assumed Jacobi was soon doing the same, or just watching the masses mingling. Some were popping in and out, but the amount of people here never seemed to dwindle. It was comical to see some conquer the dance floor while others were just as awkward as I would be if I were attempting to dance to the fast-paced song that was currently being played.

A familiar frame came into view, a shuffle to her steps as she weaved in and out of couples with someone who I assumed to be her counterpart. Rebecca had changed into a dress with a shrug, her hair pinned back into a low bun. He was dressed in a suit similar to what a lot of the men were wearing today. Not as refined and fancy as Kade's and Zan's, but still dressed up, nonetheless. He was a little thicker around the waist, but that didn't stop him from moving around the floor to the beat.

Rebecca was in full swing, enjoying herself, and I couldn't help but light up at her presence. The man was grinning ear to ear in her company, and in a flourish, they disappeared into the crowd just as quickly as I'd picked them out of it. I looked forward to getting to know her more, and hoped to meet the man who made her smile like that. I couldn't help but think about how long they had been together, and if they were just as happy now as they had been when they tethered. I never wanted them to lose that joy that I had just witnessed.

"Jacobi!" a small voice shouted from the makeshift dance floor before us, and a little boy that I recognized dove under our table and between Jacobi and me.

A bit winded, Sarah wasn't too far off, chasing after him. He was about the size of Lottie, and my heart ached at the mere thought of her. He was the perfect balance of his parents, with his father's hair and eyes but the nose and facial structure of his mother.

Jacobi's body language melted into a giant hug around the child, and the little boy squealed. "Not sick of me yet, are you?" The boy just grinned, a slight red stain on his upper lip from some punch.

"You two know each other?" I asked.

"Yeah, I babysit occasionally." Jacobi's face softened for the first time since we'd met, and I grew even more fond of him.

"I am so sorry. He's tired and fighting with me about taking a nap." Sarah was almost out of breath as she approached, and I wondered how long she had been chasing after him.

"I am not!" the little boy pouted, crossing his arms and

pinching his little brows.

"I can take him home if you want," Jacobi offered. "And Ajax if you like."

"I don't want to impose."

"Hey!" The little boy leaned away from Jacobi and snatched my necklace in his small hand, causing me to jolt forward. The quick action seized at the tightness around my waist.

"Kadriel made this!"

Sarah tried to scold him but I held my hand up. "It's fine, really." His knowledge of my necklace warmed my heart, and I returned my attention to him. "It was a gift from him. And what might your name be?"

"Brighton," he said, examining the black obsidian in his tiny fingers.

"Well, nice to meet you, Brighton. I'm Violet."

"Everybody is talking about you." His innocent admission was a fact I kept trying to suppress, but I knew it to be true. And if this little boy knew that I was such a hot topic of discussion, I now felt as if I were under the scrutinizing lens of a microscope all the more.

Just as quickly as he had latched onto my necklace, he dropped it, releasing me and returning his attention to Jacobi. Another boy, slightly older, who I knew to be his brother, came up beside his mother with his dad not too far behind.

"Violet, this is Ajax, our eldest."

"Hi, Ajax." I offered a smile but he clutched onto Sarah's side, a bit more on the bashful side from what I could tell. He was maybe one or two years ahead of Brighton if I had to guess, but the resemblance between the two of them was uncanny— they could almost pass as twins. They were adorable, both dressed up as mini versions of their father.

"Jacobi was offering to take the kids home for us." Sarah turned her attention toward Zan, who contemplated the thought as he scanned the area behind him and then shrugged.

"Honestly, I wouldn't mind getting out of here myself. It's really no trouble at all. I can tell my mom on the way out." There was a hint of desperation in Jacobi's voice that I recognized. He was being polite about his request, but in reality, he was ready to get the hell out of here. I only hoped I wasn't at fault for his plight. I hadn't been trying to make him uncomfortable or worsen his day.

Both boys began pleading to leave in their own ways. Brighton was bouncing on Jacobi's lap, rather excitedly, while Ajax was begging and tugging on Sarah's dress, asking her instead of his father.

Sarah exchanged another glance with Zan and they agreed, earning victory cheers from both boys. I grinned at the both of them, excited to get to know these two young kids that I knew Kade was so fond of.

"Um…thank you, Violet." Jacobi caught me off guard and bowed his head. I found myself frowning, and his expression changed to that of worry.

"You don't have to do that," I stammered, trying to ease his reaction, but his confusion spread further. "Bow. You don't have to do that."

"But, you are to be queen." He almost seemed appalled at the notion of going against what he thought was right.

"Doesn't matter. Not to me, anyway." I stood from my chair and he followed, Brighton hanging onto him. "Thank you for visiting with me. I hope you and the boys have fun." I offered him a genuine smile. I could tell he was resisting the urge to bow again at his exit, but he succeeded and left, retrieving Ajax as well as he headed toward the kitchen. Sarah,

Zan and I all watched him leave.

Then I broke our silence. "I wish I knew what was bothering him." I left my side of the table so I could join them on the floor in front of it. "He seems like a nice kid."

"He is. Great kid." Zan didn't skip a beat.

"I'm afraid I might know why he's upset." Zan and I turned our attention toward Sarah and she crossed her arms before looking at him. "Dimitra. And Mave."

One of the names caused me to scowl. "What did she do? Dimitra?" I found my fists balling already given our short encounter earlier.

"Have you met?" Sarah asked.

"Unfortunately, yes. At Rebecca's this morning while getting ready. Not a fan."

Sarah sighed. "I'm afraid most aren't. Mave is Jacobi's age, and she is every ounce as entitled and spoiled as her older sister. They think they're better than everybody else just because of their bloodline, and because their father is on the council."

"Their…bloodline?" I questioned, my words heavy with puzzlement.

She nodded and her voice dropped in volume. "Full line of demons. Never tethered to humans, and don't agree that it should even be an option."

I mulled over that information. Kade had said that human tetherings were rare and that you could only request one once. Was this the reason? Was that why Kade was met with pushback, especially since he seemed to have requested a human tethering earlier than usual? Or was it because of his future on the throne that the council might try to keep his bloodline "pure" so to speak? Kade had told me his world was not without its own set of problems and politics, and I had a feeling this was just the beginning.

"Do you know what happened?" I asked Sarah, but then my mind came to a screeching halt and I winced. A scream was erupting, cutting through the commotion of music and voices around us. My eyes began darting about, searching for any sign that Rafina and Staffan were close. I briefly laid eyes upon Dimitra, clad in a strappy number that seemed as if it should have been in an S&M catalog, but I didn't linger long, searching on.

"I—I have to go." I left them as the scream increased in volume. It became a stabbing sensation almost like a migraine, and I hurriedly exited toward the doorway Sarah had led me through earlier. I didn't even know if anyone was following me as the screams multiplied, others joining in.

Afraid it might send me to the ground, I all but ran down the corridor as quickly as my dress would allow. The darkness of the hall swallowed me, but I continued on and the screams began to fade.

I burst into the room that promised privacy and shut the door behind me. My chest heaved as I clenched my eyes shut, willing myself to calm down. I knew Zan and Sarah had been trying their best to keep Rafina and Staffan away, but this attack was almost at the same level as the one yesterday when I first awoke. I didn't understand the severity of it when I couldn't even pick them out from the crowd.

What was causing this? And why did the attacks vary in when they chose to surface?

I shook my arms out, trying to release the tension that had built at an alarming speed. Instead of coming and going throughout this day of celebration, I wanted nothing more than to retire. These attacks were exhausting and had no explanation, no end in sight or any indication that one was about to happen. I wanted to be as far away from other people as I could possibly be, both demon and human. I hoped Kade would understand if I made the plea to leave.

Playing with the idea of staying here until somebody found me, I decided against it. I would try to make one last appearance and attempt to leave on good terms in the hopes that I could keep up the happy charade for Kade's sake. People were going to talk about me no matter what, but I didn't want my vanishing act to be the last thing stuck in their minds about me today.

A breathy moan came from the hallway, bringing my distressing thoughts to a halt. I pressed my ear to the door in an attempt to hear more, but it had fallen silent. Carefully turning the handle, I peered out into the hall and my eyes fell upon a pink-haired beauty who had Elias pinned up against the stone wall a ways down. I was certain they had not been there when I had arrived, and their heated exchange had me blushing.

Aleena was taking control, one metal-tipped hand around his neck and the other between their bodies. Elias had one of her legs hoisted up beside him and a hand pressed into her back, securing them together. There was something primal about the way they moved, I couldn't peel my eyes away. I knew it was an invasion of privacy, but the act itself out in the hallway almost made me wonder if they wanted to get caught.

I recalled their heated exchange in the great room and wondered if it had just been a lover's quarrel, and now they were making up for it. Either way, while I hadn't pictured the two of them as a thing, now that I saw them together, I thought they made quite the pairing.

Someone cleared their throat and I jumped, trying to close the gap in the door swiftly but without noise. My hands shook as I did, worried that I'd been caught by whoever approached.

But when he spoke, I pressed my ear to the door once again.

"You two are the worst at judging the right time and place." Kade didn't scold them, but he sounded more annoyed than anything. I wondered if Kade approved of their connection, seeing as how the three of them were close. Did their coupling throw off the group dynamic, or did it add to it? Geesh, it was nice to focus on something else besides my own problems for once.

Two taps sounded at the door and I sprang back just in time for him to open it. I launched into his arms and he stumbled slightly at the abrupt motion, but soon recovered and returned my embrace.

"Everything alright?" My ear to his chest, I could feel a slight hum as he spoke, even through the thick fabric of his suit.

"I'd be lying if I said yes." There was no sense hiding it from him.

"What do you need?" His question was gentle as his hand trailed up my bare back and down again. It formed goosebumps in its wake.

I took a step back, taking his hands in mine as I stared up into his eyes. "Please don't be upset."

"I don't think you could do anything to upset me."

Sure, he said that now. But neither of us knew what was going on with me, or what the future held. I didn't care how many years he had watched me prior to our five-night courtship. We had barely been together a week, so I wasn't totally believing that line.

"I know how much importance this day of celebration holds for you, but…" I searched for the right words to use, not wanting to put him down. "I feel as if it's best for me to stay out of the limelight until we really know what's going on with me. That last episode I had I…"

I could sense Kade was trying to calm me. I could feel it all around, but my mind was made up and I had to remember that. He was in a position of power, and his actions were being called into question already. With my problematic symptoms, I didn't want to add any more fuel to that fire.

"Do we need to go?" he asked, and I blinked up at him. His face was void of any expression, not giving me a sense of whether he was disappointed, upset, anything.

"Is that allowed?"

Kade finally broke and grinned, his charm not lost on me. "It might be a party in honor of us, but we can do whatever we want."

"You really wouldn't mind leaving?" I didn't want him to regret doing so if he didn't want to.

He stepped in closer, dipping his head down toward my ear. "As much as I love showing you off, I would much rather bury myself in you right now."

His admittance went straight to my core, and I locked my knees in case they decided to give way. My cheeks heated and I teased him, "That's awfully presumptuous of you." I met his whispered words back with my own. "I'm rather fond of this dress. Perhaps I want to wear it a while longer."

"We'll see about that." I ducked out from beneath his grasp and through the doorway, retreating backward. A gleam in his eyes warned me that he had no intention of letting me escape, and my heart pounded away in excitement. His dark and predatory demeanor was one that was still new, but thrilling. I was well aware that I would be incapable of outrunning him, but I continued to back away.

"We should probably say goodbye." My mouth began to dry as he approached, and I knew I wouldn't be saying a single farewell to anyone. He was a lion with his sights set on his prey, and I didn't stand a chance.

I turned to run only to feel his hand wrap around my wrist, stopping me before pulling me to him. Our lips met and I no longer cared about my appearance. In a flash, we were back in his room, and when my fists were unable to gather his jacket and yank him closer, I let a hand wander south toward his erection. I was pleased that he was ready, and I grasped his restrained member, eliciting a groan of appreciation from him as our lips tore from one another.

He backed me up toward the bed and flipped me around, his lips finding my neck as I leaned back. I reveled in his touch as his hand found the slit in my dress. He wasted no time finding my heat, and I moaned. Ready with a need only he could fulfill. His fingers moved against my underwear, applying pressure to my clit, but it wasn't enough. I wanted more. I needed the friction of his skin against mine.

My fitted dress hugged the top of my hips and flared out from there. He withdrew his hand and tugged at the only thing keeping him from my entrance, pulling my underwear down so I could step out of it. I waited for him to rid me of my dress, but instead he raised my right leg, setting my foot on the frame of the bed, spreading my legs apart.

His hands left me for a brief moment and I remained still, heady with the change in atmosphere between us. If we didn't fuck soon, I might pass out from the waves of want washing over me. My dress began to rise and I could feel his erection press into me from behind. He wasted no time entering. His mouth returned to my neck as he cradled me to him, and my head fell back as a moan escaped.

He held me firmly around the waist with one hand, while the other found its way to my clit and he began to circle as he moved inside of me. I wasn't sure how I would be able to stand much longer as pleasure radiated through me at such a high intensity, I didn't know how it wouldn't tear me apart.

I whimpered, lost in the ecstasy of us, unsure of what to do with my hands. I scrambled between feeling myself through my gown and running my fingers through his hair. I twisted them into his tendrils, pulling the strands taut to the point I was sure it was affecting his scalp.

I was completely at his mercy as he continued to move and I became more vocal. The climb toward orgasm was on the horizon and I was afraid I would come in a blazing force that would send us both to the ground. His fingertips were relentless as he swirled around, building the pressure and anticipation for release.

I came too quickly, my body spasming around him as he continued through my eruption. I was trapped in his grasp and he didn't let my orgasm stop him from chasing after his. He thrust into me harder and harder as I writhed against him, but I was unable to protest, wanting to feel him come inside me even if I fell in a heap on the floor at the overstimulation. He began to slam into me, my rear anticipating each strike from his hips, and I felt myself building again.

"I'm not done." His voice was rough and broken in my ear.

Distorted shrieks sounded from my throat as he continued his attack on my body, and I wasn't sure how much more I could take. I trembled, unable to focus on anything but the sounds of our bodies colliding. I wanted to collapse and ride out my orgasm on the bed before us, but his grasp on me was unbreakable.

Perspiration formed at my hairline and beneath my gown. I regretted the clothing we wore, wishing there was nothing separating our bodies. But that thought was soon whisked away as my throat let out a shrill sound I didn't know I was capable of making. Kade's hold tightened as he stiffened, finding his own release, filling me.

Kade lowered his forehead to the crook of my neck as he kept me secured against him, supporting my body that wanted to go limp.

Swallowing hard, I tightened around his member, still very much aware of his presence. If he were to move again I swore I might black out. He lowered my propped-up leg to the ground with ease and slipped out of me while still supporting my weakened state. My skirt began to fall slightly, grazing my damp skin as it went, and I wobbled as I turned around and faced him.

My lips found his and we explored each other's mouths at a languid pace.

"This needs to go," I mumbled between kisses. "I can't feel you." I tried to tug at the hardened fabric that kept his chest covered. He grinned slightly and I ended up kissing his teeth, and a small giggle erupted from me.

Without hesitation or taking a step back, he shrugged off his jacket and began to undo the buttons on his vest. I became distracted by his member, protruding from his pants and wet with a mixture of us.

"Those too." I bit my lip as I tried to steady myself with the back of my legs against the bed. Kade's lips turned up in a sexy smirk and my heart did a somersault. I reached to stroke his erection without another thought and he tried to back up, but my grip only tightened.

"Ah." Kade winced as he tried to peel my hand away from him. "Too soon."

A part of me wanted to bring him to his knees before me, but I was already on borrowed time using my legs at present.

They were threatening to turn to jelly.

Closing in, I nipped at his jawline. "I don't remember you giving me a break between orgasms."

"Careful, Violet," he warned, but it only served to reignite the fire in my blood.

"Or what?" I challenged. I waited for a reply but was offered nothing but the dip of his chin and his eyes narrowing. Couldn't he just heal himself and give us another go?

Damn, when had I become so greedy?

He spun me around once more and found the zipper of my dress. Hands pulled down my straps, fast and harsh, down my arms, sides, and all the way to my ankles where I then stumbled to slip out of my flats. Turning around, I made a feeble attempt to grab at his biceps and then hauled us onto the bed.

We fell into a small fit of laughter before I pulled him atop me. Wave after wave of emotions were emitting from him and I struggled to think straight, let alone breathe.

Happiness. Lust. Gratefulness. Love.

I was swimming in a sea of Kade's feelings for me, and I was at a loss for words.

He might have wanted to bury himself in me, but I wanted to drown myself in him.

CHAPTER 12

Kade

Violet shivered and I drew up the covers around her. She hadn't opened her eyes in quite some time. Another yawn escaped her, but she was fighting to stay awake. She was exhausted, and rightfully so after our evening together. We eventually moved to the shower where we spent more time caressing and kissing each other than we did washing. Remembering her body slick with the soap foam was enough to arouse me again.

Was there ever a time when I didn't want to fuck her? Even after recovering from an orgasm, one look from her and I was attempting to gear up for another round.

I glanced down at her body curled up against me. Her wet hair had been quickly braided after we cleaned up, and now lay on her bare back. No doubt that had something to do with the shiver that coursed through her again. Sleep was trying to take over and her body temperature was dropping slightly.

"Do we get a honeymoon?" Her voice was quiet, but still music to my ears. Her words slurred slightly and if I hadn't known better, I would have thought alcohol was the cause of it. Had she drained off a few more of Aleena's drinks, it would have been the case.

A small chuckle escaped me before I could stop myself and her head bounced. "I will make every night our honeymoon if that's what you want." I knew a tethering here was the equivalent to marriage for her, and she would draw from that knowledge to make sense of my world and its traditions.

Another yawn ripped through her and now she was barely audible. "I want."

I played with the idea of putting her into a deep sleep, but decided against it. I shouldn't do it again without her knowledge. It was a simple parlor trick that some of my kind could easily use on humans, but it took more energy to use it on our own kind. She had been less than thrilled when I had done it the last time, and with good reason. She had every right to be freaked out by my appearance in her apartment, especially after our first meeting. The first time we had met face-to-face under the cover of night. The first time I could touch her, taste her, take her.

"I…love you."

Her mumbles might have been faint, but I had craved hearing those words long enough to know that they had left her lips now. I eyed her, disbelieving, taking in her soft features as she finally let herself succumb to sleep. Her lips parted slightly as the air she exhaled hit my chest. I was stunned into silence, hardly capable of comprehending her statement.

The elation I felt provided hope that maybe she really did

accept a life with me because she wanted to. That she wasn't just telling me what I wanted to hear. Perhaps she could actually be happy with me and the life we could build here.

Kissing the top of her head, I hugged her tight against me and let my other arm drift upward to prop my head up so I could admire her. There was no way I would be able to sleep now. I let myself soar on the life that her words brought me and grinned like a damn fool.

"I love you too."

Tapping stirred me and I blinked away the sleep from my eyes. I must have dozed off at some point and now my windows were dimly lit with the light of early morning. Violet had turned away, wrapping herself in the blankets, but her back was still pressed into me. I rolled my eyes as the tapping sounded again and I watched Violet cautiously as I stood, trying not to wake her. I found it odd that she was requiring as much sleep as she did. Maybe as time went on, she would need less. She was newly transitioned, so maybe I had to give her some grace.

I sifted through my pants and found my pocket mirror, and then retreated toward my watching quarters, retrieving a shirt and shorts from my closet as I did. There were so many clothes in here that I hadn't touched in ages, and I decided it was well past time to go through them. I needed to make space for Violet here, however I could. I had no idea how much she had acquired while visiting Rebecca yesterday, but I knew she was lacking in the clothing area. Her small duffle bag that Elias had grabbed from her apartment didn't have much in it, and I hoped she had taken advantage of Rebecca and the time spent with her.

The mirror tapped again and I became aggravated. It was getting on my nerves that someone was bothering me this early after our day of celebration. It had better be important. I wanted nothing more than to coax Violet awake once she started to stir and take her once more before beginning our day.

I had plans. There were places I wanted to show her, more demons for her to meet that we hadn't had the chance to talk to yesterday, and I hated the fact that she might wake up alone. I didn't want that, ever. I wanted to be the last face she saw before sleeping and the first when she awoke.

Opening the door to my watching quarters, I flipped on the light at my desk, swiping my thumb across the surface of my mirror to answer.

"What?" I stared into the compact, awaiting whoever was on the other end. To my surprise, Elias's face flashed, and before he could speak he was before me. Opening the connection by pocket allowed him entrance, and he hadn't hesitated to take the liberty of popping in here. I stowed my mirror as I read his face. I knew that his presence couldn't mean anything good.

"I wouldn't bother you if it wasn't urgent." Elias knew me well enough to not cower before me—we had been friends since we were kids and he could read me as well as I could him. He was bracing himself for the deliverance of news, his face stern.

"I know." I braced myself on my desk as I waited for him to spill.

"There's something you need to see."

What the hell was my day going to consist of now? All of

my plans to show Violet around my home today were about to go down the drain, that much I knew. Ever since I had arrived with her, it felt as if we were constantly on the go, and I was ready for things to slow down. But I knew the threat of Damian and Brett was still top priority. I was leery of pursuing the former again so quickly after Aleena's injuries, but he had to be dealt with. Him and the bastard that was responsible for Violet's death.

Elias swiped at a few mirrors and they illuminated with surveillance of Violet's world. My stomach dropped. A few I recognized as Violet's place and her grandma's. There were a few others that were familiar, and one that was not. I hoped he wasn't here to bring me grave news regarding any of her beloved family members.

I crossed the short distance to his side and waited for him to speak. He had been trying to locate the saint and the human, hopeful that their trails would meet. I feared that Violet's request for Elias to come to the celebration might have put her family in some kind of danger. She would never forgive herself, or me for that matter, if any harm came to them.

Don't get me wrong, I had wanted Elias to be there for the entire day. He would have even been the equivalent to my best man, just as Violet had said. But he took his job just as seriously as I took mine, and I was optimistic that someday I could repay him by placing him on the council, should that opportunity ever arise. If I ever got the chance to get some fresh blood by my side in that room, Elias would be my first pick.

My uncle was the only one I trusted right now, and it shouldn't be that way.

"I'm not sure what Damian is up to, but he has paid Margaret a visit and he didn't even try to hide himself. He offered his condolences and she and Cindy sent him on his way."

My jaw clenched to the point that my molars began to ache. Damian *wanted* to be seen. Visited Violet's family. But why? Was he trying to lead us into another trap?

"He then made a trip to Violet's apartment and tried to mask his appearance by shifting to a police officer."

"What was he looking for?" I asked, eyes searing through the sight of her empty apartment. The views I was granted still weren't my favorite. Nothing gave as good of a view as her standing mirror that was still a shattered mess. I could still make out the bloodstained floor from Violet's life-ending wounds, and it gutted me.

"I didn't know at first, and I had to rewatch it a few times, but check this out."

I watched as Damian's officer persona, a stocky fellow who would be your stereotypical donut-eating man, wandered about Violet's home. To the untrained eye, he was just looking around searching for clues, although it was a strange hour to be conducting police business such as this. But then he leaned down as if examining the blood on the floor, his figure obstructing most of our view, and once he stood, he retreated from the apartment and left.

"Go back again," I said, knowing that Damian had a purpose for his visit and intent on finding out for myself what it was. The uniform he wore was too snug on him, and as I watched him leave the apartment once more, I noticed a small formation in his pocket that hadn't been there before. We couldn't see him pick anything up since he was blocking most of our view, but I knew what he was doing and it made my blood run colder than the air outside.

"The shattered glass," I said, and Elias nodded in my periphery.

"How would he know?" Elias asked, and I ran a hand through my hair a bit too roughly.

"I guess this just further proves our theory that there is a traitor amongst us."

Only a mirror that had released a demon by blood would allow a saint to enter our world. There were only rumors that it had been done before, but some of those stories had truth to them.

Whoever was feeding information to Damian had an agenda. What I feared was that it had something to do with me and my impending reign. Why else would the traitor have also relayed the details of my tethering courtship, and down to the exact night we were on?

Damian had knowledge that he shouldn't, and only a demon could have passed it on. If only I could say that the circle of those who knew of my time spent with Violet was small. But the truth was far from it. With my extended absence, and the buzz Darthou generated at the possibility of a tethering, it was impossible to know how far the news had spread.

I loathed Staffan, and the disdain between us was mutual. But as much as I wanted to place the blame on him, I knew that I couldn't. I still had no proof.

It also felt too easy to think that the traitor could be him. But the screams that Violet had encountered in his and Rafina's presence since becoming a demon now had me looking at the both of them in a whole new light.

While I didn't expect Rafina to have anything to do with Damian, she could very well have something to do with Violet's unusual transition. Who would suspect that the almighty healer would have an ulterior motive? What would she have to gain by bringing Violet back from death? And while the people of Darthou were struck with shock and awe at Violet's rebirth, there was also gossip of Rafina's healing powers and just how far they could go.

But even I had trouble believing that. The last transition, Jacobi's father, had ended in tragedy. Why would Rafina let him die but let Violet come back?

None of it made any sense.

"And I hate to be the bearer of more bad news but…" Elias drew my attention toward a woodsy cabin sort of place that I knew I didn't recognize. Its walls were made of lumber, and antlers and taxidermy lined its walls to the point that it looked tacky. I never understood the need to place dead carcasses around as decorations.

"Damian was a distraction and I took the bait." Elias ran through some footage, and Brett came into the picture as an older woman answered the door to the cabin. Before the frail human could hold her hands up in defense, he shot her point-blank. No remorse registered on his face as he crossed over the threshold, stepping over her lifeless body as her head began to bleed out. He dragged her away from the door far enough to close it and locked the bolts.

"I caught up to Brett while he was driving. But then I got a hit on Damian and followed after him. I've been trying to get ahold of you for the past half hour." Elias gestured toward the screen and I knew he was taking this personally, which was a weakness he rarely exhibited.

I couldn't help but wonder when he'd last slept, and realized I would have to relieve him of his extra duties, and soon. He needed a break, and some rest. Even if he had found himself entangled with my sister for a short while last night, I knew he would have kept that time with her to a minimum so he could return to work.

"What is he doing now?" I waved at the mirror to bring it current and found Brett in another view, sprawled out across a bed and fast asleep. He hadn't even bothered to cover up or hide the woman's body. Brett was a loose cannon, and I didn't want to entertain the thought of what further damage he could do before he was apprehended.

Two lives. He had taken *two* fucking lives now.

"Should we tip off the police in the county?" Elias asked. Normally I would have agreed on the spot with that action, but I was eager to put an end to him myself.

I knew Brett hadn't done enough damage for the council to approve of his assassination. I knew I was too involved personally to see straight, but dammit he was responsible for the death of the woman I loved. Images flashed through my head of Violet broken and bleeding, her lips moving but nothing but blood filling her mouth. It twisted my insides in the most agonizing way, its viselike grip making me see red.

"Kade?"

Elias and I exchanged glances as Violet stepped into the room. She had found one of my shirts and wore a pair of my pajama bottoms I hadn't seen in years. Her figure didn't drown in them, but her curves were evident and my eyes traced her body. Once she realized Elias was here she crossed her arms, covering her breasts and pebbled nipples that were free from the restraints of a bra.

"Oh. Hi, Elias." She didn't hide her embarrassment well and color crept into her cheeks. "Is everything okay?"

I tried to suppress my blinding anger, afraid that she might catch wind of it as she began to enter the room. But before she could join me at my side, movement on the mirrors before us caught her attention and I held my breath.

I hadn't had the chance to show her any of this yet. In fact,

I had escorted her out in the hopes of revealing all of this to her soon, just not at that time. Her curiosity about everything, and my life in particular, was a breath of fresh air that I never knew I needed.

I had fully intended to share everything with her.

"Good morning, Violet. I'm sorry to have disturbed you." Elias exchanged another glance with me and I knew he was just as concerned about her arrival as I was. She wasn't going to be able to go back to bed after this, and she was going to ask questions and demand answers. That is, if she didn't throw the both of us into a repeat of her death.

"What…what's going on?" She closed in on the mirrors, examining them, and I wasn't sure which she would inquire about first. I decided to let her choose the direction the conversation would go.

Still, I didn't like it when she came to a halt in front of the mirror that showed the cabin. She had found Brett, and the silence that filled the room was deafening. But what happened next was something I never could have anticipated.

Violet stilled and a roiling anger began to take over, coming at me in droves so hard I stumbled back a step as if I had been shoved in the chest. Rage was on the horizon, and I could taste it on my tongue.

"Violet?" I called to her, but even as I tried to push the anger away, I couldn't find a calm within me to combat it.

"Ah!" I stumbled back again, as if a bullet had become lodged in my chest, and then another in my abdomen. I struggled to breathe, reliving the same experience I'd had after our tethering and before our celebration but worse. Much, much worse.

I wheezed, gripping at my chest in search of bullet wounds, but there was nothing there. Violet stood motionless before the mirrors. I tried to call out her name, but I had no voice that I could hear. The agony that I was experiencing was at a level I had never encountered before, and I fell to the ground.

"Kadriel?" Elias took a knee beside me, eyes focused on my incapacitated state, and I tried to direct him to Violet. Her hand was reaching up to the mirror and she vanished in the blink of an eye, taking root in the very cabin that housed her murderer.

At once, my anguish was lifted and I hunched over, bracing myself on the floor with my hands as I coughed and gasped for air, attempting to fill my lungs.

"We…have to…go…after her," I sputtered as I tried to stand.

"Are you alright? How the hell did she do that?" Elias was beside himself—no doubt my weakened state was nothing he had ever witnessed before. In all my battles with him at my side, I had never been rendered to a state of such uselessness.

Violet was approaching the bed where Brett was sound asleep, and Elias and I transported there only to be met by deafening screams. I shrank away, covering my ears. A chorus of varying screams at all different pitches and tones filled my head, and I couldn't tell where it was coming from. I searched my whereabouts as Elias studied me, clueless.

"Can you not hear it?" I hollered, unable to hear my own voice as I did.

When Elias spoke, I couldn't make out from his lips what he was saying, and I turned my attention back to Violet and Brett. He was now scurrying up from the bed, fear consuming him. His ruthless killer persona was gone and it was replaced by a man begging for his life. I tried hard to concentrate, but the screams were overpowering me and I couldn't move. It was as if they were physically holding me down, the weight of them debilitating.

Violet closed in on him as he leapt from the bed only to be backed against a space on the wall between two deer heads. I tried to tell her to stop, but it didn't faze her in the least. Brett's mouth opened as if he was shrieking himself, and he began to claw at his ears. His eyes were wide as she drew nearer and blood began to leak from them.

I watched as Violet's hand shot forward at full force and into his chest.

Elias shot across the room, but it was too late. She withdrew her hand, and in it, she held his bloodied heart. Or at least, the remains of it.

Brett's lifeless body slid down the wall and came to a stop at her feet, a gaping hole in his chest. And as much as I wanted to rejoice that he could never take another life, what Violet had just done had me fearing for her life as much as mine.

As deep crimson began to drip from her hand, she dropped the heart to the floor beside her bare feet, and the screams that had consumed me ceased. A bit dizzy, I took a moment to get my bearings, then lunged forward to catch Violet as she fell back. Her eyes remained open but vacant, and her body was limp. I shook her gently at first, trying to wake her, but she remained unmoving.

"Violet!" I called out, and shook her harder, but it didn't faze her.

"What the fuck just happened?" Elias's voice was strained.

We had seen a lot in our time together, but everything we had encountered before now paled in comparison to this. Whatever was going on with Violet wasn't human or demonic. It was something else entirely. She might look as if she had transitioned to a demon, but something else was developing inside of her and we had to find out what. And fast.

Scooping her body up, I cradled her against my chest and her head fell back.

"Find Zan and meet me in my quarters," I ordered.

Elias vanished before I could. I returned us home, propping Violet up against the corner of the couch that sat before the mirrored wall. Her bloodied hand stained my shirt and I couldn't stop myself from replaying the scene that had unfolded before me.

I had been powerless against the voices in my head, unable to reach her, unable to stop her. Was that what she experienced each time she was in close proximity to Rafina and Staffan? I hated the very thought of it. Loathed myself for putting her in any situation that would ever cause it. No wonder she had been overwhelmed. And that was putting it mildly.

"Violet, can you hear me?" I cupped the side of her face, willing with everything I had for her to wake up and face me. But she remained still and silent. The steady rise and fall of her chest made me wonder if she was asleep, but with her eyes open. Nothing about this was normal.

"What's going on?"

Elias returned with Zan, who looked like he had just gotten out of bed with his disheveled hair. He knelt beside me, examining her.

His question was geared toward me, but Elias responded first. "That's a good question." He crossed his arms and stood behind the couch. I had never seen him in a panic before and it didn't suit him.

Zan pushed, louder. "Kadriel."

I was having trouble pushing frantic thoughts away as Violet lay lifeless before me. As much as I didn't want to leave her side, I needed to put some distance between us so I could try to come to my senses. I stood and crossed the room before running my hands through my hair, focusing on how to begin.

"Violet crossed into her world and killed Brett." Elias spewed the words so quickly that I shot him a cruel look for being so callous in his wording.

"And you did nothing to stop it." I met him with enough bite to my words to match his.

"Neither did you! How was I to know she was going to fucking kill him!" Elias yelled back.

"Boys!" Zan stood as his voice carried through the space between us all.

Zan was usually levelheaded, the voice of reason among others. When he used this tone, we knew it was time to shut up and listen.

"Now, start from the beginning. Tell me everything that transpired up until now." Zan's face was firm as he waited for me to begin.

"Elias came over to show me some happenings that took place tonight, and Violet found us while we were talking."

Elias butted in. "I drew up these views." He gestured toward the mirrors that still harbored feeds of Violet's world as he approached them. "This one caught her attention. Everything else that followed was a shit show."

I was agitated at his candor, but he was right. The speed at which the events had unfolded was maddening.

"And what caught her attention here?"

Elias swiped at the mirror to find another reflective surface that just so happened to overlook the dead body. "Brett."

Zan studied the image for a moment before looking at Violet. Probably trying to figure out just how she had happened to rip the man's heart from his chest with her bare hand and no weapon.

"And then what happened?" he asked, and I stepped

forward.

I took a beat before responding. "Violet was…angry. More than angry, she was livid. I was powerless against it." I felt weak speaking it aloud for others to hear. "Then I felt as if my body had been riddled with the bullets that took her life, and I couldn't breathe."

"Like the other night," Zan stated, and I nodded my head. Elias was confused, his platinum bun wobbling as he shot a look my way. He had a right to be, since I hadn't caught him up to speed yet. He could have my ass over it later, I didn't care at the moment.

"Much worse. I felt as if I was choking on my own blood. And then once she crossed over, it ceased. So Elias and I went after her. But when I arrived, all I could hear were screams. Voices so loud that I couldn't hear anything else. Elias looked at me as if I were crazy."

"I did," he agreed. "I heard absolutely nothing of the sort."

"It wasn't until she killed Brett that the screams stopped. And when I approached, she collapsed. She's been in this state ever since. I sent Elias for you and I came straight here."

Zan was deep in thought, avoiding eye contact with Elias and myself before turning toward the mirrors at his back. He swiped to the left, and I knew he was going to replay the moments that had just transpired. I couldn't shake the dread of watching it happen all over again, yet my eyes remained fixated on the mirror, watching it unfold once more. I was stunned when I couldn't detect a single scream, now witnessing it all from a new perspective.

A part of me wanted to take pride in the fact that Violet had removed his heart and killed him. Fucking murderer had it coming. I was just a bit perturbed that I wasn't the one who got to do it.

But when the heart dropped to the floor and Violet tried to follow it, that perception shifted and sank. How would she react when she came to? Was she even aware of what she had just done?

Instead of turning away after the replay of events, Zan began searching for another view and another angle. The one he found first must not have been to his liking, because he swiped in another motion to find another. I wasn't sure what he was searching for, but I kept my eyes glued, studying each scene as I would any other scenario that required extra attention.

He settled on one that caught Violet's face as she appeared in the cabin. Her jaw was dropped in a menacing manner, as if she herself were screaming. It didn't look natural, the way it stretched, like her mandible was going to tear away.

"You said you didn't hear anything, Elias?" Zan asked without taking his attention away from the mirror.

"No screams. I didn't hear anything else besides Kadriel yelling and Brett begging for his life."

Collectively, we all turned our heads toward Violet. She remained as she was, almost in a vegetative state. It was unsettling.

"Should I call on Rafina?" Elias asked.

"No," Zan and I answered in unison.

"Not yet, anyway." I shot Zan a look of disbelief that he would even consider it.

"For all we know, she could be the cause of all this. We don't know what happened with Violet's transition, and what transpired between them when we left for council and she brought her back to the infirmary."

"Sarah was there waiting for her to return, but I'm not sure how long it was," Elias stated. "I retrieved her and then went to check on Aleena."

Zan returned to Violet, sitting beside her on the couch and picking up her wrist to check her heart rate. I used this moment to catch Elias up on everything that had taken place in his absence, since he had been inadvertently left out of the loop. It was never my intention, but I knew he was maxing out his watching capabilities with my load added onto his, and I'd been waiting for things to settle down before I threw more shit at him.

No, this wasn't the best time, but it had to be done.

"And not a word of this to Aleena," I warned him. I knew their relationship was a constant battle of hot and cold, and I couldn't keep up with the two of them. But I would decide when the time was right to bring her in. *If* we could bring her in.

"Kadriel?" Zan's voice pulled me away from my conversation and I waited for him to continue. "When was the last time you felt your connection?"

"It was…" I combed through my memories at hyperspeed and settled upon the image of Violet taking a life. "I felt her up until she killed Brett. I haven't since then."

His lips pressed into a thin line and he vanished, only to appear again not five seconds later. "I have an idea, but I don't think you're going to like it."

"Go on," I pressed. I was out of ideas right now.

He produced from his hand the very dagger that had been used for Violet's and my tethering, and I stilled as I put two and two together.

"You don't mean to…" I shook my head, taking a step forward. "No."

"I need to make sure it's still intact." My uncle was trying, I'd give him that, but I didn't believe this was the answer. I hated that he had come to this conclusion, and it pained me to lose her in this sense. But if Violet really was something else besides a demon, we might have already lost our tethering.

"But surely if it was gone, I would *know*." I refused to face the fact that I might not.

"With what you've been through this morning and what you're currently experiencing now, which is nothing, we have to be sure."

"But it could hurt her." I dragged my gaze over her body. I didn't want to inflict any more pain on her than what she had already been through. What if she was conscious but trapped inside her own mind?

She had been awake enough when I had sliced her hand in the infirmary in an attempt to tether and save her. She remembered that. She *felt* it. What if she was still in there but just in shock? She did brutally kill a man, after all.

I closed my eyes a beat before I raised my forearm toward him. "Don't do it to her, do it to me."

There was a moment of hesitancy and I waited to be met with pushback, but to my surprise he held his tongue.

I watched Violet instead of the blade that dipped into my skin at the base where my palm and wrist met. It sliced into me and a sizzling blaze began to awaken at its intrusion. My teeth ground together as I began to fist both hands at the pain erupting from the site of impact. I wanted to raise my voice in screams like those that had taken over me earlier. The burn felt as if I had shoved my hand into an inferno, and it was moving up my arm, consuming it. I had to focus on the fact that it could be worse. It *had* been worse when those last bullets struck me.

"Concentrate on Violet," Zan said, and I attempted to do just that.

My eyes watered as I tried to adjust my view on her. I wanted to see her smiling back at me. Her radiant energy and loving touch were all I craved. I knew she blamed Brett for stealing her life, but I still felt at fault. I didn't know if the Violet I knew and loved was still in there or not, but I would do anything and everything in my power to get her back.

My body began to shake uncontrollably and Zan's grip on my arm tightened. "Steady, Kadriel."

The blade moved further up my arm and I tried to twist away, but Elias stepped in to secure me. I wanted to hurl my best friend across the room but I fought it off, keeping my eyes on Violet.

Surely it wouldn't hurt this bad if we had lost our tethering. Why would anyone in their right mind submit themselves to this torture? Perhaps this was why requests for tethering removals were so rare. This was literal hell, and I was beginning to think I might trade it for the bullets.

Her right arm twitched, and I let out a scream that ripped through my chest. I was sweating through my shirt and I could feel it drip down my forehead as Violet shot up from her position and let loose a bloodcurdling scream that intertwined with mine. A flood of emotion rushed through me at her return and I fell to the floor but scrambled to her side.

Black tears streamed down her face as I embraced her. I was immensely grateful to feel her again, both by touch and our connection. She was a whirlwind of feelings that had me on edge in a split second trying to keep up with them.

Fear. Pain. Anguish. Betrayal. Remorse. Worry. Satisfaction. Dread. Confusion. All overlapping to the extent that it was almost unbearable.

"I'm here, Violet. I'm here." I knew that calming the storm within her wouldn't be easy, but I had to try with all that I had.

She clutched onto my shirt as she sobbed with a hoarse voice. I might as well have been stabbed given the guilt that overtook her, and I had to focus my thoughts to find something peaceful, tranquil, to think of. I squeezed her hard, trying to push the serenity I found into her being.

I looked up to find Zan and Elias still present, not that I thought they would run off considering what had just transpired. As Violet started to settle, I gestured for Elias.

"Turn them off, please." I was referring to the reflections behind me, afraid of two things. One, how she might react to Brett's dead body that she was responsible for and two, her ability to pass through another mirror again without getting lost in crossing over. It took some demons years to fully master travel through mirrors, and she had successfully done so twice. While a part of me was impressed, a greater part was concerned.

"I don't mean to sound insensitive, but we need to discuss what happened while it's still fresh in her memory."

Zan was right, and while Violet had quieted some, she froze in my hold as he spoke. She began to feel distant again and I released her, studying her eyes. "Hey, Violet. Stay with me."

I gave her tethered hand a squeeze and noticed that the very spot where Zan had cut into me was mirrored on her skin as well. Our tether was still intact, and while I was grateful to know she had demon in her, I wondered what else there was. My glance didn't go unnoticed as Zan cautiously approached, observing what I was looking at as he knelt.

The room fell eerily quiet and Zan peered up at Violet. "What did you feel when you looked at Brett?"

Violet's heartbeat quickened beneath my hold, and her jaw tightened. "Focus, Violet. Stay here."

My words came out more as an order than a plea. Her earlier anger began to rise to the surface and I squeezed her hand harder, trying to contain it.

"She's getting angry. Very, very angry," I answered for her. I could feel her hatred for Brett as if it were my own.

"And after you killed him?" Zan asked, and just as quickly as her feelings of anger had appeared, they began melting away into something else.

"Triumph, maybe. Then…peace." I could feel my eyebrows furrow as I studied her face. She inhaled deeply, closing her eyes as if she was reveling in the victory of taking his life. It was something I didn't want to share with this audience, no matter how close we all were. "Then nothing."

"Because she avenged her death. And that of the woman in the cabin," Zan said as he straightened, his face becoming stern. It aged him.

"But she's a demon. Our tether is still intact," I stated. That earned a look from Violet as I released her and stood to face my uncle. Where he was going with this didn't make any sense.

"With the screams of a banshee and the vengeance of a fury."

CHAPTER 13

Kade

"Furies and banshees are not in our realm. Not anymore." Elias spoke what I knew to be true as well.

They, among other creatures, had been banished to another realm long before we were born. They were too unpredictable. While we tried to adapt to the world Violet lived in, they were set in their ways and their own beliefs about how to handle and carry out justice.

They also did not have the shifting capabilities that we had as demons and did not disguise themselves amongst the living. With today's technology at everyone's fingertips, they would cause more chaos than good. They were a liability to all of the different species and had been forced away long ago.

"Have you ever met one?" I asked Zan, knowing full well

that Elias and I never had.

My uncle's face fell at that small query. "I guess you could say that I did once. A banshee. With your father and mother."

At the mere mention of them I became melancholy. Nobody spoke about them. At least, not anymore. If anyone did, it wasn't while I was around. I knew my uncle had been close with them, and he and my dad were thick as thieves growing up just as Elias and I were.

Perhaps that was why I viewed Zan as a parental figure. He reminded me so much of my dad. Together with Sarah, they treated Aleena and me as if we were their own.

Violet squeezed my hand, and I couldn't bring myself to look at her black, tearstained face. It reminded me of the black waters of Obsidian Falls and her death.

But she shouldn't be crying black tears in the first place. That had been a red flag, along with her coming back from the dead. How could I have pushed these things off until now? Until she had taken a life?

It wasn't the explanation I had been hoping for, but it was all the more reason to believe that there was more to Violet than becoming a demon. Be it banshee, fury, or both, it was a complete mindfuck. How could she have more than one creature stirring within this body of hers?

"What was it like?" Elias chimed in. I returned my attention to Zan, who had crossed his arms, chin in hand.

I was to be king and I myself had never entertained the idea of crossing into that realm, as it was forbidden. From what little I knew, the creatures had been sealed in there and that was that. If it was ever brought up in conversation, it was shut down almost immediately. It was for the safety of humans, demons, and the remaining creatures of our respective worlds.

"Why did you go?" I asked when Zan didn't proceed with

an explanation right away.

"We were curious. A bit rebellious. We thought we were invincible, and with your father's upcoming reign, he thought he should know firsthand what was in that realm. Of course I wanted to go. He didn't have to ask me twice."

Knowing that my father hadn't quite begun his reign yet meant that he had been close to my age now, and I wondered if he had tethered to my mother yet when they made the decision to explore that realm. They would have been stronger if so, but I knew I couldn't compare my tethered partner and experience to theirs.

There was so little I remembered of my parents anymore. My memories of them were few and far between, though there were little things that would remind me of them occasionally. But this revelation of their act of defiance was an intriguing insight into the lives I never knew they led.

"The sky was overcast and there was blood in the air. A metallic smell and taste that lingered in your senses. You would have expected to find rivers or streams of blood, but they had the same water as us. From the moment we arrived, we knew we were being watched from the shadows and we were constantly on guard. There were sounds, rumblings, and shrills in the distance that would make the tiniest of hairs stand on end."

I hung onto each word he spoke, envisioning this region that I had never seen before. Sure, I had wondered plenty about that realm, but it never seemed like a place I had to worry about. It was almost as if it didn't exist. A myth, even.

"We moved in silence, cautious of every step and sound. Heads on a swivel and weapons at the ready. We didn't want to start a fight, but we'd be damned if we didn't plan to finish one should the situation arise."

He began to pace away from us as he revisited his past in his mind. "It wasn't until we came to a large river overtaken by brush with needlelike branches that we finally came in contact with anyone there. On the opposite side of the water stood a woman in rags. Her hair was so white it looked as if it were glowing beneath the darkened sky. Her face began to imitate the same expression Violet had when she was approaching Brett. It was as if she was screaming, but I could hear nothing. Your parents, however…"

"Heard them." I swallowed hard.

He dipped his chin down to confirm. "But here's where that banshee conflicts with Violet and her symptoms thus far. Although they could hear her scream, it was just that. Singular. There was no choir of voices, and it didn't consume them into a state of helplessness. They could still communicate, and they tried to plead with the banshee, telling her that they meant no harm. We began to cross the river, but she fled. We left before we could explore Xandor any further. It wasn't until we returned and began to peruse the library that we began to realize the seriousness of the situation."

Predictors of death.

At least, that was what little I knew of banshees.

"Now, they went on to live a few more decades before they met their fate, but all the same—it was predicted that day. But Violet's eyes, her hair, and the screams all differ from what I saw that day. And I'm sure you know we have very few texts about banshees and their appearance. We have more knowledge of furies than of them."

"What about her eyes? I have never heard of any kind of demon or creature that cries black tears," Elias butted in.

"That is something I have never encountered before. Or read, for that matter. I am certain I would remember something like that."

"Should we be concerned that Kadriel can hear them? The screams?" Elias was solid in posture, but his face showed how he truly felt. Worried.

I knew that a banshee could sense death, and what my parents heard was the prediction of theirs. Was Violet tapping into something in that regard about Staffan and Rafina? Was I interpreting all of this wrong in thinking she was sensing something negative about them?

Perhaps they weren't the enemy after all. I was conflicted about everything.

"I can't say for sure, but a part of me believes he is only hearing it because of his tethering. Their bond, their *connection*, is growing, and seeing as how Violet's ordeal this morning didn't break it, I think Kadriel has somehow tapped into Violet's banshee side."

"And the fury side?" I asked him as I watched the wound on Violet's arm close in tandem with mine. Zan pulled me from my watchful gaze as he questioned me.

"Did you feel the need to seek revenge and punish Brett?"

I scoffed, amused that he would think there was a possibility that I wouldn't.

"How could I not? He was responsible for her death."

"But that aside, did you feel a blinding rage to kill him yourself?"

"Yes," I spouted, then swiftly switched gears. "No. Maybe."

Had I only felt that through her?

I let my thumb graze across her skin, rubbing off some of the dried blood from her victim. It felt wrong to call him that, knowing that he had claimed two lives within such a short time frame.

I had wanted to deal with him myself, but it was

controllable. Violet had seemed almost in a trance of some sort as she took matters into her own hands. Exactly as Zan said—blinded by rage.

"I..." Violet's hoarse voice was barely a whisper as she struggled to speak. Her other hand shot up to her throat, alarm in her eyes. "I..."

"Don't force it." Lifting my hand to her neck, I gathered whatever energy I could. My hand began to warm but my touch did nothing. I couldn't feel the energy passing through to her, just as when I had attempted to save her body from the bullets that claimed her.

Feeling like a failure, I left her for my desk, grabbing a pad and some paper and then returning. I sat it upon her lap, and she paused before writing a message.

What happens now?

I swallowed hard, unsure of what answer I could give. The council was going to have a field day with this if they found out. My tethered mate was an assassin, of sorts. One I couldn't control or get a handle on. An unexplained hybrid that they would feel threatened by, and they would use it against me. Would they choose to banish the both of us, or would they go to the extreme and execute us? I didn't like the possibility of either.

Zan widened his stance, a newfound alertness prominent in his features. "I swore to myself that I would never go back to that place. Especially after losing your parents. But I think we need to pay it a visit."

Everyone in the room stilled. I could feel apprehension flowing between Violet and me. As much as I wanted to witness what Zan and my parents had seen, it was also unnerving not knowing what we were going into. Just because they had ventured out the last time and were never attacked, it didn't mean that we would be dealt the same hand.

"I'm coming." Elias stepped forward, adamant in his declaration. Like a soldier ready for battle, he was braced for it.

Zan nodded in his direction, then glanced between my best friend and I before he issued an order. "Dress in your protections and pack light but smart. Let's meet at my quarters at the top of the hour."

And with that, Zan and Elias left us.

What am I supposed to wear?

Violet's scribble was a quick flourish, and I could tell she was nervous by the shake in her hand and the air between us. I had dressed in my black armor that hugged every inch of me, but the hardened material at my chest felt like it was pressing too hard. I wasn't sure if it was just snug or if it was the waves coming off of Violet. I couldn't get my head on straight enough to differentiate between the two.

I retrieved my personal stash of weapons from a box in my closet and began strategically placing them all over my body. I had no idea what creatures we might encounter, but I had to be ready at any given moment should our lives depend on it.

I didn't like walking into unknown territory with the woman who had stolen my heart so many years ago. While I was mostly worried about Violet's well-being, I knew that we would all be walking targets.

And I hated that Violet had to come with us, as she had never been trained in combat. I knew she had to in the hopes of finding some answers, but the worry of her not being able to defend herself in the face of danger made a knot form in my stomach. Because she was part demon, I knew she was stronger than a mere human, but it was the banshee and fury parts of her that I wasn't familiar with and that sent my inner thoughts spiraling.

Would they be to her benefit or demise? If Violet somehow became more powerful than me, then so be it. I didn't care. But if it fucked with her somehow? If Violet was going to suffer because of everything that we had yet to understand?

I had been the one to take her to Obsidian Falls in the hope of a damn miracle. I hadn't cared about the consequences for me, but I hadn't even stopped to think about whether there might be any for her. Just when I had stopped beating myself up over one decision, the wound was reopening before my very eyes.

Knocks sounded at my door, and my chest tightened as the air around us thickened. I cast a look at Violet, who was already shrinking away from the sound and hugging the notepad into her chest.

As my heart rate spiked, I waited for my body to react to the remembrance of bullets. Spacing my feet apart as if that might help with the impact, I waited.

And waited.

Violet and I exchanged glances, neither of us looking forward to reliving the moment that had taken her life. I imagined her old green eyes, how bright they would be had they not changed to black, and the terrified look they would be giving me right now.

More knocking, this time harder and with more space between each to draw them out. I retrieved my pocket mirror and swiped to discover the guest who had decided to show up. My shoulders sagged a bit as I found Rebecca standing in the hall with several bags in hand. She looked as if she were humming a little number to herself.

Impeccable timing, I thought.

I instructed Violet to hide in my closet, and her back straightened slightly. "Just for a few minutes," I begged.

It felt as if I were going to get in trouble for having a girl over. Stashing her in my closet in the hopes that no one would find out. The humor wasn't lost on me, but I would rather not be riddled with questions as to why Violet's voice was currently out of order. We had gotten her cleaned up from her bloody mess, but her voice was still practically nonexistent.

I opened the door and was met with Rebecca's warm and gracious smile. "Good morning, Kadriel."

"Rebecca, please come in." I glanced about the hall, ensuring it was empty before letting her come inside. I offered to take some of the bags from her and she unloaded a few before stepping in. I quickly shut the door behind her as her short frame made its way into the bedroom area.

"I got these done a bit earlier than expected so I thought I would just go ahead and bring them by."

"Of course, thank you," I gushed as I hurriedly set the bags I had on the bed. Rebecca was eyeing me now at this point, taking in what I was wearing, and her face fell, creating lines around her chin.

"I'm sorry if I've interrupted anything."

"Nonsense, I need you actually. But this is delicate and requires discretion."

She tipped her head to the side as her eyes slanted, crinkled at the edges. "Anything for you, dear. Of course."

"I need protections for Violet, and fast."

"How fast?" she countered, looking about the bedroom, possibly in search of Violet. Little did she know Violet was peering out of the closet behind her back.

"Like, now." I tried not to seem pushy, but my tone was betraying me. "Please." I tried to cover it up with my manners.

"Is everything alright?" She crossed her arms, suddenly unsure of the task I was giving her.

I bit my tongue. The less she knew the safer it was for her. "It's too soon to tell. But I can try to petition the council to give you a longer stay with your family on your next return if you can help us right now. We're on a tight deadline."

Rebecca's immediate family had been gone for some time now, but she still visited during the summers to see the grandchildren of her siblings. They were unaware of who she really was, but she used it to her advantage, posing as a member of the community who had a winter home in Florida, renting out her home while she was away.

"Must be serious then." Rebecca had been here long enough to know when to stop asking questions. I only hoped that the draw of seeing her family for an extended amount of time was enough to buy her silence, if only for a little while so we could see this mission through. I trusted her discretion and that of her husband.

"I might have something that will work. Take me to the back room of my shop."

And I did just that. Rebecca hurried off, rummaging through racks or armored protections. I began to double-check that all of my weapons were secured as I waited. There was a thrum coming alive within my body. The very same one that took hold of me each and every time I found myself getting ready for battle. Adrenaline began to pump through my veins, readying my limbs and mind for the events of the unknown.

The same occurrence had happened only days ago when Elias, Aleena, and I were about to take on Damian. The mere thought of him made me want to punch a hole in the wall. As soon as we got to the bottom of this matter with Violet, that saint would get my full attention. The fact that he now had the capability of crossing into Darthou with that shard of glass was a matter that needed to be brought to the council as soon as possible.

And when I did so, I would have Elias at my side. He deserved recognition for catching such a crucial detail that would have impacted us all should it have gone unnoticed. I looked forward to watching Staffan's face as I delivered the news.

We still had no idea who had been feeding Damian information. Who would have told him that I was courting Violet for a possible tethering? The nerve someone must have had to betray their own was maddening.

"Now, you may not want to hear this, but you should know." Rebecca returned with an outfit that differed slightly from my own, and a pair of boots.

I cracked my knuckles with two rolls and waited for her to continue. The release of built-up tension faded away slightly with the sounds.

"I think this is the only one that will work for her figure. But the material is composed of different fibers. I have been toying with different techniques to try and reinforce the protections and make them stronger."

I could tell she was biting the inside of her cheek. Something like this would ordinarily need to be tested during training before being taken out on a mission of any kind.

"Is it weaker than what I wear?" I asked as I extended an arm to feel it. It was firmer than mine, and thicker.

"The goal is stronger." She was worried about her own creation being taken out of her possession, and on a newly turned demon, no doubt. Rebecca was smart, and her skills in building protections had surpassed any demon's knowledge decades ago. She had been responsible for making them ever since.

I honestly didn't know how she ever slept. Between dressing people for their day-to-day and making sure our protections were always in order, the woman certainly kept busy. But she was proud of what she did and she loved it. This craft was hers, in her past life and now.

I knew she meant well, and that she only had the best intentions at heart, but if this was the only piece that might work for Violet, we had no other choice.

"Kadriel, I'm not sure what's going on." She placed the garment over my arm but let her hand linger. "Please be careful. *Please* protect yourself and Violet."

She spoke with such sincerity that it had me blinking away from her momentarily. She was the only one to have dressed Aleena and I since we were kids and had followed us through our lives. She may not have been family by blood, but I knew her care for us ran deep.

"Thank you, Rebecca." I placed my hand over hers and offered a light squeeze. Rebecca and her tethered mate—husband, if you asked her—had never had any children of their own, and I had never thought to ask about it, knowing it wasn't my place. But I couldn't help but feel as if she treated us as her own, although in a different sense than Zan and Sarah. Aleena had worked with her for years and they were still close. And if she could put up with my high-maintenance sister for so long, she deserved high praise for that alone.

Returning to my place, I found Violet sitting on the edge of the bed. I apologized for leaving her so abruptly, but she remained quiet, fingers twisting together so tight her knuckles had whitened.

She held up her notepad, a longer message scribbled out.

Just how many things are real? First, demons and saints. Now, furies and banshees? What in the actual fuck, Kade?

Tension was rising before I could even finish reading. While I wanted to brush it off, I knew that this was a much larger conversation. While the feud between demons and saints was a big one, our troubles with them greatly outnumbered those with other creatures.

"Violet," I began, unsure of how to navigate through this news, "if demons and saints are real, is it that big of a stretch to know that there's more?"

Her eyes widened as her stern face sank with that realization.

"Our worlds are much bigger than you might have anticipated. And I look forward to teaching you about them, their inhabitants, history and so on."

As if a light bulb went off, she snatched the notebook again and in big bold letters wrote a word that brought a grin to my face. It was a welcome feeling in the heaviness of the situation we had found ourselves in.

MERMAIDS?!

"There are many underwater creatures," I said, purposefully skirting around an answer, and her lips began to pout when I didn't provide any further information.

Violet held up her hands as if she were going to beg and plead if she had a voice to do so.

Sighing, I gave her what she wanted. "Yes, they're real."

Her jaw dropped, and all I could think of was the menacing manner in which she had done the same thing in Brett's presence. I cleared my throat, trying to push that image away.

My mind was full of the painful scenes of her death, and now a newfound terror of what might be to come after seeing that look on her in the cabin. Violet's innocence was gone. And while I knew Brett's murder hadn't wreaked havoc on her up until this point, I feared that now that she had the taste of blood, what if there was no stopping a need for more?

Violet wasn't even acting like she had just murdered someone. A human might have felt remorse. Hell, a demon who had just made his first kill might have felt it as well. But now I didn't sense a single drop of it. There was a fleeting moment of it when she came back from her comatose state, but nothing since then.

I helped her dress, my hands intrigued by the feel of her protections. They hugged her curves and smoothed over her body with such ease that I thought it was too good of a coincidence that Rebecca had this in her size. I wondered when she had started working on this piece to begin with. The black material was similar to mine, but had a red sheen to it when it hit certain lighting.

Violet slipped her fingers through the fingerless gloves and stretched her arms out. Stepping behind her, I began to close the back, latching the hooks embedded in the material before pulling the zipper up. I placed a kiss on the space between the high points of her shoulder blades before finishing, and she turned.

Her eyes bore into mine, and quicker than I could anticipate, she launched herself into my arms, taking me around my middle. I held her for as long as she needed, not wanting to end the embrace until she was ready. I felt as if she needed the closeness as much as I did.

When we finally parted, I made my way back to the closet and retrieved another weapons box. While dressing her, I had noticed she had the same placements for some. While she hadn't been trained yet, I couldn't let her travel with nothing. I would send her in prepared, but with the hope that she wouldn't need to use them.

Setting the wooden box on the foot of the bed, I unhooked the silver clasp and opened it. Some of these were the very first blades I had used when I began my combat training. I hoped these might be more adequate for her hands. They were lightweight, which was good for traveling, but the blades were still sharp as a scalpel.

I could feel her hesitation as I began to collect a few to hide on her. "It's better to be prepared and not need them, than to go empty-handed and wish you had them. Prepare for the worst, but hope for the best."

I slid a palm-sized blade on the inside of her calf, the color of the handle blending in. I grabbed another and placed it on her upper arm, on the opposite side of her dominant hand. She eyed each one with apprehension and I tried my best to quell it.

Violet reached for the pad of paper and scribbled down another message.

You've really never been there before?

My heart sank at that. My father saw to it to explore this realm before his rise to the throne, and the thought had never even crossed my mind. Granted, he did so without permission or the knowledge of the council, but was I fit to run Darthou if I had never even seen this place? After all, we demons were the primary ones who had locked away these creatures in a realm of our creation, with the help of witches.

"I am not pleased to admit that I haven't." I secured another blade at her hip and looked her over. "Xandor is sort of taboo. I'm not even sure how to get there."

That admission out loud made me feel even worse.

"But we won't be alone. And at least Zan has visited, so this will be a learning experience for you, Elias, and me." I kissed the top of her head and took her hand in mine. "Come, we should get going."

CHAPTER 14

Kade

We appeared in Zan's watching quarters to be met by him, Sarah, and Elias already waiting for us. The grim expression on Sarah's face was one that many humans wore when their loved ones were getting shipped out for military duty. She came over to Violet and gave her a squeeze.

"I hope you find the answers you need." She held her at arm's length as she spoke, then backed away so she could view the four of us dressed in our protections. She seemed out of place amongst us all, wearing her usual attire for when she was home with the boys—a sweater, jeans, and her hair pulled back and up out of her face.

"You boys take care of her," she almost scolded us three men with a look in her eyes that I had seen her use on her sons. "Be smart and be safe." She placed a kiss on Zan's cheek just as something crashed in the background.

Sarah let out an agitated groan, her face scrunching as she hurried out of the room, closing the door behind her. If I had to guess, my cousins were roughhousing, and now probably trying to scurry away to try and hide whatever damage they had just caused.

Violet pulled me from my thoughts, placing her hand in mine in a tight hold. I was doing my best to try and stay levelheaded, providing her with any ounce of comfort or ease that I could, but I was nervous myself. I felt weak, knowing there was a possibility that I was showing her that this brave face I wore hid so much beneath it.

Crossing into Xandor while tethered was going to present a new set of challenges that I wasn't ready to face, but I had to. Not only did I have to combat Violet's and my own warring feelings while trying to navigate an unknown realm, but I had to protect her from any harm that might come our way. With our connection still figuring out whatever the hell it was doing, we had no idea just how far it would take us. If one of us was injured, we had no idea how it would impact the other. I only hoped it wasn't any hindrance physically.

"Now—" Zan's voice became like that of a commanding officer, readying his troops for battle. I only hope it didn't come to anything like that. "I think it goes without saying that once we arrive in Xandor   we will flank Violet and I will take the lead. We will remain soundless and move cautiously. Stay away from the shadows if you can help it, and stay on high alert."

"But how do we get there? Better yet, how did you find out that you could?" Elias was asking the exact questions I wanted to know. I had never seen the place, nor did I know much about any of its occupants, so I couldn't bring up an image on a mirror even if I wanted to. You had to have a rough idea of who or what you were searching for.

"There was a journal your father claimed to have found long ago with hand-drawn images of it." His gaze fell to the floor as if recalling a memory that he had to focus on. His face reminded me of my father when he became pensive. "He might not have gone about finding it in the right way, but he gathered enough information to take us there."

"And where is this journal now?" I asked, never having heard of such a thing. I didn't like that my uncle had kept this from me. That it had taken Violet coming to Darthou and becoming whatever she was for me to find out about it. How long would he have kept this from me?

"I'm afraid that is one thing that Tarnon never would share. He said that when he went back to find it again, it was gone."

Would the mysteries ever cease? Where on earth would my father have been to discover something like that? Did someone find out that he had? I knew a resource like that would never be found in our library, and I wondered what kind of snooping around my father was doing that brought him to it.

Zan took a blade from his side and sliced the top of his finger as he approached his wall of mirrors. "For this passage, we'll need to walk through. But upon return we can do so by pocket."

That earned a quizzical look from Violet, and I tapped at my chest. "Our pocket mirrors. We shield them beneath our armor."

She nodded in understanding as we returned our attention to Zan who was marking a series of mirrors. I wondered just how much information my father had come across to know that crossing into Xandor required blood. I wouldn't have been able to cross there without knowing that tidbit.

With a swipe of his hand from the floor up toward his highest marked mirror, an image began to form. Barren trees and cracked grounds began to fade into view. Patches of dead grass that were few and far between showed a wasteland that looked as if it had no life. If there was any kind of sun, it wasn't doing its job of illuminating very well.

"Hm…darker than I remember," Zan mumbled as he took a step back, studying the lifeless picture before us all. "May fortune be on our sides."

With that, Zan was the first to cross over, and Elias followed him without hesitation. I could feel Violet's heartbeat quicken in my palm as they began to appear in our view of Xandor. I knew they were trying to scope out the surroundings and I waited for them to signal us to cross.

A bit hastily, I pulled Violet's view away from the mirrors and pressed my lips to hers. I didn't know what awaited us there, but I had to taste her one last time before we traveled there. She met me with equal desperation, pulling at the back of my neck to secure me to her. But we were soon interrupted by a tap on my pocket mirror. It was the signal for the all clear.

"I love you," I said as I reluctantly broke away. Her eyes opened with a sense of fear as I led her toward the mirrored entrance. I knew she had spoken those same words to me on the verge of impending sleep, but whether she could recall it or not, I didn't know. I didn't want her to feel as if she had to say it now, especially if there was a chance she didn't fully mean it. But I couldn't leave here without saying it to her one last time.

I stepped through first, pulling Violet in behind me. We were met with a cool, dirt-ridden breeze that passed by us, carrying with it the scent of blood. Zan had been right about that. I scanned the area as I placed Violet between Elias and me, and behind Zan, so we were a V-formation around her.

There was a crack from my right and my head snapped in its direction. The shadows in the naked woods seemed too dark considering there was no greenery around. While it was indeed cloudy, it wasn't dark enough to be considered night. I should have been grateful that the trees and bushes were bare, giving less of an opportunity for something to hide, but I was well aware that some creatures wouldn't need cover to do so.

The wind howled past my ears, picking up its course as we began to move. The metallic taste was evident on my tongue, and I caught the scent mixing with something I could only describe as rotting corpses. It was a foul smell that made me begin to take shallow breaths, and it was affecting Violet just as much.

She was worried but on high alert, just like the rest of us. She was quite the sight among our group, and to the untrained eye she fit right in with her apparel. The way her body moved in her protections was something I never knew I needed to see. She exuded an appearance of power and for that, I imagined her upon my mother's throne.

If we could just get to the bottom of this banshee and fury business, she could be a force to be reckoned with. Even though she had ended Brett's life, I still didn't fear her, but feared *for* her. I wondered what all she was capable of and if she could control it. If she could learn to.

There had to be a reason why Violet had come back like this. I just didn't know who would have anything to gain by her doing so. Nothing had been done to Violet prior to her being shot. Elias and I both had been through the footage so many times, and there was no foul play. It had me circling back to the only plausible explanation.

Rafina.

My eyes widened as I tried to shake away my straying thoughts. This wasn't the time or place—I had to get my head on straight.

Another snap to our right drew our collective attention, and I knew something was following us. I felt its presence even though it couldn't be seen. I withdrew a blade from the underside of my forearm and readied myself. I wouldn't be the first to start anything, but I would be ready if something else made the first move.

Zan and Elias prepared themselves as well. My adrenaline was fueling me, gearing up for whatever hid in the dead forest that stretched on for who knew how far.

The wind stilled and the only sound to be heard was the crunch of the ground beneath our feet. Zan held up a signal to halt and we did so, forming a circle around Violet with our backs toward her.

It was too quiet. This was the calm before the storm, and I was eager to meet whatever thought it could ensnare us.

A shriek cut through the silence, a rallying cry that had us all bracing ourselves, but it was as if the one sound was coming from different directions. We had only been here a few minutes, but whatever was nearby wasn't going to let us explore any further. I couldn't tell where the sound originated from, but its cry filled my ears and resonated in my chest. The shadows from the trees seemed to grow outward and toward us, darkening the ground on our path.

Snapping twigs and branches began to close in but I couldn't see a single creature. A gray mist began to emerge from the tree line and rolled out into view. It let out a sizzle as it approached, and I took a step back just as the rest of us did to close in around Violet. I had no idea how to defend myself against this mist, had no thought of what it was capable of, and I was ready to bolt back to Darthou before Violet's voice rose into a piercing scream that split into two.

How in the hell could she scream when she couldn't get her voice out to speak?

I ducked at the sound she made, trying not to topple over from the impact on my ears. I shot looks at Zan and Elias, already knowing they couldn't hear her. But the mist quickly began to retreat and then to take form.

Violet's voice didn't cease until the mist created a wicked-looking woman before us, just a few yards away. She wore a mixture of materials that were shaded to blend in with her surroundings, and her features were sharp and pointed, her gray hair matted to the point that it probably needed cut off.

Her power was a dead giveaway that she was a witch, and I knew we all were gravely unprepared for the likes of her.

"State your business here!" She raised her voice, aggravated by our arrival. This certainly wasn't the greeting that Zan had experienced with my parents. What had transpired here since then to bring this on? And how was Violet able to stop it?

"We mean no harm. We are only here to seek answers," Zan spoke up, voice firm and unshaking. He moved, rotating our positions in our formation around Violet so he could face the witch straight on. I hated tearing my gaze away from the witch, but Elias and I had to make sure nothing else crept up on us in the wake of her distraction.

A shrill laugh erupted from her in her amusement. "Like I haven't heard that before. Liars!" She practically spat at us. "And you think bringing her will grant you passage? How dare you!" Lightning cracked in the distance as her anger elevated.

The same shriek from earlier shot across the sky, and I had the sneaking suspicion that this witch before us was not the cause of it.

"What do you know of her?" I swiveled in my post so I could see her again. Violet had never stepped foot here until today. Until only minutes ago. "We mean no harm, we are only here to—"

"Seek answers, yes. And yet you come armed and with this—this thing!"

My blade began to heat in my hand, sending sparks into the air. Within seconds, a flame ignited. The same happened to the ones in Zan's and Elias's hands, and we all dropped them to the ground at the same time. I healed my hand in seconds from the sudden and harsh blaze, barely letting the pain register.

"And you—" I could see her eyes fixated on Violet. "You could be powerful enough to lead, and yet you hide behind them like some child. You will be used and then thrown away when they can't control you anymore."

The witch's words angered me. Was this the purpose of Violet's transition? Of the fury, banshee, and demon within her? This was nothing she asked for.

"I am not a child," her broken voice cracked from behind me, and I could feel her wrath at being called such.

The witch snapped her fingers and Violet was before her and within arm's reach. A gripping panic overcame me that I had only experienced once before. The thought of losing her after she had been shot came to the forefront of my mind, and I began to lurch forward.

The earlier mist left the witch as if caught in a gust of wind, skirting around Violet and headed straight toward us. I braced for impact, but it stopped only inches from my face, creating a barrier and caging us.

"Violet!" I shouted as I let my fingers graze the mist to test it before I could barrel through it. It singed my skin, creating burn marks that quickly began to shape into boils.

"Fuck!" I jumped back, assessing them. They were slow to heal, but I could feel them fading already.

"Not to alarm you two, but pocket travel is useless," Zan alerted us as we frantically searched for some way out that we had yet to see.

I tried to leave myself, trying to escape. But nothing happened. We were fish in a barrel at this point, awaiting whatever the witch had in store for us. I had been hoping to try and return home, so when I came back, I could put myself behind the witch. But that plan was quickly squashed.

She let out a devilish laugh as the mist continued to box us in, closing off our view of the clouded sky. Zan, Elias, and I backed against each other, shoulders hitting as we did. If I so much as took a deep breath, my chest would make contact with the mist, and I didn't want to take the chance of it ruining my protections. Then again, if I could heal my hand that quickly, would I be able to make it through the box that held us captive?

The witch began to circle Violet, eyeing her as if prey had just fallen into her lap. Her smug look was the last straw, and I stepped forward into the mist.

CHAPTER 15

Violet

Excruciating pain erupted through my body and I felt as if I was burning. I pivoted on my feet to find Kade caught in the mist, and I could feel his struggle against it. It was an inferno that overtook us both.

"Stop it!" I shrieked at the woman. Whatever witchcraft this was, it was brutal and unrelenting as Kade remained suspended in it, the toes of his boots barely touching the ground beneath him.

"Make me!" She met me with equal rage.

Fearing for my life, Kade's, and those with us, I sprung at her. Knocking her to the ground, I let my throat burst with a cry that I wanted her to hear. I wanted to make her fear me, wanted to make her eyes bleed, and if I had to rip out her heart just as I had Brett's—so be it if it meant saving us. I would not be made fun of, and I would prove to her that I was no child. I had no idea what I had become, or the extent of my so-called fury and banshee sides, but I'd be damned if I was going to let her come between me and the answers we sought.

And if she took Kade from me, her head would fucking roll.

The whites of the woman's eyes began to redden, creeping in from the outer corners and taking over. I could feel my influence over her as her strength on me began to diminish. The rags she wore reeked of body odor, yet it still paled in comparison to what the air of Xandor smelled like.

I let a hand pull back, ready to plunge into her and take another life today.

I could sense that she had wronged others herself, that she was a killer. As the whites of her eyes vanished and blood began to pool, I could see reflections of those who had died by her hands. It was as if I were her in those moments, carrying out horrible deaths with her bare hands or with magic. It was infuriating. Hate seeped into every pore as I watched each life get taken.

I would be doing a service to those very lives that were lost.

"Stop!" A bony hand wrapped around my wrist, and my lust for revenge faded away almost immediately. I stumbled back and scrambled away to find two women in shreds of clothing staring back at me. If I didn't know any better, I would say they were homeless. They were tattered, dirty, and nothing but skin and bones, as if the wind could carry them away like blades of grass.

I panted as I realized the mist was evaporating, and I rushed to my feet and over to Kade who was hunched over. Only his face and hands were uncovered, but the burns and boils were fading at a slow pace.

"Are you okay?" My voice was hoarse again and it irked me. I could scream but I could barely talk?

Elias and Zan helped me bring Kade to his feet. "Never better," he groaned as his complexion began to surface through his marred skin.

"Why are you here?" One of the skinny women spoke and I turned my attention back to them, carefully placing my hand in Kade's.

"We don't mean any trouble," Zan said gently. "We came here looking for answers, for her." He gestured toward me.

The two exchanged a look I couldn't decipher, then looked to the woman I had almost killed as she began to stand and compose herself. She was swiping away at the red on her face, wiping it off on her sleeves.

"Anyone who travels here either makes promises they can't keep or decides to kill us." The woman swept away the blood on her cheeks. "And you—" She gestured at Kade. "You remind me of the one who promised to release us and never returned."

Kade exchanged a glance with his uncle as Zan stepped forward. "Tarnon was my brother, Kadriel's father. But he only visited once, with his tethered mate and me."

The woman shook her head. "You are wrong. He visited many times by himself. Brought food, clothing, and gifts. He was no stranger here."

A stunned silence fell over all of us before Zan spoke again. "I...I never knew. We barely spoke about this place after we left."

I could feel Kade's confusion and sense Zan's over this news. He seemed to have been close with his brother, from what little he had spoken of him. What made Tarnon decide to keep him in the dark over his comings and goings? Why the secrecy from his own family?

"I thought the banshee's cries were enough to keep him from coming back." Zan shook his head, his hurt evident on his face as he scrubbed at his chin.

"I assume he has met his end then?" The woman asked as if she already knew the answer, and I could tell there was a sadness behind her words. How well had she known Tarnon, to care about him? Her display of emotion was fleeting before she put on a sour face again.

"About twenty years ago, yes. He and his mate, Audra. By the hands of saints."

The woman's face grew grim and the two other women spoke one right after the other.

"Filthy creatures."

"They should be trapped here, not us."

"Along with your demon friend."

The air began to grow tense around us and the wind picked up. The women who were made of skin and bones continued to hiss through their teeth, a sound that made my skin tingle.

"You're furies," I said, drawing their attention. My voice cracked and I swallowed hard. They appeared nothing like the depictions I had seen in any show or book, but I could feel a draw toward them the longer I was in their presence. A familiarity that pulled at me.

"And you—" They approached me in unison as if they were twins, even if they only resembled one another by their skin and bones physique, but perfectly in sync. "You were born from the blood of our sister."

Their words made my blood run cold. "Wh…what?" I could feel a panic building. I couldn't decide which of them to focus on as I searched their eyes. One had blue, the other light brown.

"You really don't know, do you?" The woman who I could only identify as a witch stepped in closer, and I could feel Kade tense beside me. "Come here."

Kade tugged on my hand as I tried to leave his side, but I shot him a look. We came here for answers, and I intended to get just that and by whatever means necessary. Besides, I almost killed her once, and if I had to, I could probably do it again.

"This might hurt a little." Her hand shot forward, landing on my forehead, and my eyes turned to the darkened sky. Images began to fire through my mind as a numbness radiated through her touch. We were going backward through the events of the past few days. Brett's murder, Kade and me messing around, the day of celebration, the screams, Kade, tethering, council, screams, waking up in the infirmary, pain, my murder, Kade, the tethering courtship, and all the way to my life before I'd even known about this world.

She released me and I felt the dizzying aftermath of her sifting through my memories. I blinked my eyes, hard, trying to focus. My breath became shallow as I tried to compose myself.

"What did you do to her?" Kade rushed to my side to steady me. I could tell in his voice he was ready to fight for me and I had to talk him down.

"I'm fine, really," I tried to assure him. "How did you do that?" I asked the woman, embarrassed by the croaks coming from my throat.

"She's a witch," Kade offered. I had already come to that conclusion myself after seeing what she was capable of so far.

The witch eyed the furies and they approached her. "She is indeed innocent. She was a human until two days ago. She knows nothing of what happened here or to her with the block in her memories."

"Again, we only seek answers. We mean no harm," Zan said again. I looked at Elias. Up until this point, I had almost forgotten he was even here. He remained on guard but quiet, taking everything in and continuing to scan our surroundings.

"Come," the witch instructed Zan. He cautiously moved toward her and I observed as the witch proceeded to do the same thing to him as she had done to me. I wondered what she was searching for, knowing she had stopped skimming through my memories a while before Kade had entered the picture.

She placed her hand to his head and he clenched his fists. Veins began to become more pronounced in his neck and he grimaced almost in pain. I wasn't sure if it was the witch's touch that produced it, the sifting through his memories, or both. My turn was over so quick that I recovered fast, but it seemed to take longer with Zan and I thought he might pop a blood vessel. Her focus remained on where her hand met his skin the entire time. And when she finally released him, he was gasping for air.

"Two days ago, a demon returned. One we thought to be a friend. She left a path of destruction in her wake. She annihilated several different creatures and some, the last of their line. By the time I finally caught up to her, it was too late. The damage had been done, lives lost. We weren't prepared for an attack." The witch shifted her stance and crossed her arms.

"Even though our realm is dying, I vowed then that I would do whatever necessary to protect those of us that are left, no matter the cost." The witch spoke with such hurt, and I could only imagine the carnage she had seen.

A friend's betrayal and no warning of the tables turning. Who could do such a thing? Why slaughter the ones who were banished here? It made no sense, and I struggled to wrap my head around it. It was cruel. Too, too cruel.

"That's why you attacked us." Zan had recuperated from the assault on his mind and shook his head. He looked exhausted.

She nodded. "When you arrived with this…*girl*. This being that has been derived from the loss of others, I lost it. These were creatures I cared for, that I considered family. We've been cleaning up the mess and giving them proper burials ever since." Her voice began to break, emotions cutting through her hardened exterior. But even with her display, I couldn't help but wonder about the images I had seen in her eyes. Could she really be trusted?

My heart sank for those I didn't know, for the lives lost. I couldn't help but feel responsible for some of it. I was created from the death of others. It made my stomach roll.

I separated myself from Kade and the group, needing a moment to comprehend. Just how many had died? How many lives were lost because of me?

Demons. Saints. Furies and banshees and witches. Oh fucking my. This was too much.

"Our prison is dying." The witch looked about at the wasteland around us as she continued. "I am siphoning off bits of magic here and there to try to protect and feed us."

"I thought it looked different here," Zan said. "It's bare. Like a forest turned into a desert."

The witch nodded, and the furies at her sides kept their heads hung low. They weren't much for eye contact, which made it easier to study them. They looked like they'd been starving for some time. It was evident even through the rags they wore.

"Walk with me," the witch instructed Zan as she pivoted to leave. "We must talk."

I could hear footsteps as they began to leave and I kept my eyes away from the rest of the bunch. The witch's clothing dragged against the dry ground, meddling with the sounds of their departure.

I placed a hand to my throat, willing my chords to heal enough so I could speak. I felt ridiculous being rendered to this state in the presence of those who could provide insight into what I was and what all I was possibly capable of. I never knew what was going to come out of my mouth when trying to speak.

"You've killed."

I could feel the statement directed at me and I froze in place. I knew one of the furies was speaking to me, but I didn't know which one. Their voices were too similar. They both had darkened hair, but their eyes and complexions set them apart.

"Your first." The other one spoke this time, and I detected a slight airiness to this one's tone.

"And recently."

Kade's voice cut through. "She did. Her murderer."

I shuddered at Kade's words. Adding murderer to my list of identities was something that I had trouble comprehending. Everything had happened so fast this morning, it felt like a blur now.

I looked down at my hand, envisioning Brett's blood upon it, the weight of his massacred heart after being torn from his chest. How I'd ended his life without a second thought. I should have been troubled that I had committed such an act, but in reality, what really scared me was that I had no regrets about it.

"And yet you have demon eyes."

"Precisely why we came here. We didn't feel as if we could trust anyone back home." I knew Kade had struggled at first with the fact he couldn't turn to the powerful healer he claimed Rafina to be. But once he had accepted my plea and heard me out on the matter, he never questioned me again.

"Trust is earned."

"And easily broken."

"We were tricked."

"Never again."

"Do you know who killed your sister?" Kade tried to ask. "Who caused this devastation?"

"We do not use names."

"Names can be used against us."

I returned to face everyone still present. Zan and the witch were nowhere to be seen.

The way the furies spoke made me wonder if they shared a brain at this point. The way they moved and spoke made them appear as if they were almost the same being but split in two. They looked more human than I thought they would. I couldn't explain how I even knew they were furies; I only felt a strange connection that I couldn't put my finger on. I felt it when one touched my hand, almost as if I already knew them.

"What did she look like?" Kade prodded, trying to get some sort of helpful information from them.

"She wore many faces."

"Many frames."

Kade was clearly perturbed by this and he began to pace back and forth. "If you saw her again, you would be able to identify her, correct?"

"Yes…" they hissed in unison, and the hair on my arms rose. I could sense their vengeance. It mirrored my own that I had felt earlier. Their features turned dark, eyes hollowing as their loose hair whipped around them. "We want to end her."

They wanted to seek revenge for their lost sister and the

lives of others. I, myself, wanted that for them. I wanted the murderer to suffer a slow and agonizing death. I wanted to draw it out, make them beg for their life, and twist them until they came undone. I wanted to see life slip from their eyes as they succumbed to death. My body began to vibrate as I focused on an unknown and faceless predator. A ruthless killer who had taken so many lives that these furies were still dealing with the aftermath and burying their friends even days after the event.

"Violet?" Kade's voice sounded distant, and I began to descend into a madness that welcomed me with open arms. "She's doing it again, she's slipping away." Kade crossed in front of me and I could taste the return of a blinding rage.

The furies exchanged a look of mischief before corrupted grins crossed their faces. Their very presence fed me, as if it were fuel to the fire blazing within me. There were so many teeth present when they smiled, their sinister glee belonging to some sort of horror flick.

"She is powerful."

"*Very* powerful."

I knew Kade was hanging onto the sides of my arms, but I couldn't feel his touch. He was trying to calm me down with his influence, our connection, but it wasn't strong enough to pull me back.

I pushed it—and him—away as if making my way through water. I knew he only sought to protect me, regardless of what I had become. He didn't care what I was, he only wanted to understand and help me navigate through it. It was why I loved him.

And I did love him. I knew it in my core.

"Violet, stay. Please. Don't go," he pleaded, his voice becoming more pronounced as he fought to hold me again. As if he could root me here in the dehydrated earth we stood on.

I began to cave beneath his touch, feeling the high that overcame me begin to subside. The anger that was tearing me open at the seams began to melt and fade away as I focused on his eyes.

Images flashed through them, much the same as I had seen in the witch earlier. Lives that had been taken by his hands and the weapons in them. I studied each one as they flitted through.

The first had Aleena and Elias in the background. In some building I didn't recognize.

Then another scene. Kade held a beaten man over the edge of a bridge late at night, snapping his neck before letting his body fall into the waters below.

Again and again, I witnessed the man before me taking life after life. All different places and with different faces. But there was one thing that separated the lives taken from what I had seen in the witch's eyes.

I couldn't explain how I knew, but they were evil. Souls that were as black as I could imagine they came. Even as they were begging and pleading for their lives, it fell on deaf ears. Kade had a code that he lived by. That demons were supposed to live by.

The watchers found the wrongdoers and the seekers punished them. And in each image I saw, he was doing exactly that.

"She has the sight."

"She does."

CHAPTER 16

Violet

I blinked away, shaking my head to clear it of the images as I tried to register the words from the furies and come to terms with what I had just witnessed. I hated to think how long it could have gone on, had I not been interrupted. Just how many had Kade killed over the years?

I knew he had taken lives before, by his own admission. But seeing it was like seeing a whole new side of him, almost an entirely different person. The worst I had seen him do was punch Brett, and later drag him out of my apartment building by the back of his shirt.

"You've killed," I stated bluntly, rubbing my throat as if it would help my voice become clearer. "A lot."

The amused looks from the furies didn't go unnoticed, and Kade stumbled back, alarmed at my words. I could feel his shock as he tried to stifle it, putting on a mask before his feelings caught up to cover it.

"Your voice will heal." One fury stepped forward and the other followed a fraction of a second behind.

"Claiming the life of the one who wronged you is always the hardest. Mentally and physically."

Elias stepped toward the furies and they eyed him curiously. "What is this sight that you speak of?"

Thankful that he had asked the question for me, I returned my attention to the women. Until today I had never experienced this before. *This* was new. Along with my apparent strength, and the will to assassinate the human who wronged me and the witch who posed a threat to the demons I had arrived with.

"You were going to kill the witch." One spoke and the other followed. I was about ninety-nine percent certain they shared a mind at this point.

"Why?"

I began to shrink in my pose as I crossed my arms. Everyone's eyes were on me, and the thought of them waiting with bated breath to hear my squawk of a response was unsettling.

I had seen images reflected in Kade's eyes, just as I had seen in the witch's earlier. But the lives she had taken outnumbered Kade's by an astronomical amount. It begged the question once again of whether we could really trust her. About anything.

And how close were the furies to this witch? If they were a close-knit bunch, seeing as how the population here was apparently dwindling, I had to choose my words carefully. They had no reason to trust me, just as I had no reason to trust them.

I swallowed hard before speaking. "I could see death in her

eyes. The lives lost by her hands." I stared at the ground between the feet of the furies. Whatever they wore for shoes was flimsy and worn. You couldn't tell me it shielded their feet any more than a sock would.

"Just as you could see it in him?"

"The one you cling to?"

My head shot up to them, only to then glance at Kade. "Yes."

I hadn't asked to see it in him. Didn't even know what I had done to bring it on. It felt like going through personal belongings that I had no right to see, and I felt guilty for it.

I could sense apprehension flowing out from him at the admission. Telling me was one thing, but I was sure he hadn't expected me to be able to visit those memories.

"What is so special about him?"

"Why *do* you cling to him so?"

They both cocked their heads to the side, eyeing the both of us. I was going to start calling them Thing 1 and Thing 2 if they didn't give me any names to go by.

"We...we're tethered." Kade's words did little to vanquish the uncertainty in his voice.

"How unusual."

"How intriguing."

Their scrutinizing gazes traced over us and I wasn't sure what they were searching for. Their beady stares swept us from head to toe and back again, studying every nook and cranny. I might as well have been naked, getting sized up by the frail women and their stares.

When they turned to each other, it was as if they were speaking amongst themselves with their thoughts.

"Attempting to tether with different creatures was prohibited long ago." The witch had resurfaced to my right, along with Zan who wore a grim expression that made my stomach sink. "I can't recall a single encounter where the tethering proved successful, either. It is imperative that you keep these abilities hidden. Your life and the lives of those around you will be gravely impacted if this information falls into the wrong hands."

A chill ran through me and Kade wrapped an arm around my side, pulling me closer.

"She can't exactly control when she hears these screams. Sometimes, the force of them when they hit her is…alarming. Distance is the only thing to give her some relief, but we can't exactly keep her sequestered away from everyone. It would be too suspicious." I was grateful that Kade was speaking up for me.

"The only way to rid yourself of the screaming in your mind is to let it out. But if you do that you will expose yourself." The witch approached and held out a fisted hand. Hesitantly, I placed mine beneath hers. She dropped two silver coins into my palm. The warmth that came from them was unusual. They harbored more heat than they should have. Either the witch had a high fever or something else was at play here.

I raised an eyebrow as I flipped them in my hand. They were worn and slightly bigger than quarters, but there were only rune-like engravings on them. It reminded me of those coins in textbooks about ancient civilizations —the ones that would be put on the eyes of loved ones after they had passed. If I was remembering correctly, it was the Greeks that did that?

"I have never done this before, but I hope they will prove a useful aid in Darthou. Keep these with you at all times and they will suppress your fury and banshee senses."

"But will her demon side remain intact?" Kade asked.

"In theory, yes. Just make sure to have them on you when you are in the company of others and keep them hidden. Tell no one of them and keep your circle small." The warning in her voice was evident, and the look upon her face was serious.

"What about Kadriel? When Violet screams, he can hear it," Elias butted in, and everyone's attention turned to him.

"How odd."

"How curious."

The witch stepped forward, studying Kade. He acted as a buffer between her and me and placed himself between us. "Is it directed at you? Her screams?"

I shook my head no as Kade responded. "I don't think so. It was toward her murderer and toward you." I could sense he was nervous even though his response was calm and level. While I had never been one to read Kade well, his emotions provided more insight than what showed in his exterior.

"May I?" She lifted her hand and Kade stilled. I had hoped that when she sifted through Zan's and my memories that would be enough. But apparently with this new information, she needed to see things for herself.

Squeezing his hand, I dipped my head down to urge him to let her in. Reluctantly, he stepped forward and she placed her palm to his forehead. I knew the instant she began her work as Kade's grip tightened. The earlier numbness I had felt from her touch started at my forehead and began to work its way back, spidering off through my head in a dizzying manner. I felt like a bobblehead without her hand steadying me this time. My neck was unable to keep straight as my ball of a head swayed side to side, and just when I was on the verge of toppling over, she released him.

The witch didn't wait for Kade or me to recover before she moved on. I was still trying to find my bearings as she did.

"You need not worry about hearing her screams unless they are for you. Your tethering is so strong that you are tapping into her, just as she is into you. Only time will tell the extent of your abilities."

I should have been as relieved as Kade was, but I couldn't help but contemplate what she meant by the extent of his abilities. She didn't speak to us as a pair when she said that last bit, she was looking at him and only him.

"I'm afraid we have to cut this party short," Zan cut in.

"Not much of a party," Elias tried to joke.

Kade was spilling words out of his mouth at the thought of leaving. "Already? We haven't even—"

Zan drew up a hand to stop him. "I'm afraid we have to return, and quickly." He turned toward the witch and the furies. "My apologies for the quick exit and I do hope to return soon. We thank you for your time." He bowed in their direction and then turned his attention to us. We must have all looked dumbfounded at his abrupt eagerness to leave.

"Should you find yourselves visiting again, I'd like to meet this Aleena."

I was momentarily thrown by the witch's request. But I realized that since she had sifted through the memories of everyone but Elias, she probably had a plethora of information. The thought that she now knew more about Kade than I did was unsettling.

"We will take that into consideration." Zan's face was void of any emotion or confusion. But when he turned his attention on us, his head dipped down in seriousness. "My quarters, now."

Without a blink, we were back in his quarters, my eyes settling on the sight of Sarah, concern etched on her face as she all but leapt into Zan's arms. My eyes fluttered, trying to sort out the drastic and sudden change in scenery.

The fresh air that I inhaled was a welcome return to Darthou. I had gotten used to the rotten smell of Xandor, but now that we had returned, I was a bit relieved.

"How much time do we have?" he asked her as she released him. When I'd been here before, I hadn't allowed myself the chance to take in my surroundings. I wondered if Zan's quarters were in his place of residence like Kade's. He had a monstrous desk with papers and files stacked and a computer amongst it all. He had several bookshelves that were filled to the brim, some of them bowing at the weight of the books on them. It looked more like a mini library here compared to Kade's.

"Maybe fifteen minutes. I tried to buy you more time, I did. But Staffan was rather adamant." Sarah was beyond flustered, stumbling over her words.

"I'm sure he was. He didn't waste any time." Zan was beginning to remove his weapons, placing them on a small table that had only two chairs at it but was big enough for about six.

"What is it?" Kade inserted himself into the conversation.

"Council will meet shortly to discuss your actions from Sunday."

"Already?" Elias jumped in. He was really good at being a silent partner, as I kept forgetting that he was with us. He was the fly on the wall that you forgot about, but he was still very much present.

"Afraid so," Zan said as he kept removing blades from his person. "Elias, thank you for joining us today. Carry on as usual, and I might call on you later."

Elias mumbled good luck and left as Sarah retrieved a box from a chair at the table, one that resembled the box Kade had pulled out of his closet to find some blades for me. She made quick work of putting them away, knowing which one went where as they were nestled into their homes.

"I'll take Violet home. She can wait there until I return." I perked up at Kade's mention of home. I hadn't even been here forty-eight hours yet and he was referring to his place as *our* home. While I liked the notion of it, I couldn't focus on it for long.

"I'm afraid that won't be an option." Sarah's voice was a bit perturbed. "Rafina has been instructed to perform an examination on her while you're at council."

I clutched the coins in my hand so tight that I could feel them forming indents in my palms.

"They are separating us…fuck." Kade walked off, both hands running through his hair. Anxiety was flowing off of him and it did nothing to help ease mine.

Zan agreed as he removed a knife from his ankle. "They are. No doubt that was their plan. I'm sorry I wasn't here to fight it off. Violet, I think it goes without saying, but keep those coins hidden on you. Do not divulge any details regarding our trip to Xandor, or Brett. You are trying to acclimate to your new life as a demon, but don't elaborate on the extent of your abilities. Common side effects of transitioning to a demon are headaches, nausea, and fatigue, but they will have usually faded by now."

Funny. Those were side effects of any and all medications or prescriptions, so they should be easy to remember. That aside, I was still concerned about one thing. I pointed to my throat to draw attention to it. This was one thing I wouldn't be able to explain away. I cringed as I croaked again, "This?"

"Right." Zan retrieved what I hoped was the last of his weaponry from his opposite ankle and handed it to Sarah. He was armed just as much as Kade was. Returning his foot to the ground, he met me with an even stance. "Kadriel, try to heal her."

Kade looked like he was resisting the urge to roll his eyes. "I've tried, Zan."

"Try again," he practically ordered this time, and the room became hushed, although I wasn't sure how that could be possible. When voices didn't fill it, it was pin-drop silent. Zan struck me as an elevator music kind of guy. Something to just play in the background to offset the quiet.

Kade took a deep breath as he came to stand before me. I offered a half-hearted smile as he lifted a hand to my throat, and I knew he didn't have high hopes that his healing abilities would work any differently on me this time.

His touch began to heat, warmth spreading from the palm of his hand and outward. It spanned the entirety of my neck and wrapped around the cords that I had put through the wringer today. The sensation was welcoming and I let my eyes close, feeling my vocal cords settle at his touch.

Too soon, he removed his hands and I took a second to compose myself before finding three sets of eyes watching me. Waiting to find out if it had worked. I knew our time was fleeting, as both the council and Rafina would be expecting our arrivals and quickly.

"Thank you." My voice was whole once again, and I smiled at Kade. Everyone seemed to let out a collective sigh of relief, bodies relaxing from their rigidity.

"Hopefully that serves as proof that those coins are working. Each one should be able to suppress your abilities as banshee and fury." Zan gestured toward my hand and I let my fingers reveal the silver coins.

Was that the reason Kade couldn't heal me before? Were

the other parts of me—be it fury, banshee, or both—not allowing him to fix my voice? It was unnerving, to say the least. Of course I didn't plan on getting injured in the future, unknowingly self-inflicted or not, but I didn't like the fact that Kade couldn't do something as simple as healing my voice. I didn't blame him in the slightest for not being able to save me when I was dying, that was an entirely different scenario.

But it still begged the question, what part of me was denying the help he was trying to give?

I had been a human when he healed my injured foot and bruised wrists. It probably wasn't fair to compare a human's afflictions to whatever the hell I was now.

"We should all change. Let's get through this council and examination business and hopefully we can revisit today's events later." Zan came to stand before me, words on the tip of his tongue as he inhaled. "Violet, be careful."

I nodded as Zan began to take his leave. Sarah began to follow but placed a hand on my shoulder before exiting with him. I could tell she was uncertain about what all was transpiring, but knew it wasn't the right time to question it all.

Kade returned us…home. I wanted to bring attention to that little detail, but Kade was already darting toward the closet and rummaging through it.

I began to sift through the multitude of bags Rebecca had brought earlier. They varied in size—some were quite large and I was puzzled at how she managed to bring all of this here by herself. She was human, after all, and didn't have eight arms. I knew she couldn't just pop in and out like the rest of the demons. Or maybe her husband had brought her, a husband I hadn't had the chance to meet yet. I made a mental note to make that a priority for a later time.

I found a pair of black jeans and a button-up blouse I had

picked out yesterday. The silky green material was a comfort compared to this black attire that Kade had made me wear to the other realm. It wasn't that it was uncomfortable, but it was a little more formfitting than I would have liked and I wasn't crazy about the way it hugged me. I felt like I was dressed to go to some cosplay convention. Just give me a mask and a sword that attached to my back like the ones Elias had.

Kade had already rid himself of his weapons and was beginning to peel himself from his attire. What were these outfits called again? Protections? His muscles were taut as he pried the fitted material from his body. I admired the view of his profile and my mind started going in a direction that neither of us could afford to go right now. I bit my bottom lip, wanting nothing more than for the two of us to hide away in this room. Biting harder, I tried to quell the need that was beginning to take its hold on me.

He stilled for a moment, and I feared that he was picking up on my longing. I hurried off toward the doorless bathroom and straight to the sink to splash some cold water on my face.

Today I had killed Brett, had almost done the same with the witch, and had been to another realm. Why in the hell was I getting turned on by Kade undressing? My emotions were all over and I was upset with myself for even thinking about succumbing to the lust I felt for Kade after all that had occurred so far today.

My upcoming meeting with Rafina should have been at the forefront of my mind, and nothing else. I did *not* want to be alone with her. The very thought of Kade and me being separated for these meetings was enough to churn my stomach.

I did as I had observed Zan and Kade do, beginning to remove the few blades that were hidden on me. I examined each one briefly as I laid them on the marbled counter next to my coins. We had been in such a hurry when he was dressing me earlier, preparing me for the unknowns ahead. Each blade had nicks and scratches on the handles, yet the blades still shone brightly when they caught the light. I tried to use my imagination as to what they had seen. How they had arrived at the state they were in now.

I knew I had eyes on me from behind, without a glance or glimpse of a reflection. My breath hitched, knowing Kade was devouring the sight of me just as I had observed him in the closet.

"Care to help me?" I asked as I pulled my strawberry-blond hair to the side and tried to reach for the zipper at the back of my neck. I could imagine the intensity of his gaze as he made his way into the bathroom. I could smell him before he even laid a finger on me, and I was afraid if I looked into the mirror, we would be late for our ill-timed meetings. His pace as he drew the zipper down, slow and steady as my back began to come into his view, was agonizing. The coins on the counter caught my attention as he came to a stop at the base of my spine.

"Do we really have to go?" I knew the answer, but I wanted to hear him say he was fighting the urge to stay alongside me here and say fuck it to the lot of them.

He began to tug at the fabric on my shoulder, exposing more bare skin that only had a sliver of a bra strap on it. He pressed a kiss to my skin there, and I let my head fall back against his chest as I reveled in the smallest touch. The way he still wanted me after everything was just what I needed to feel.

I wanted him to continue, but I feared what might happen if we stayed here. I didn't know the council or Rafina like he did, and to be honest, I really didn't want to. I hated that they all seemed to carry an immense amount of pull around here. I thought that Kade was supposed to become king, did that not count for anything right now?

It was certainly not a knock, more like a beating that came from Kade's door, and we both snapped our heads in the direction of the sound. "Finish getting ready," was all he said before slipping out from behind me and out of sight.

Getting this thing off of me was no easy task. My heart was racing as he left to see what all of the commotion was about, and I hated that I had no privacy with the lack of a door. There were fastenings around my elbows, knees, and waist that were held by something stronger than velcro yet still pliable enough to allow movement. I could hear Aleena's voice in the distance and wanted to be relieved, but her accusatory tone was one that had me racing to finish so I could join Kade before he had to leave.

She was questioning his whereabouts and why Elias had disappeared. Kade told the truth, saying that they had met this morning to discuss some things about his watching, and that he had no idea what Elias was up to now. The ease with which he spoke when his hotheaded sister was grilling him with question after question was a talent that I admired. He spun things in a way that meant he didn't have to lie about anything, but it seemed as if his answers weren't good enough for her. When she began to inquire about our early leave from the celebration yesterday, I knew I had to get out there.

Retrieving the coins from the counter, I placed them in the small inner pocket of my jeans before retreating from the bathroom. I was about halfway up the buttons on my blouse when I whipped around the doorframe. Luckily, I had a cami beneath it so I didn't end up flashing anyone my breasts.

"I'm afraid I may have taken the whole consummation of the tethering thing a bit too seriously, so I'm probably to blame. I'm still a bit bummed that we don't get any kind of honeymoon." I was hoping that my disheveled appearance might lead her to believe that Kade and I had been together all morning in that sense, minus the small encounter with Elias. "And I'm really not much of a party person. Not a big fan of crowds."

Her eyes narrowed, studying me as I smoothed down my blouse. Her pink hair was drawn up into a sleek ponytail and she wore shorts so tight you could see the definition of her legs. I was pretty sure she could bench-press me and still look feminine while doing so. Her crop top hung off one shoulder, showing off her toned stomach that made me feel inferior to her. She oozed strength and sexiness all wrapped into one.

"We should get going," she said, a bite to her voice. Was she really so perturbed that she couldn't get ahold of Kade or Elias this morning? What was so urgent that she needed them so bad?

"Aleena is here to take you to Rafina," Kade said as he joined me at my side, placing a hand around my waist.

I nodded at that. I hated that we had to part ways and go into the unknown without each other. I had no idea what this examination entailed, and I feared for what lay ahead for Kade in that council room. They seemed like they wanted their own control around here and I didn't like it.

"Well, I don't exactly know my way around here so, I appreciate that. Thank you."

Aleena's face remained unchanged at my words, and I couldn't tell if she was going to keep up this hardened exterior while she escorted me to the infirmary or not. What had changed in her since yesterday? Was she onto us and suspicious that none of us could be found this morning?

"I'll see you soon." Kade placed a kiss on my cheek and

vanished before I could speak. Not that I knew exactly what to say, given that he was going to a meeting to discuss himself, his actions, and no doubt me.

Good luck? Break a leg? Hope they don't decide to deal out some punishment for the choices that you made? Nothing that came to mind felt right. I pulled my thoughts away and focused on Aleena, who was studying me.

"What exactly am I supposed to do for this examination? Because I already had a pap smear last month and I am not consenting to that."

Aleena rolled her eyes before she smirked. Her previous anger started to dissolve and she shook her head. "Not that kind of examination."

CHAPTER 17

Violet

Rafina's blond hair was cascading down her back in a luscious manner that made me want to touch it. It looked too perfect.

I asked Aleena to stay if her time allowed, and although she hesitated, she agreed. Rafina had a fleeting moment of protest, but then asked her to remain at a distance. I thought it was a strange request, but if it meant I didn't have to be alone with her for this examination, so be it. I could manage.

My nerves were getting the best of me and I tangled my fingers together. I was thankful to not have heard any screams yet, and hoped these coins had enough magic in them to keep doing whatever the hell they were doing until I could get out of here. I sat on the very slab where I had awoken after my so-called rebirth and resisted the urge to swing my legs as I waited for her to begin.

Aleena had busied herself in a book that she had retrieved from the corner of the room with a red and tattered binding. I had no idea if she was genuinely interested in it or if she was just roaming through it to appear occupied.

"How are you feeling, Violet?" Rafina left her standing desk and came into view at my front. She was wearing a deep blue dress that stopped just above her knees. It was fitted around her waist, making her appear as if she were corseted.

"She thinks you might give her a pap smear," Aleena expressed, head still buried in the book as if she had never made a peep.

My eyes shot open at her remark. I had sort of joked about it, but I really didn't want another one. I had no clue what all Rafina planned to examine, and that was the first thing that came to mind. I didn't think she had any reason for me to spread my legs for her.

"I just had one last month and everything was normal," I gushed as my face began to turn red.

Rafina smiled sweetly, but I wasn't buying it. I might have the coins to thank for suppressing the screams, but there was still something in my gut stirring with the instinct not to trust her.

"No, none of that."

"So, what is the council looking for then? Why do they get to determine that I need an examination? Is this a normal request for anyone that transitions?" I tried to pose my questions as mere curiosity even though I was kind of pissed at the situation and their demands.

She paused, as if contemplating how to answer me. A politician plotting their response before they opened their mouth. "They just want to make sure you are accepting your transition without complications."

"Should I be experiencing complications?" I countered, wanting more info than she was willing to give. She wasn't very forthcoming.

Rafina took one of my hands and pressed her two fingers to my wrist, checking on my pulse, and we both quieted. She focused on the touch for a few seconds before returning to face me head on.

"What do you remember from when you first awoke here?" I knew she was referring to my first experience with the screams, and I fought off the urge to show any reaction to her question.

"I was…confused." I reflected back to what I was told earlier about common side effects and Kade's ability to skirt around the truth. "My head hurt really bad. Like, the worst splitting headache I have ever experienced."

I knew I couldn't write off my experience as if the screams had never happened. It would put me in an even worse light if I tried to lie about it, so I tried to embellish a little.

"I felt as if I was reliving the last moments of my life all over again. Screaming for Brett to stop and fearing for my life. It's like I could feel the bullets hitting me all over again. I could even taste my own blood." I shook my head, trying to lean into the performance, willing it to be real at that point in time. If there were ever a moment to put on a show, it was now.

Rafina didn't need to know that I had experienced this more than once and that my tethering with Kade had led him to experience it with me. I had to do everything I could to hide anything that could lead her to believe I might have something else within me. I was so incredibly grateful for these coins right now, knowing full well that if I hadn't had them, I wouldn't have been able to be in her presence for this long to begin with.

"And have you experienced that again since?" She pried, urging me to continue.

"Thank goodness, no. I mean, a few headaches, but that's about it." I shook as if trying to shake away a bad memory and its grasp on me.

"Which is normal for someone who has transitioned." She placed her fingers beneath my neck and felt around my lymph nodes, working downward on my neck. I would have to thank Kade again for healing my vocal cords. Had he not, I probably wouldn't have much of a voice to answer her questions and that wouldn't have looked good for anyone.

"And how have you been since your tethering?" She stepped away, leaning against another slab at her back as she laced her fingers together at her front. "Have you two consummated?"

I bit my lip at the personal question, eyeing Aleena who I doubted was reading anything of interest. I had admitted to her earlier that Kade and I had been screwing around, and quite a bit at that, so I had no choice but to answer honestly.

"We have, yes…a lot." Deciding to push it a little further so there would hopefully be no doubt, I added, "Human men have nothing on demon men."

That earned another smile from Rafina. Had it not been for the unsettling feeling in my stomach, I might have been falling for it. "This phase of the tethering is definitely a special one. Senses are heightened, and everything around you pales in comparison to the link that you are forming. Embrace it and enjoy it."

"Maybe we're enjoying it a little too much? I guess we were kind of hard to reach this morning. I take responsibility for that, and I hope Kade isn't in too much trouble with the council for it. If it were my choice, he wouldn't leave the bedroom for a week."

"Sounds about right," she mused. She looked as if she was reflecting on a memory of her own, a fondness in her eyes before she continued. "Do you have any concerns about anything so far?"

I thought about that for a moment, trying to spin things in a positive light. "Actually, since I'm a demon now, I should be able to change my hair color, right?" I didn't want our focus to go toward anything negative, and I had been curious about this potential talent.

"You will, in time. Just as you will be able to shift and change your appearance however you see fit. You may learn from instructors or those closest to you."

They had instructors for shifting? Did I have to enroll in some sort of demon/wizarding school?

"Could Aleena teach me? That is, if you want to." Her head had popped up too quickly, confirming that she was hanging onto every word of our conversation.

"Could be fun, sure." She hopped down from a slab and returned the book to its shelf.

"Very well. Now there is one more matter we need to discuss." Rafina motioned for me to follow as she led the way toward the only mirror that acted as an entrance and exit to the infirmary. I still found it odd that this place had no doors. Every other room I had been in so far had them, so why was this one different? You would think an infirmary would be easily accessible to everyone. The fact that Sarah had been trapped here after my escape seemed problematic.

My reflection joined Rafina's in the oversized mirror. I was shorter than her by a few inches, and her slender frame paled in comparison to the muscled stature of Aleena who remained at a distance but still closer than she had been before now.

"Have you traveled alone by mirror anymore since you first arrived?"

There was no way in hell I was going to admit that I had. I knew everyone was concerned that I had traveled by myself for the first time and didn't get lost in the process. Apparently, this skill was one that was not so easy to come by. In reality, I had done it twice, but I couldn't tell her about the most recent time, when I was passing through to kill Brett. Mentioning that would be to my detriment. I shook my head from side to side, unsure of what she was after next.

"Either Kade or Aleena have escorted me. And like, freaky fast. Doesn't anybody just walk around here?"

The thought must have amused her, as her face spread into another grin. "Do you think you could do it again? Take yourself to the council chambers?"

I was uneasy at the thought. Was this really a part of her examination?

"Um…I don't know. Last time I was a mess, and not in my right mind considering I had just been murdered."

"Understandable. But would you be willing to try?" she pushed, drawing closer.

I wasn't sure if I could, but I didn't think I was in any kind of position to deny her this request. I wanted to come off as sincere and honest, trying not to give her any indication that anything else lay beneath the surface.

"Would we get in trouble for going there? Kade was meeting with them," I asked. I was afraid he was going to be in the hot seat, much like he was when I had first arrived there after trying to locate him.

"Not at all. I am to report to them after we finish."

Oh? Were we done then? That wasn't so bad. In fact, it felt too easy at this point. That was cause for concern in itself.

What information was she going to relay to the council members? She didn't administer any tests, and only had her hands on me two times. Was what little time we'd spent here really enough for her to come to a conclusion on me? The thoughts swirling through my head were alarming. Would the council members ask any questions regarding me, or would Rafina simply state her findings?

"Go ahead." She gestured toward the mirror and I reluctantly stepped forward.

If there was ever a time that I wanted this to not work, it was now. I didn't think it was possible for a demon to be a "natural" at crossing through mirrors, so I didn't want to be the one to do so. Kade and I already had so many eyes on us and were unable to really know who to trust, so I didn't need the added spotlight of being abnormal in this case.

My eyes closed and with every ounce of will I had, I wished for the wall before me to be solid glass. If I could channel my life as a human and imagine the mirror before me to be nothing more than an inanimate object, maybe, just maybe, I could stop myself from passing through. I didn't want to get to Kade on my own, not now. I wanted to fail at this, wanted to admit defeat in the face of this trial.

When my fingers made contact with the hardened surface, I wanted to be relieved. And I was, until my fingers passed through. I felt betrayed by my own body, but then the glass hardened around them, locking me in place.

"Um…" I was hit with confusion, then panic as I tried to yank my hand free while my knuckles cracked at the pressure. I peered over my shoulder to find Rafina staring intently, perhaps a bit perturbed that it hadn't worked.

"W-what do I do?" The rising fear within me was very real at the realization that I was stuck. While I had wanted to fail, it wasn't supposed to be in this manner.

I wondered if the coins in my pocket had anything to do with it or not. Was passing through mirrors just a demon thing, or could other creatures do it as well?

Aleena seemed to be fighting off her amusement while Rafina stepped forward. Her hand entered the glass and it rippled as she freed my hand. She let go as soon as my hand came into view.

"I'm sorry," I muttered as I examined my hand. How humiliating would it be to get stuck again, especially if my ass was hanging out on the other side?

Rafina's expression hardened, like she was about ready to scold me.

"I-I don't know how I did it before," I admitted, and began to question myself on whether I really knew how to cross or not. But instead of dwelling on that, my head switched gears rather abruptly.

"I did die, right?" The words were out of my mouth before I could contemplate how the conversation might go. "Kade said my heart stopped."

She blinked at me. Her expression fell into an unreadable state. Aleena seemed surprised at my words, the total opposite of Rafina as the blond healer responded, "You did."

"So how am I alive when you have to be living to transition to a demon?" It was a question that no doubt was on the mind of everyone in Darthou. And while I didn't expect her to answer, at least not truthfully, if anyone had had the chance to do something to me after my death and before my rebirth, it was her.

But there was no way to prove it. And even if she had, did that mean she was the one to cause the destruction to those banished in Xandor?

"That is what we intend to find out." Her use of the term "we" didn't go unnoticed. Did she mean her and Staffan? Her and the council? Who was the *we* she was referring to?

"Aleena, you can see yourself out. Violet, let's go to council."

I was equal parts grateful and embarrassed that I had proved successful in my plan to thwart my crossing, but those feelings quickly receded as Rafina and I exited the darkened hallway and entered the council chambers.

All of the men were seated in the same places where I had witnessed them the last time I was here. There was a heaviness to the room as we approached the center, which was directly in front of Kade. He sat in the chair that was previously empty, his eyes dragging from mine to my escort. He appeared to be the youngest and seemed out of place between them all. His face was unchanging as Rafina and I came to a stop.

I wanted to be relieved that Kade wasn't in our spot on the floor this time, but there was a low hum of a frequency radiating from him that told me his visit so far hadn't been anything pleasant.

Rafina bowed before she began, not waiting for anyone else to speak up first as their whispers amongst themselves hushed. I found Zan easily, his mood unreadable, and I tried not to linger on him.

"I have finished my examination."

Again, I was incredibly grateful that I had heard no screams leading up to this point, and I looked forward to my return to Xandor so I could thank the witch for her help. Had

I killed her after witnessing the lives she had taken, I would have ruined things for myself without ever knowing it.

Staffan extended a hand as he urged Rafina to continue. I wanted to turn my nose up. No encounter with him thus far had been a good one.

"Considering she has had a less than ideal transition, it is indeed that. A transition." The way Rafina commanded the room as all the men hung on her every word was an artform I'd never possessed. It was one I could appreciate, even if I didn't trust her.

"Violet is a demon who has experienced some light symptoms, some of which could be referred to as post-traumatic stress disorder. I would like to request a weekly examination so I can monitor her."

Monitor?

"And what do you say about her ability to cross over unassisted?" A man to my right who looked to be the oldest of them all—at least by appearance—asked. I recalled seeing him at the celebration yesterday, but we hadn't formally been introduced yet. I had met a lot of demons, but I was certain he wasn't one of them.

"Nothing more than beginner's luck. She failed to pass through on her own in my examination. I would suggest that she begin instruction as soon as possible."

A different man to the left chimed in this time. I was certain I had made his and his significant other/husband's acquaintance, but their names were so far-fetched they escaped me. "Do you have any preference over who to appoint as her instructor?"

"She has shown an interest in Aleena. I would like to make a motion for her to instruct."

There were a few glares exchanged among the men before

us, as if they were unsettled at the mention of Aleena. I couldn't help but wonder why that was.

"Does someone have a problem with my sister and this task?" Kade remained unmoving, but his voice carried through the space around us as they all averted their eyes away from him. "Speak now."

After a few beats of silence, the man to my right spoke up again. "Can she remain unbiased in her instruction and reporting?"

"Are you implying that she cannot?" Kade met him with greater disdain, and I swore he was shooting daggers with his eyes at his fellow demon. The man straightened and leaned back into his chair. His peppered hair was a strange choice for someone who could choose whatever appearance he wanted.

"Of course not." His voice began to fade, but I could tell by the look on his face he was fighting the urge to say more and biting his tongue.

"Does anyone else have any objections to this motion?" Kade's eyes moved side to side and down the lines of men surrounding him. I half expected Staffan to butt in, but he remained still and silent in his seat.

Last time I was here, he had appeared to be running the show with Kade standing where we were now and in the hot seat. What had happened in my short time in the infirmary until now to cause such a shift here? Regardless, it was kind of exciting seeing Kade assert his dominance.

"Violet," he said my name in a tone I hadn't heard before. It was commanding and demanded my attention as I met his stare. "Do you accept Aleena as your instructor?"

I was a bit shocked at even having a chance to speak. I didn't think I really had much of a choice in the matter, as I didn't know who else could even be a consideration for the task. "I do, yes."

Kade's jaw tightened before he leaned forward in his seat to address the room. I had a fondness for his presence in the moment, and admired his ability to control the room just as he had before with the countless number of people who were in attendance at our celebration.

I hated any group setting bigger than a handful of people and remembered the countless presentations I'd cowered away from. Pretending to be sick to get out of school, and faking injuries when that failed. Dare I say it, I even skipped school entirely some days when it got too bad. When you already felt like an outcast, what was the harm in that?

"Rafina, thank you for your time and expertise. Your motion and requests are granted. You will report to the council at the end of the month. I will meet the both of you in the infirmary shortly. That will be all."

Kade's dismissal was swift, and at the slightest touch on the shoulder I was back in the confines of the very room he was to meet us in. I was perturbed by the whole situation at this point, and again found myself with more questions than answers. It was starting to eat away at me.

"Well, that was…weird," I said as I crossed my arms and began to meander away from Rafina. "Are other newly transitioned demons met with such scrutiny, or am I the only one?" I already knew the answer, but figured it wouldn't hurt my case any to vent to Rafina about this. I hadn't exactly been met with a warm welcome when I arrived. "If this Obsidian place is capable of killing some when they fail at the transition, why is it not possible that it can bring some back from the dead as well?"

I pivoted and waited for Rafina to respond.

She proceeded to cross the room at a leisurely pace, closing some of the distance between us, but stopped two slabs away. Her blue dress swayed to a stop before she responded.

"The council doesn't do well with the unknown. They want concrete evidence and answers—"

"I want answers!" My voice rose and her blond brows shot up. "Why am I being treated like some enemy when this is just as new to me as anybody else? Do I not deserve to be treated like any other newly transitioned demon? Why am I being given the third degree?"

I really wanted to give my piece of mind to the council—they deserved the steam that was coming off of me. It seemed at this point that Rafina was just carrying through with their will. And while I believed that the council was calling the shots on this matter, I knew Rafina wasn't exactly innocent in all of this either. I believed she had an agenda of her own, I just didn't know what all that entailed.

"Because they fear you." I stilled at her words.

A part of me knew exactly that. They *should* fear me. They sat all high and mighty in that council room, happy to bark orders and demand whatever they wanted, but in reality, they were scared of the unknown. I was more than a demon, and if they ever found that out, it would be disastrous for Kade's upcoming reign and for my life here that I hadn't even begun to live.

"And why on earth would they fear me?"

"Because they don't know what you're capable of." Her voice was clipped as she replied.

And she did? Was she really behind all of this? If so, why was she covering for me if she knew otherwise, and why did she give the report that she did to the council? My fingers went through the glass, did that count for nothing?

"Why do they think I'm capable of anything else besides

shifting and normal demon-type things?" I was going to try to keep playing the innocent card. Hell, as long as I had these coins, hopefully my other abilities could remain undetected.

"Because Obsidian Falls has never, ever in our recorded history, brought someone back from the dead like it did with you."

But what about her? Could the mighty healer that Kade had known his whole life produce such a result?

"Have *you* ever brought anyone back from the dead?" I met her eyes and took my even-heeled stance, unfaltering as I awaited her response.

"I am a healer," she stated, her mood darkening as her chin tipped down.

"Remember, I'm new here. I don't exactly know what all is included in your definition of *healer*."

Something lurked beneath her surface and it made my nails dig into my palms. There was a shift in the air, a thickening that made my throat ache. I knew there was more to her than that.

She was hiding something, and I intended to find out what.

"What happened after Kade left?" I rounded the slab that I stood behind and began to approach her. "What happened to me before you brought me here to the infirmary?"

"I don't know what you mean."

I scoffed at that. Playing ignorant didn't suit her. Not in her position of power. "I think you know exactly what I mean. What I don't understand is why you're trying to hide it. This is *my* life."

"That you have been given yet another chance at. You should be grateful." Her voice grew with the latter part of her statement. I had touched a nerve. If she was expecting me to thank her, she was sorely mistaken. Not when I didn't know what her agenda was in all of this. What use was I to her, whether I lived or died?

"I never said that I wasn't. But I would like some clarification and understanding as to why I have been given this chance, when kids like Jacobi lose their dad to a transition. Why me? Why do I get to take another stab at life?" I jabbed a finger into my chest when I was about two feet away from her.

"Change," she said, as her mouth twisted into an unsettling smirk. She turned away from me and began retreating just as Kade popped in. "If I am no longer needed to babysit, I shall find Aleena and tell her of her duties."

Kade eyed her suspiciously before glancing at me, then to her again. "Thank you for your cooperation in the matter."

She bowed her head and left with a few parting words. "Training begins tomorrow at ten. See to it she's not late."

It frustrated me that she acted as if I wasn't even there as she spoke. It was one of the things that annoyed me about the council. Rafina did the same, so callously, and vanished before I could object to her demand.

Anger overtaking me, I pounded the floor like a child in a tantrum as I made my way over to him. "Kade, she—"

He held a hand up to stop me, eyeing the room. "Not here."

Kade whisked me away from the infirmary, and back home.

CHAPTER 18

Violet

I lifted my hands toward my head, exasperated by Rafina, the council, everything. I began pacing back and forth, wanting out of the four walls that felt as if they were closing in on us. I felt trapped in this place, and at the mercy of the demons that surrounded me.

"She's hiding something, Kade. I know it!" I retrieved the coins from my pocket and turned them in my hand. "She won't even speak about the moments when I was reborn. Just give me one minute with her. One minute to look into her eyes so I can see for myself if she's behind the devastation in Xandor. It's far too big of a coincidence that these people died the same day I did, and I came back. She's the only one who would have been able to pull something like that off."

"I understand that, I do. But we have no proof, and you are

not going to reveal yourself in the hopes that we might get some."

"Then why can't we bring the witch here? Have her identify the one who slaughtered those who had no other choice but to call that shitty realm a home."

"Because she would be killed before she even had a chance to speak."

I grew louder. "It's not right!"

"I know, Violet!" His agitation came off quick, as if he had shot an arrow. He pried my hand open and snatched the coins from me, hurling them across the room. They made high-toned clinking sounds as they bounced and then skidded across the floor.

"Why the hell did you do that?" I turned my attitude on him and went to reclaim them.

His shoulders sagged slightly and he ran a hand through his hair before placing both hands on his hips. His eyes widened as he fixated on a spot on the floor. "There has been a ringing in my ears ever since we returned from Xandor." He swallowed as he shook his head. "It was subtle at first, but when you arrived at the council it multiplied. Even more when I met you at the infirmary. Whatever magic is in those is affecting me somehow."

"Are they hurting you?" I had kneeled, but paused before I could pick up the coins.

Kade's failure to answer made my mood plummet.

"But...they're helping." I felt defeated at the realization that the coins might be too good to be true. "I wouldn't have been able to meet Rafina or stand before the council if I hadn't had them."

Another thought crossed my mind and the idea was spilling from my lips. "What if Rafina was responsible for the destruction in Xandor? I probably would have killed her. I almost killed the witch."

It was one thing to think that Rafina had something to do with my rebirth. Another to try and blame her for the deaths in Xandor without any proof.

The severity of my own confession should have scared me, but it didn't. And to think, I had judged Kade just days ago when I first learned of the lives he had taken and the decisions he had made. Decisions I didn't fully comprehend until now. I supposed I wasn't much different than him.

"I know. I might have been in excruciating pain, but I knew you were going to. That is, until the furies stopped you." He shook his head as he approached me. I loathed seeing him in pain. Powerless against that mist that burned him, causing burns and boils that ravaged his skin. I wondered if it had been doing the same beneath his protections or if it was only his exposed skin.

"A bit creepy, really. The furies," I declared as I tried to cover up the thoughts of Kade in agony. *Thing 1 and Thing 2.*

I really had to come up with some better names for them.

"They definitely weren't what I was expecting. But then, they've been living in Xandor since long before my sister and I were born."

The mere thought of living in that desolate and depressing land was unnerving. Granted, I knew we had seen very little within the short time we were there, but I failed to see how it could have been much better if we'd made it any further in our exploration.

"Come here." Kade held out his hand and I let him lead me down the hallway. Instead of turning toward his watching quarters, we went in the opposite direction. I hadn't had the chance to snoop over here yet and was curious as to what lay past the door we were approaching.

I wasn't expecting to be welcomed by the outdoors, and the cooler temperature as we exited. He closed the solid door behind me and led me down a narrow stone path, the stones resembling those of his shower.

The winding path began to widen as we approached what looked to be some sort of garden area. We reached the end of the overhang from the building we had exited. Now that I could look up, I couldn't even begin to guess how many stories high the concrete fortress might be.

Returning my gaze forward, I took in the sight of the many plants, bushes, and greenery that filled the large circular area. We were encompassed by a wall made up of thick gray bricks higher than I could reach, and vines attempting to cover them. I couldn't make out any other entrance or exit, just a water area that looked more like a giant, inground jacuzzi with steam sifting into the air.

I was quick to make the connection to the citrus smell that Kade wore. It was here. I would have expected to find orange trees or some sort of fruit growing around us, but there wasn't an edible thing in sight. I wondered how much time he spent out here to make this a part of the sweet concoction of cologne that he wore so well—citrus and liquor.

In the distance, I could make out frost-covered trees. It reminded me of the winters back home in the Midwest after we had a hard freeze. The drastic difference between the tree line and the gorgeous surroundings I was now standing in was mesmerizing.

In awe of the aesthetics of the scene before me, I released his hand and explored everything, letting my hand touch and feel the life of the picturesque environment. I had never had much of a green thumb, but I could definitely appreciate the beauty that could be found in something so simple. The air was filled with that sweet citrus scent that wasn't too overpowering. Green was predominant in the area, but there were strategically placed splotches of color that decorated the scene. A collection of yellow flowers at the water's edge caught my attention and I beamed.

"Are these…?" I knelt and felt their petals on the back of my fingers.

"The flowers I brought you? Yes." He flashed his boyish charm as he stuffed his hands in his pockets, along with a coy smile that made me want to melt. He had told me that yellow was his favorite color, and if these flowers had been in existence in my world, I was pretty sure it would be mine as well.

"This place is…beautiful." I stood and took in the sight of it once more. It was quiet, quaint, and utterly stunning. "What else are you holding out on?"

I playfully nudged him with my elbow, but he snapped an arm around me and pulled me in close.

He drew in a large breath as I laid my head on his chest, savoring the closeness and the comfort that only he could provide. I let my eyes close as I relaxed into him, savoring the moment. If only this could last. If only we could hide away here forever, I would be happily content.

"I'm sorry I'm such a mess," I confided. I was just that. This new life I'd been thrust into was a chaotic mindfuck and there was no better way to put it. And we had tethered, so I guess that meant he was a mess because of me too.

"I don't place an ounce of blame on you, Violet. I'm sorry that Darthou is a fucking mess." His agitation grew. "This isn't the world I wanted to bring you into."

"For better or for worse, am I right?" A nervous chuckle escaped me as I joked about our marriage-like tethering. "More or less."

"I would still choose you every time. I can't imagine a life without you." I could feel his genuine love as it whirled around and through me. I knew he only spoke the truth, firmly believing it myself. I wondered if he could feel the affection I had in my heart at the same level as I could feel what he felt for me. I still wasn't able to utter the words yet, but I had to believe he knew.

"So what are we going to do about our respective messes?" I gazed up into his dark eyes, still in awe of them even though I now had the same ones.

"We…" He began to unbutton my blouse and my skin began to warm. "Are going to enjoy ourselves out here in this little oasis and try to forget about all of our problems. Even if only for a little while."

"You want to have sex?" I began to tug at his shirt as he finished with my buttons. I had to wear a cami under any kind of button-up shirt. Otherwise, it would gap when I sat down and reveal a bit too much underneath.

He beamed from ear to ear and a lighthearted laugh escaped. "Wasn't my intention, but if that's how you want to spend your time out here, I'm happy to oblige. I just figured you would rather relax without your clothes…in the water, that is."

"Uh-huh…sure," I teased as I let my top drop to the ground. Turning my back, I removed the rest of my clothes as he did the same. He was entering the water before I could and began to drift away toward the farthest side from me. I dipped my toes into its heat, a momentary sting as I acclimated to it. Submerging my body, I sighed in the relief it provided. My eyes closed as I settled into it, succumbing to its calming effect.

"How do you know somebody won't bop in while we're

here? Can we really afford to disappear right now when there's so much going on?" The heat radiated off the water and filled my nostrils and I breathed in deeply.

I was met with his smile as I reopened my eyes. "Afraid somebody might catch us?"

"Maybe. It's not exactly like people announce themselves before popping in," I expressed. "What's stopping them from coming and going as they please?"

"I apologize for not telling you sooner. But in our living quarters, we have enchantments that protect our home. As long as the doors are closed, no one may enter unless invited."

Well that was intriguing. "Kind of like vampires?"

He laughed, the sound melting away my stress. He didn't mock me, but I thought maybe my naivety was refreshing for him.

"I suppose it could have been rooted from that myth," Kade stated, then continued as if he were reading my thoughts on the subject. "They are very much real."

"Have they been banished, or are they like…here?" I asked, growing even more interested. I didn't know why the thought of them was so riveting. Maybe because of my fascination with them in high school, the fictional versions, anyway.

"Some have been banished, sure. But we do have them here in Darthou."

"Where? Have I met any?"

I seemed to amuse him as he sank a bit deeper into the water, settling against the back wall until his neck and head were all that was above the surface. "You have not, no. Guess it's time for a little geography lesson."

I raised a brow. That class in school was one I didn't care to revisit.

"Darthou is where you are currently. Our own city, so to

speak. There are four others that are home to demons as well."

I blinked at him. There were more?

"Are you going to become king of all of them?" The thought that there were more demons and humans than what had been present at our celebration had my stomach twisting in knots.

"No." He shook his head. "Each city has their own leaders. We will only be crowned here in Darthou."

As if that made me feel any better. I couldn't stand to dwell on this whole king and queen thing at the moment. It would make the reality of it too real. And there was too damn much going on right now to even try to consider myself as a future queen.

"But these other creatures," I started, trying to circle back, "can I meet them?"

Kade's heartbreaking smile returned. "In time, yes. I think you would agree that we have a lot on our plates right now."

I pursed my lips, a bit disappointed. I knew he was right, and even though the coins provided me some relief around Rafina and Staffan, how would they do when I came face-to-face with other creatures who were normally depicted as killers and monsters? If I could see death in the eyes of demons and witches, surely it would work on them too. I was beginning to wonder if this sight thing the furies referred to was a blessing or a curse.

I hadn't played witness to Kade's murders since he had thrown my coins to the ground and honestly, I was grateful. I wasn't going to question why right now. I only wanted to focus on us, this garden, and how damn good this hot water felt on my body.

Making my way toward the yellow flowers across from Kade, I stood straight to inhale their scent, then examined our surroundings once more. This place was exquisite, and I could see this easily becoming my favorite spot to come and hide. The seclusion, the aromas, and the serenity of this little oasis had me relaxing beneath the yellow flowers and lowering myself deeper until my chin skimmed the water.

"Have you always had a green thumb?" I was curious about this welcoming space. Everything out here was lush and full, while inside his home was almost bare and neatly organized, and almost everything had its place. "This garden is just so…beautiful."

Kade didn't answer immediately, and when I opened my eyes I found him gazing at the scenery around us, as if remembering something. I let him take his time, wondering if I just needed to shut my mouth and let us bask in the silence.

"My mom loved gardening. So much that my dad tried to help her with it, but he was a bit, well, challenged in that area. The earth here is not the same as your home, and it takes a patience and persistence that he didn't have. But nevertheless, he kept trying because it meant so much to her." A sadness fell over his features and I pushed off the wall, wanting to comfort him.

"That's really sweet," I acknowledged. "This was all their doing?"

He nodded, unable to look at me.

I didn't know when I might get the chance again, and while we were on the subject of his parents, I decided to ask him about what Aleena had told me yesterday.

"Does it bother you at all that I call you Kade?"

This drew his attention toward me and I froze. I found it weird that I was the only one to not call him by his full name here. And while I loved being the only one privileged to do that, if it caused him any grief, I would make it a point to call him Kadriel from now on.

"Aleena told you." His statement was quiet and the earlier light in his eyes had diminished.

"If it bothers you at all, just say the word. I didn't know." My brows furrowed as I awaited what he might say next. Yes, it would be strange for a while calling him Kadriel, but it would be a new habit I could form and I would do it in a heartbeat for him.

Scooping my hand up in his, he rotated me around so my back fell against his chest. My body slackened as he held me close, albeit a little tighter than our normal embraces. My wet braid was a nuisance and I pulled it over my shoulder to my front before settling again. Kade held me with one arm across my waist and another above my chest, a hand resting on my shoulder.

"You can call me whatever you want, Violet. I'll come running."

The thought was warming, even though I had yet to see him run. I still didn't know what he did to stay in the shape he was in, but I had no doubt he would live up to his words. Popping in—now that seemed more accurate.

We stayed like this for some time, plastered to each other as if we were breathing statues. The silence that filled the air mixed with the scents around us, allowed my mind to go blank. I didn't pry anymore about Kade and his name, and decided against all lines of questioning, letting us enjoy the reprieve this oasis provided. I didn't want to ruin the break we undoubtedly needed given the stresses of everything going on around us. I knew that as soon as we left, the realities of our lives would come crashing back in, and at full force.

Or right now, as I could hear the faint tapping from Kade's pocket mirror from the pile of clothes he had discarded.

CHAPTER 19

Violet

After arguing with Kade about whether or not to take my coins with me to Zan's place, I finally caved. The fact that they created a ringing sound to him the longer I had them on me was enough cause for concern. Now that I was aware, I was ready to battle him on the subject.

While I was sure we would be among those we trusted, he didn't want to take the chance that something else might arise and I would need them. I made him swear to me that if they became too much, he would tell me. And should we find ourselves in the presence of others and unable to speak freely, he needed to tug on his ear or something to signal to me that he was unable to combat the sound any longer.

Zan had called on Kade and me to come meet him once we were available, and our short escape to the garden came to a screeching halt. As we arrived, I noticed Sarah shutting the door to leave and I frowned. I didn't even have the chance to offer her a greeting. She was one of the few I knew we could trust, and the comfort of having another woman by my side would have been nice. I could only assume that she was taking care of the kids instead of joining us.

I couldn't help but wonder why we hadn't brought Aleena into the fold yet. If Kade trusted her and Elias with his life, and she was to begin instruction with me tomorrow, why hadn't she become involved yet?

"Will Aleena be joining us?" I asked innocently. This earned heads snapping in my direction, and I wanted to shrink away but held steady in my stance.

"Aleena will not be accompanying us, no," Zan said, face firm while his voice was laced with an authoritative tone.

"Is there any reason as to why? I thought we trusted her." I shot a look at her brother, confused.

"We do trust her, to an extent," Kade said. The avoidance of an explanation didn't sit well with me, and I pushed some more.

"Either we trust her or we don't. Which is it? Some clarification would be nice, since I am going to be seeing a lot of her."

The three men in the room exchanged glances, and I was about to lose my cool if somebody didn't provide me with any information on the subject.

Zan was the first to break the silence. "Normally we would include her, yes. But since Rafina is involved, I'm afraid it complicates matters."

"Why, are they like besties or something?" I questioned further. These vague answers weren't cutting it.

Kade stepped into my direct line of sight in front of his

uncle, and I focused on him as his voice lowered. "From time to time, the two have been known to…enjoy each other's company."

The manner in which he spoke the word *enjoy* gave the impression that they might have been romantically involved in some way. But only yesterday I had observed Aleena and Elias enraptured with one another in the hallway, so I shook my head in confusion.

"But I thought—" I peered around Kade to find Elias recoiling at the mention of the two women, and Kade's eyes widened. He shook his head and mouthed *not now*, and I dropped the subject instantly. I couldn't help but cringe, thinking about the possibility of the two women together.

Rafina was tethered to Staffan, wasn't she? Were they not committed to one another? I couldn't care less what Aleena's sexual preferences were, but the thought of Rafina and her together made my skin crawl. Why couldn't it have been anybody else but her? And what did Elias make of all this? He was visibly uncomfortable at the mere mention of it. But how deep did his feelings go for her?

I recalled the brief conversation I had with Aleena yesterday about tethering. She had mentioned she wasn't tied down yet. Perhaps this was why.

"Right. Well, Violet, how are those coins holding up?" Zan pushed the conversation in another direction and I dragged my eyes away from Elias.

"Fine for me. I can't say the same for Kade." I looked at him as I said his name.

"What does she mean, Kadriel?"

Kade looked perturbed that I had even mentioned it and tried to wave it off. "It's nothing."

"Bullshit," I retorted, thinking back to the little argument we had just had before arriving. Elias stifled a laugh at my comment. "The longer I have them on me, the stronger he can feel some sort of side effect. He described it as a ringing in his ears that started once we left Xandor, and it only got worse as time went on. By the time we got back to his place after the council meeting, it didn't cease until he hurled the coins across the room."

"Hm…maybe the witch underestimated the tethering part of your relationship." Zan spoke aloud but it seemed as if he was thinking to himself. "Can you hear it now, Kadriel?"

He didn't speak when his uncle posed the question, but I knew by his grim expression and silence that he could. That, and the fact that he wouldn't look anybody in the room in their eyes.

"It may not be as strong as it could be, but he can hear it," I answered for him, and he shot me a look. I didn't give him the satisfaction of acknowledging it. They needed to know.

Zan nodded as if he was contemplating something, loosening the tie around his neck. He was dressed more business casual compared to Kade's and Elias's more comfortable day-to-day attire. He took a beat before he spoke again.

"If you are comfortable, Violet, you can remove the coins while you're here."

"Done." I pulled them from my pocket and set them on the table for everyone to lay their eyes on. I could feel the ease that came over Kade once they were out of my possession, and I was grateful that he could rid himself of the effects so quickly.

"Is that why you were irritable in council today?" Zan returned his attention to Kade and I couldn't help but contemplate what I'd missed in that room before my arrival. I hoped it was a good sign that Kade had been seated amongst the council members instead of before them like someone on trial, but I still had no idea how things worked around here.

"No comment," Kade mumbled, but his words were still clear as day. He shifted his posture, propping himself up against the wall and crossing his arms. It was as if he was pouting, and to be honest, I found it amusing. And a bit cute.

"What happened in there? I know I was kind of late to the party, but things seemed different than the last time I was there."

"You mean besides Kade putting them in their place and reminding them that they do not run Darthou? To question him and his actions is to question his future reign. Which, by the way, as you so delicately pointed out, Kade, begins with the next Blood Moon."

Again with the blood? I wanted to roll my eyes but resisted the urge to do so. Of course it had to be a Blood Moon, why wouldn't it be?

"Oh, shit." Elias guffawed at the mention of it. "Wish I could have been there for that."

Zan exhaled before sitting down in the high-backed chair before him. He let a hand rest on the table amidst all of the items on it. He had seemed quieter since we'd returned from Xandor, more reserved than usual. Although his time spent with the witch was short, I had the gut feeling that their exchange of words might have been troublesome, and a pit began to form in my stomach.

"Actually, can we back up a minute?" I sat at the opposite end of his table and clasped my hands together in my lap. "What did the witch talk to you about? Does she have any clue as to who caused the destruction there? We didn't really get much out of the furies." I shuddered as I remembered them. I might have fury in me, but their freaky unity made me uneasy.

All eyes turned toward Zan and I knew we were all waiting with bated breath to hear what he had to say. He focused on the stacks on the table as he stilled, his posture stiff. Even though he wore a high collar, I could see a vein protruding as his jaw clenched.

"The woman who caused this destruction is younger in years, so that would rule out Rafina."

That tidbit was a blow I hadn't been expecting. With the screams I heard in her presence, I wanted to believe that she had done it. That *she* was responsible.

"So how young is young here? Because my definition is no doubt vastly different from yours." I glared at him.

"She has a thing about age," Kade quipped.

"Shut up." I allowed myself the grace of an eye roll before I returned my focus to Zan.

"Probably two hundred years old or less. Old enough to have mastered her craft in changing her appearance and traveling to their realm. But young enough to still find anything and everything in Xandor fascinating and intriguing. She was adamant to learn all about the creatures there, by name and their abilities, claiming that she was never taught anything about them. They were as good as forgotten."

"She's not totally wrong," Elias began. "We've been in the dark about it ourselves. The creatures that were completely banished are basically bedtime stories now."

"And anytime we would try to question anyone who might know something, they would just wave us off as if it were all nonsense," Kade added.

"But these creatures, these *people*, they have lives, and they are obviously suffering there. Who can blame them for meeting us with such force when we arrived? They don't know what could happen next. Where or who the next threat may be." I shifted on my chair and looked at Kade. "Your father somehow figured out how to get to their realm, and now this woman. Who else is going to go after them until there's no one left?"

"Time is something they don't have much of. As you heard her say, their realm is dying," Elias added, further raising my frustrations.

"Then we have to get them out of there!" I sat forward in my chair to meet the stares of the men around me at my outburst. "Haven't they lost enough?"

"We don't know anything about them," Elias countered as his voice grew louder.

"So we should turn a blind eye and let them die?" I shot back as I rose from the table.

"We're not saying that, Violet. We don't know them." Zan was trying once again to bring tensions down, but it wasn't enough.

"There has to be something we can do. That place is a disaster. They can't continue living like that. Why can't we bring them here? Can we hide them somewhere?" I pleaded, refusing to believe that the only choice was to let them stay there like pigs to the slaughter. I didn't know them either, but I didn't think they deserved that.

"We don't have the means to hide an unknown amount of creatures. We don't even know who is left besides the three we met today. The witch might have trusted me to an extent, but she is still keeping her cards close. And I don't blame her one bit for not trusting anyone."

"So when can we go back?" I asked in a rush, wanting to return with the first chance I had.

"We can't. Not yet anyway."

"Why?" I demanded, anger beginning to take root inside

of me. If I really was born again from the deaths of those in that realm, I owed it to myself and to them to fight for them when no one else would. I couldn't let this chance at a new life mean nothing. I had to give those lost lives a purpose, a meaning. I had to avenge their deaths, and I would make it my personal mission to do just that.

Zan's face became stern as he began to scold me. "We have too many eyes on us! The council was already suspicious enough of our combined absences this morning, and we can't have them snooping around on us anymore than they already are. We must lay low and keep our meetings brief so we can establish a routine that seems normal to outside eyes."

I shook my head. How could we go about so-called normal lives knowing that the people of Xandor were suffering? I shot a glare at Kade, waiting for him to speak on the matter, but when I was met with silence it only fueled my growing temper.

"Did the witch say anything else?" Elias questioned Zan, and I bit my tongue, waiting. "Any more clues as to who betrayed them?"

He exhaled deeply, eyes darting back and forth a few times before he spoke up again. "Only that her fascination with the creatures of Xandor revealed her own set of concerns that no one else seemed threatened by. She was curious as to their origins and beginnings. Every ability they possess and how they wield them. She said there was a shift of power coming. That change was on the horizon and that they would be a part of it."

My gaze snapped to Zan and I felt as if my blood had been drained from my body. "Ch-change?" I stuttered as I recalled my last moments with Rafina.

"Her exact words," he confirmed, and I stood from my seat to leave the table. The pit in my stomach was back and I knew she was involved. Even if she hadn't directly slain the people of

Xandor herself, she was a part of whatever was in the works, unbeknownst to the rest of us.

"What is it, Violet?" Kade let a hand rest on my shoulder as he joined me at my side. I knew he was aware of my emotions that were getting the best of me, and my head was a mix of images and words from the last few days that were scrambling together. But Rafina's mood as she had uttered that exact word before fleeing the infirmary made my nose turn up in disgust.

I whipped around, fury blossoming within me. "That is the last word Rafina spoke to me today before we parted. Before Kade arrived at the infirmary."

Zan cast his eyes down. "The witch assumes that you are a creation made for this change, and fears there might be others. Especially with the number of lives lost in their realm. She said she wouldn't be surprised if more hybrids came from this."

"So what am I? Some sort of experiment?" I was appalled by the notion but pissed that this piece of the puzzle fit. It didn't make sense to me, or to the other demons, that I had come back from the dead. While I wanted answers, this wasn't what I had anticipated.

"That's what the witch meant by control. Someone plans to use her." Elias shook his head. "At least, until they—until she—fulfills their purpose."

Zan built upon Elias's words. "Obviously, a change of power could mean a few different things. But if we're talking about Darthou, and the connection that Violet has with Kade, then that would most likely be him and his upcoming reign. What better way to take him down than through the one he's tethered to?"

"And if anyone stands to gain something from that happening, it would be Staffan," Elias added. "He would be next in line."

"But why Kade?" My face was growing hotter at the thought of someone using me. "He's not a king yet, so why would anyone have it out for him?"

"Why does anyone want power? They want control. They don't care who they have to take it from." Zan's words only infuriated me more.

My disdain at the mention of Staffan and Rafina was reaching its tipping point. The thought that someone had created me for control left a bitter taste on my tongue, and I wanted to rip their throats out with my bare hand. I wanted to drain the life from their bodies. To feel their blood spilled by my hand and mine alone.

I was tired of being lied to and used, and for what? So they could take down the man I had chosen a life with? The man I'd chosen to tether to?

No. I would not be used as a weapon against Kade. I wouldn't let them get the chance. The joke was on them, because I would fucking kill them before anyone or *anything* could land a hand on Kade.

"Violet?" Kade's voice seemed distant, but I knew he was approaching my side with trepidation. I was slipping into the madness of my mind that welcomed me with open arms. Did they really think I would kill him? Did they believe they had some way to force me into doing so?

"Violet," he said louder as he tried to take my hand. I jerked away and recoiled from him and from the men in the room. Zan stood and together with Elias, they advanced toward me.

There was a familiar pull from behind me. One that I had felt before when I was in a desperate search for Kade, when I had first awoken in Darthou. Again, when I set my eyes upon

Brett sleeping soundly in that hideous cabin. I glanced over my shoulders, eyeing the wall of mirrors that could take me to Staffan and Rafina.

I could put an end to this.

Now.

"You have to control this, don't let it consume you," Kade pleaded. The fact that he was trying to talk me down only ticked me off more. Why wasn't he upset about this? He should be pissed off! This affected the both of us!

A small part of me was hesitant to try and sprint off toward the mirrors, seeing as how I had succeeded in failing to pass through earlier during Rafina's pointless examination. But now, that appeared to be my only way out of here.

I knew now that my meeting with her was just a ruse to put the council members' minds at ease for the time being. She had an agenda of her own, and who would question the mighty powerful healer that she was?

The time for talking here was done. I wanted action.

Bounding from the cornered position they were aiming to put me in, I raced toward the mirrors. My heart thumped as adrenaline coursed through my veins, and just as my fingertips sank into the surface of the glass, I was yanked back and into Kade's hold.

"Let me go!" I shouted as his arms restricted me. My body thrashed against him, furious that he would keep me here against my will.

I was trying to save him! To save us!

"The coins," Kade said, and even though his strength was overpowering, I didn't relent in my fight against him.

"Don't you dare!" I spewed, angry at how he would hold me back. I wanted to stop whatever threat lay ahead and put an end to it. How could he not want to do the same?

Kade secured my wrists in one of his hands, and the pain of him doing so was minimal compared to my agitation and the increasingly foul mood overtaking me. I knew he had slipped the coins into my pocket, and I fought to keep the vengeance but I could sense it fading away. I didn't stop fighting him until my body began to weaken without my consent.

Alarm set in as my body began to slump against my will and fatigue began to take over. I had only felt this one other time, and I couldn't fight it off, it was happening too fast.

I drifted off to sleep.

CHAPTER 20

Violet

Son of a bitch.

My eyes popped open and I saw light filtering through the stained glass windows of Kade's bedroom, much like when I'd first looked upon them. I shot up in bed and surveyed the area, furious that he could apparently still put me to sleep like that. I had no idea how much time had passed but knew that he wouldn't leave me alone at a time like this.

Admittedly, I was a loose cannon and was formulating an agenda of my own. If he wasn't going to get on the same page as me, we were going to have a whole new set of problems. And I'd be damned if he ever put me to sleep like this again.

The space around me was quiet and empty and I heard nothing even as I stood from the bed. For once, I was grateful that Kade wasn't by my side when I woke. If he had been, I might have slapped him and given him a few choice words for knocking me out. I knew he was stronger than me, but it was infuriating that he would stoop to that level.

Leaving this room to wander around this castle-type place would be a stupid idea. I didn't know what hallway would lead where. It could be a maze that I'd lose myself in, and I didn't want to take that chance.

Now that my head was thinking a bit more clearly, as much as I wanted to find Rafina, I didn't know where to start. I wanted to believe that the earlier pull I felt would have led me to her, but what if I failed? I'd been able to locate Kade without knowing exactly where he was, but I was unsure I would be able to replicate that to find her. And what if she wasn't alone? What if I had to take on Rafina and Staffan at the same time?

I knew Kade couldn't have gone far. I highly doubted he'd leave me for long. I padded to the closet and checked it thoroughly before moving on to the bathroom. Once there, I moved soundlessly down the hall and made a right. I could feel him in there even though the door was closed. I crept away, leery that he might figure out I was now awake. I felt trapped here, knowing that the other hallway only led to the enclosed garden.

I only had one option left.

Flipping the bathroom light on, I entered and examined my appearance as I drew nearer to the mirror. My green blouse was crinkled and my braid had seen better days. I removed it from its binding and ran my fingers through it, opting for a low ponytail to the side. Waves gave my hair volume, and its coloring against the green material was a flattering combination.

I shook my head as I realized I was getting sidetracked. I

had more pressing matters than my appearance. Hell, my first time meeting the council I was in a robe and covered in black stuff. Why did I care what I looked like to those around here anymore?

I toyed with the thought of Rafina again, but then my mind drifted to Xandor. Our time there had been cut short, and my voice was now healed so I could speak freely without sounding like a chewed-up dog toy. I couldn't help but feel protective over that realm and its people. Maybe it was because their deaths had occurred so that I may live, but I owed it to them to help. I had to find my purpose in this life, and I strongly believed that this was it.

But I needed blood to cross over.

The blades I had removed from my protections earlier lay in front of me on the counter, and I picked up the closest one. If I did this, I would have to move quick and cross over fast. Once I injured myself, Kade would no doubt come into the picture. I only hoped that he took the chance to walk the short distance instead of popping in. I was on edge as I played through the order of events that needed to happen.

Retrieving the coins from my pocket, I set them on the far corner of the marbled top. I pushed the rest of the contents on the counter to the side and hopped up to stand on it. I had seen this realm with my own two eyes, and I had to believe that I could get there if I wanted to.

My heart began to pick up speed as I tried to envision the desolate land, the furies, and the witch. Glancing down at my skin, I lowered the sharp blade to it but paused before I could drag it across my flesh.

The failure to act quickly was my undoing. I could feel Kade's presence the moment he arrived.

"Don't you dare try to stop me," I commanded, still

furious with him for holding me down and forcing me to sleep. I hoped he could sense every ounce of resentment I had for him right now. How hurt I felt from his actions.

I caught sight of him in the mirror as he gradually entered the bathroom at a snail's pace, arms crossed as he examined me with his head tipped to the side.

"You're forgetting your protections," he said nonchalantly.

I rolled my eyes. "I can take care of myself. And don't you ever fucking touch me like that again."

"I'm sorry, but it was for your own good. We have to be smart about this, Violet."

I scoffed. "And your idea of being smart is inaction. Or better yet, it was your uncle's idea. I can't just sit on the sidelines and pretend that everything is alright when clearly, it's not."

"I'm not asking you to do that," he declared with a clear voice. He uncrossed his arms and his stature grew.

I met him with an increased volume of my own. "Then what are you asking me to do?"

He took another step closer and I put the blade back to my palm, ready to cut in. I wasn't going to back down without another fight. I didn't care if Kade and I stumbled into Xandor in a brawling fit of our own making, but dammit I was going to make it there regardless.

"I'm asking you to put on your protections."

I came to a halt and lowered the blade, eyeing him suspiciously. "You're not stopping me?"

"I'm not. And you're not going alone." He pivoted and exited the bathroom without another word. I stood on the countertop, stunned at his amenability for a moment before I sat and hopped off.

Had I just gone to him with this request, would he have agreed? I highly doubted it.

I made quick work of removing my outer clothing and began to submit myself to the confines of the protections that hugged every curve of my body. They seemed tight around the spaces where Kade had messed with some of the straps earlier. I peeled off the one at my right knee and tried to adjust it to fit so it was more comfortable, so I could bend my joint better. But then the one on my upper arm began to pull at me and I started to become irritated.

"Need some help?" Kade sauntered in and I let out an exaggerated puff of air.

"Why must I wear this?" I didn't think it was really necessary at this point. The witch had sifted through my memories and knew I meant no harm to them. Why did I need to wear all of this stuff when I didn't pose a threat? Once we had settled and began to talk like adults, everything calmed down.

"You haven't had any training yet, in travel or self-defense. Please do me this one thing, that's all I ask." Kade removed the strap and placed a finger between the fabrics before securing it for me. I flexed my arm out and back again. It felt better already and I gave him the other arm to fix as well. His eyes traced my body as he finished and he took a step back. A wave of want overcame me and I tightened my legs as I stilled.

"Don't do that," I warned.

"Do what?" He took a step back and crossed his arms, guarded. The sight of him dressed in this attire again almost made my knees buckle. He looked lethal and—even while ninety-five percent of his body was covered—sexy as sin. I tried to squash the want that I had for him, but I had trouble denying the need to strip him out of his protections with my own hands. It would be difficult, but I would rid him of them somehow.

"What do you mean, what? Don't try to distract me with your lust, I'm mad at you." I had meant for my words to come out harsh, but instead they sounded more like a pout and I was angry at that betrayal.

He shrugged, his boyish charm sweeping across his facial features. "Can't help it. And I don't think I'm alone in my lust."

I hated to admit that he was right. Heat began to bloom at my core and I turned my back on him so he could zip me up. I had only been able to raise it about halfway, but it felt as if it was caught on something. His fingers grazed my skin along my spine and I resisted the urge to shiver at his touch. I knew whatever expression crossed my face he would be able to view in the mirror before me. As much as I tried to focus on my loathing of his actions and the events of earlier, his close proximity was making it difficult.

My throat was dry and my face heated as I swallowed before facing him again. "Is this normal?" I gestured between us as I took a step back, bumping into the counter. "Feeling everything there is between us like this?"

"I think we're navigating some uncharted territory in more than one area of our tethering. It's going to be a learning experience for the both of us." He focused on me as he spoke, and I noticed how he didn't directly answer my question.

"So…not normal," I acknowledged. The thought that I couldn't hide anything from him was annoying. I wanted him to know I was furious with him, but I was distracted by my swaying thoughts of sex. That tidbit should have been kept to the confines of my head and nothing more.

"To my understanding, the levels at which we feel each other's emotions are probably heightened because of your other attributes."

I couldn't help the amused laugh that escaped me. "Attributes? That's a nice way of putting it." It felt more like I had multiple personalities with their own abilities. I had no control over the banshee screams, although according to the witch the only way to deal with those was to let it out myself. And my fury side wanted blood and vengeance. I was in control to an extent, fixated on the subject of my wrath and well aware of my actions in the moment. But it was my demon side where I didn't know what I was capable of. That part of me was still a bit of a mystery even though I had their eyes.

"Come, we should get going." Kade pivoted to turn and I followed him into his watching quarters.

I found it strange that he was so ready to return with me to Xandor and didn't try to question me about it. Perhaps he was just relieved I wasn't trying to go off and kill Rafina and saw this as a necessary distraction for me in the meantime.

"I'm assuming you want to do the honors?" Kade beckoned me toward the wall of mirrors and I became hesitant. "Or, I can do it if you like."

I nodded my head slowly. While I was nervous that it might not work for me, I had to know if I was capable of crossing over. Had my desperation to thwart Rafina earlier worked because I simply wanted it to, or had I truly failed at the task? I wanted to believe that I was capable, that this being I had become was powerful in more ways than one.

Traveling through mirrors was a skill that could take great lengths of time to perfect, but I didn't want to fall into that category. To anyone I trusted, anyone who mattered to Kade and me, I wanted to be strong and go against the odds. Blaze my own path.

With a flick of my wrist, I sliced my palm. Blood began to

pool and I fought the urge to react.

"What the hell, Violet?" Kade met me at my front and placed his hand beneath mine. It began to heat, but my open wound remained just that. Open. A gaping slice that had panic setting in between the two of us. "We're not trying to tether again, we're just trying to open a connection."

He said that as if I should know the difference between the two. They both required blood, didn't they?

"Dammit, where are your coins?" I could tell he was exasperated. I told him they were in the bathroom and he left to retrieve them.

I bit my bottom lip as my palm began to ache. I dipped my fingers into the pooling substance and began to touch the mirrors before me in the same pattern that Zan had earlier. As I finished, I eyed the puckered skin and tried to recall what it had felt like for Kade to heal me. The warmth that it provided as he healed my throat earlier. The heat that radiated from his touch when he healed my injured foot the very first night we had met. The comfort it had brought me when his touch healed my wrists after he had restrained me for sex.

My hand began to heat at the thought of it all and I studied it as Kade reentered. "I seem to only be able to heal you when you have these."

My head tilted as my parted wound began to close and seal itself. I thought my jaw might drop to the ground as Kade approached, no doubt observing the very thing that had me waiting in anticipation. When the wound completed its course of closure, the warmth faded away and I examined my hand, stunned.

"How...how did you do that?" Kade stuttered as he searched my hand for himself, in disbelief of what we had just witnessed.

My forefinger of my dominant hand dragged across the healed spot. I couldn't feel any trace of the mark that had just been there. It was as if it had never happened, minus the bloodied mess that lay on my skin.

"I don't know, exactly. I just thought of you and the times you've healed me. What it felt like and…" I didn't know how to finish.

Kade blew out a slow and steadied breath, just as stunned as I was at my ability to heal. Was this something I had arrived at on my own, or did I have our tethering to thank for this? Just another piece of the five-thousand-piece puzzle that was my new life now.

"You are…a wonder." His astonishment made my heart skip a beat as he gazed upon me fondly. I was grateful that he never feared me with each new revelation that I came upon. Instead, he seemed to share an equal interest in each new detail that shed light on who I might be. On who I might become. But even so, it scared me that the woman standing before him now was not the same one he had been watching for six years. The one he had fallen in love with.

Kade eyed my markings on the mirrors before he began to wipe my hand clean of my blood with a dampened washcloth before placing it and my coins on his desk.

Envisioning the place we had visited this morning, I tried to recall what Zan had done. Did he actually touch the mirrors, or did he just do the swiping motion?

I focused on the furies and the witch once more and the place they were exiled to. The barren land that didn't look like it should be able to sustain life as I knew it.

There it was again—the pull.

Closing my eyes, I touched the glass and repeated the motion Zan had made. Instead of my fingers dragging across the glass, it felt like nothing more than skimming across the surface of water.

When I opened my eyes again, I found the imagery of the land of Xandor unfolding and revealing itself to me. The wasteland they had no choice but to use as a home became as clear as day. Or at least a cloudy and depressing one.

"Well done," Kade said, and a sense of pride came over me at my accomplishment. "Lead the way."

This time, I took his hand in mine and led him through. We passed quickly, our feet crunching with each step into the dry and cracked earth beneath us. However, I could sense a change in the atmosphere around us, and a cry pierced the sky as lightning flashed above.

Kade and I exchanged looks of worry as smoke began to fill the air in the distance. To my right, rising swirls of it could be seen, and I feared that another attack might be taking place. It looked as if something was on fire, or multiple things for that matter, and I took off in that direction.

My pulse raced as Kade and I ran through the trees side by side. I went as fast as my lungs and legs could carry me. I was sure Kade could have left me in the dust, but he remained close as we dodged branches and twigs snapped beneath us. A bare branch scraped my cheek and I knew it drew blood, but I continued on. I was just thankful that it didn't try to take my eye out.

I couldn't help but notice how soundless Kade was compared to my steps and envied his ability to move in such a way. He could have an element of surprise if I wasn't here ruining it.

Another voice cried out, but in agony, and I picked up speed. I waited for my lungs to burn with the exertion but carried on in its absence, thankful I hadn't experienced it yet, knowing it would hold me back.

A clearing began to form in the distance beyond the trees and I could make out piles of smoke and figures up ahead. We slowed our approach and I caught my breath, but my heart continued to rattle on in my chest.

"What brings you back so soon?"

I whipped my head around to find the witch forming from the very mist that had caused chaos earlier. This time, however, instead of venom in her words, she was different. Despondent, even. Her once wicked face carried a sadness that moved me. I was conflicted by it, knowing, *seeing*, that she had murdered before.

Sobs sounded from the clearing and I found myself torn between talking to the witch or following our pursuit of whatever lay ahead on our path.

"Is everyone alright?" Kade asked the witch, and I began to feel a strange tug toward two figures over my shoulder. I left Kade's side to follow the sensation, recognizing that I had felt it earlier with the furies.

A high-pitched ringing emerged and came to the forefront of my mind as I closed the gap between the figures and me.

As I left the tree line, my breath caught as I focused on the rows of funeral pyres up ahead. Some were lit and burning at full force, while others had already been put out with nothing but ash remaining. There had to be dozens of them, and I grasped at my chest at the sight of it all, but the hardened exterior of my protections didn't cave one bit.

My legs almost gave out as I realized where the ring in my ears was originating from. On one of the few pyres that had yet to be burned lay a woman who resembled the two furies I had met earlier, and they were mourning over their loss.

One clutched the dead woman's skirt and buried her face

in it for a brief moment before revealing a painful expression on her face that spoke volumes. The other held her lost sister's hand and touched her face, wrought with a suffering that I could feel in my bones. Her lips moved in words I could not hear. Sobs erupted from them once more as an unknown man approached with a torch in hand, ready to light the pyre that housed their lost sister.

A few rows down, a flame burned over the body of what looked like a child, and my stomach rolled in anguish. Someone who I thought might be a parent was on the ground a few feet away, his fists beating so hard on the dry ground he might create a crevice of his own making. Tears streamed down his dirt-ridden face as he let out a guttural howl.

I didn't know why I was surprised that there were children here, but the fact that they weren't even spared for this massacre…it was blood that never should have been spilled. I didn't care what kind of creature they were—it was unacceptable and unfathomable.

None of them had to die. But none of them had a choice in the matter. Countless lives had been ruthlessly taken just to fulfill some unknown agenda at their expense.

Somehow, someway, I had been thrust into the middle of it.

I slowed as I drew nearer to the scene, the high-pitched tone drowning out all other sounds until I came to a stop. The woman fury on the pyre showed a massive laceration to her throat and trauma to her chest. She had met a tragic and violent end, and the realm of Xandor fell away as I was brought down to my knees with such force that I thought my kneecaps might snap, if that were even possible.

Someone would pay for this.

Anyone who was involved would.

The loss of my human life and everything I had left behind paled in comparison to this annihilation.

I didn't care what became of me in the process, or if I died trying to carry out my mission. This was now a war I was willing to lay down my life for.

I would become a weapon indeed, but if someone thought for one moment I was going to be used against Kade, they were sorely mistaken. They had no idea just what they had created, and I would see to it that they found I was their greatest regret.

EPILOGUE

Kade

"**A**gain!" she ordered as she spit blood from her mouth and wiped her face with the back of her arm.

Elias looked at me warily, unsure if he should obey her command. I knew he was taking it easy on her, his movements drawn out and exaggerated throughout their combat session.

Elias and I had trained for this our whole lives, and Violet was trying to take everything on as if she could learn it in a month. A few times a week, Violet trained with Aleena for the purpose of satisfying a warring council. But on the other days, she requested training with Elias, so she would have nothing holding her back.

And as much as it pained me that she didn't want me involved in these sessions, today I had made it a point to see her progress and observe how she was doing with his instruction.

"Pretend I'm not here, Elias," I said through gritted teeth. I could see why he had been hesitant to inform me of their work so far. She didn't know when to quit or to tap out. She was using her newfound skill of healing, although it was sketchy at times whether it worked or not.

Violet had her hands up and at the ready. Her frame had become leaner and more fit in the time since she had begun training, but she still kept that delectable curve to her that beckoned to be held, to be touched.

That is, if she didn't get herself killed first.

If she went out into the real world with this attitude, she wouldn't get very far. I knew the extent of Elias and his strength, and he was trying to quell her thirst for a fight while still trying to teach in the process.

She avoided his attack as he came up on her right, but he was swift in his movements and swiped her legs out from under her. She fell but caught herself before her face could hit the ground.

I could sense her frustrations and knew that me being here was a distraction. She rose and her top fell off her shoulder, exposing her bruised skin. I nudged toward the front of my seat on the bench. Violet swung with such force, a right hook that caused her to stagger when Elias dodged out of the way. She tried to recover quickly but his elbow came down on her and she went to the floor in a yelp of pain. It radiated off of her—the blow had been damaging.

"That's enough," I ordered as I stood. "Thank you, Elias. That will be all."

"What?" Violet panted as she scrambled to her feet again. Her braided hair was falling apart and her chest heaved as she stood, grasping at her side as if she was trying to inhale deeply. "We're not…done."

"Yes, you are." I raised my voice and her lips thinned into a hard-pressed line. She was pissed, but I wasn't about to let her madness consume her.

Ever since we had returned from Xandor, witnessing the lives lost, she had been different. Guarded and distant, and intent on learning everything she could. Be it physical forms such as combat, or knowledge that she and Sarah buried their heads in books to find. We barely had time for each other anymore, and when we did, we usually ended up fighting. Which was why I was adamant to see how she was progressing with Elias.

"Talk to you later then." Elias left with nary a scratch and I was met with Violet's piercing gaze.

"We weren't done." She spat her words at me as if it would matter. Her hands were fisted as her eyes bored into mine, expecting me to apologize, but I was far from it.

"What have you gathered from Elias and his fighting techniques?" I began to circle around her, knowing it would cause unease.

"What?" She whipped around to face me, but I continued my pace. She winced at the act, grabbing hold of her side again. I suspected she had done something to her ribs with the dull ache I felt in mine.

"Are there any repetitive moves he uses? Any side he favors? Tell me, what have you learned from him besides taking on beating after beating?" My words angered her, and I went on. "Come on, you've been training with him for weeks now, what have you deduced from fighting him?"

She placed her hands on her hips as she stilled, and her irritation only grew at my words. We were in one of the smaller rooms used for sparring and hand-to-hand combat. There were no weapons in this room and no windows, just lights along the ceiling and markings on the floor from fights of the past. Divots here, scratches and dents there. There were splotches of uneven surface which could raise the difficulty of your stance if you didn't balance yourself correctly.

"He likes to send me to the floor. A lot." Violet's chest puffed in agitation.

I nodded. "He is quick and he likes levels, especially lower. And for as tall as he is, you wouldn't think he would literally stoop to that, but he uses that to his advantage. You have to be light on your feet." I ducked down and swung a leg in her direction, and she responded to the attack, just narrowly missing the hit. Shock ran through her momentarily as she raised her arms to guard herself.

"Good." I recovered as I began my route around her again. She turned with me, eyes fixated with an urge to fight me, and I was happy to oblige. Stepping into her zone, I swung and she ducked out to miss it, landing a blow to my side. The power behind the punch was a pleasant surprise as I whirled around her.

"You're getting stronger," I mused, and she cut me off as she tried to draw back for another hit. She was too slow, and I grabbed her arm and pulled it behind her, back against my chest.

"Doesn't feel like it," she said through gritted teeth. She attempted to ram her elbow into my torso but I blocked it with my free hand. I knew she had a lot of anger bottled up inside of her, and I had hoped that this extra combat with Elias would help, but it seemed to be more to her detriment.

"Squats, jump rope, and running," I muttered into her ear, and her anger peaked.

"What?"

"Elias. Those are a part of every workout regime he ever does. It's not all combat, it's about strengthening and conditioning your body. I don't think jumping directly into combat is your best approach."

"But that's what I want. I *want* to fight." She struggled against my hold but didn't give up, and I only tightened my grip on her.

"But there's more to it than that."

Her body all but vibrated beneath me, and before I could respond to it, the back of her head made contact with my nose and I released her. She then proceeded to copy my previous move, sending me to the floor where I landed with a thud.

Ignoring the throbbing sensation coming from my nose, I tripped her. She fell to the floor beside me and I pinned her down. Her face was distorted with another shriek of pain as she tried to fight her restraint.

"Let. Me. Go!" Her face was reddening as she yelled in mine, and instead of trying to suppress her anger, I just did as she asked. I was afraid for her and the path that she was on, and while I hadn't openly admitted it yet, I thought it was time.

Releasing her, I stood. She found her way to her feet as well, tucking loose hair behind her ears.

"Our place." I approached her, and before she could protest, I took us back to our bedroom. She had scolded me on more than one occasion for not giving her a heads-up before traveling by pocket, so I tried to make it a point to do so. Even if it was only mere seconds before our departure. She was still aggravated and let out an exaggerated exhale.

"I wasn't finished," she spat.

I inhaled deep before I began. "I'm worried about you."

"Why? Because I'm lousy at fighting? I'm sorry I didn't

have the same upbringing as you."

I waved off her words. "No. Not at all. What you've learned in your short time training is impressive, but you're not giving yourself credit for it."

She rolled her eyes and turned her back to me as she faced the stained glass windows of our room. A halo of light illuminated her hair and I tried to commit the image to memory. It was still surreal that she was even here, that we had been given this chance, even if it wasn't of our own doing.

"You come *one* day to see me train and call it off within ten minutes. Then you take me down and make me quit altogether. Either I'm doing fine, or I'm not, which is it?"

The harshness of her words should have given me pause, but if I didn't say this now, I was afraid she might continue down this destructive road and endanger herself.

"Violet, I don't want to stand in your way, but I feel like that's all I am anymore. I've tried to give you space and the freedom to study and train as you want, but you're not allowing yourself time for anything else. I understand that what we witnessed in Xandor was tragic, and we will find those responsible, but letting yourself get beaten over and over again in the process is doing more harm than good."

"Says you." Her posture stiffened and I hoped I didn't regret my next words.

"And Elias. Aleena. Sarah. Zan."

"Aleena?" she questioned, confusion dripping from the name she spoke. I hoped I wasn't pushing too far as she flipped a switch. "So everybody is against me?"

"No." I was adamant in my response. "It's because they care for you that they are worried. Aleena may not know everything that's going on yet, but she knows something is up with you. She didn't want to say anything to Rafina, because you are under such scrutiny already."

"But she talked to you about it." Her voice cracked, and I could sense her anger falter for a moment. I hoped I was breaking through.

"She did. And I'm all for you finding out who you are and becoming who you want to be, but you don't have to get yourself beaten to a bloody pulp in the process." I couldn't keep track of the countless outfits that were disposed of because of her bloodied sessions. The fact that her trainings even went that far was worrying enough.

Her head tipped down and she hugged herself but flinched again in the process. It was a subtle movement, but I knew she had an injury to her ribs that she hadn't been able to heal yet.

We stood in silence for a few moments, and her body started to soften in its stance. Emotions began to flood through her. She was processing something, and I decided to give her some alone time so she didn't feel as if I was crowding her.

"I'm going to go out to the garden for a while. I have some time before I need to be on watch. You're more than welcome to join me if you want." She stood there, unmoving as I left, and I continued down the hall until I reached the garden.

The soothing aromas from the flowers out here welcomed me, and I began to undress so I could enter the water. Its heat was a welcome sensation that I hadn't felt since I had first introduced this place to Violet weeks ago.

I didn't know how to get her to open up, didn't know how to get her to understand that these changes she was after weren't going to happen overnight. The limits she pushed herself to were alarming, and after seeing her today I knew that Elias and Aleena were right to come to me. I knew it would look to Violet as if they were betraying her, but she had to see that they cared enough to say something.

And why was she placing distance between us? It was like a light within her had been snuffed out and hadn't been lit since we witnessed the carnage in Xandor. She was quiet and reserved around me, but then practically begged to be punished in training. What was I missing?

The door to the garden opened and Violet stepped out, black tears streaming down her now puffy face. I rose immediately from the pool and met her at the door, water running down my body. A ringing was forming in my ears and I knew she had her coins on her. That, and the droves of increasing discomfort coming off of her were impossible to ignore.

She lifted the side of her shirt to reveal raised skin and an indent where she had been struck in the ribs. I couldn't crush my distaste at the injury she had sustained and wondered if I had made it worse.

"I can't." She inhaled sharply as I reached out a hand, placing it on the point of impact. She tried to stumble back from my touch but I let my hand remain fixed on her. Warmth began to spread across her side and I could feel the crack of her rib as it snapped back into place.

Violet shuddered away from me but was only met by the door at her back as I continued to heal her. Her pain tolerance had certainly increased immensely in a short time frame, but she still hadn't mastered the healing aspect of her abilities. The fact that she was coming to me for healing was proof enough that she was biting off more than she could chew.

I drew my hand back and she released a sigh of relief, her skin now void of any markings or signs of what was once there. She was giving off mixed signals—regret, sadness, anger, and hesitation—and I took a few steps back from her. I had already offered once for her to join me out here, and I wasn't going to push for it if she didn't want to be here. I only hoped that she would allow herself the grace to rest and let herself relax.

This wasn't the first time she had needed the use of my healing, and I was sure it wouldn't be the last. But at least we knew that when she was in possession of her coins, I was able to heal her. For some reason, when her fury and banshee sides were not being suppressed, I was unable to do so.

But to be fair, I had no knowledge of whether or not my healing worked on anything besides demons and humans. I had never needed to know until now.

Without another word, I made my way back to the pool and began to enter it again. Keeping my back to her, I sat on the steps, keeping my upper half out of the water for now. The steam rising off of the surface filled my lungs and I closed my eyes.

Violet had yet to leave, and even a short distance away I could sense her inner turmoil. I willed her to stay, to accept that her body and her mind needed a break from everything. Hell, if she needed to be out here alone, I would grant her that if it meant her having even the slightest respite. I wouldn't be offended if that was what she wanted, even as I longed for her presence for myself. I craved the connection that our tethered bond had created. We hadn't even been intimate in any way for far too long.

The shuffling of clothes could be heard and I assumed she was undressing. The dull ache coming from the coins subsided, so she must have removed them as well. I wished I could say that I had grown accustomed to the sound they emitted, but it still affected me just the same as the first day she had been given them.

It felt like a small victory that she was undressing, and I caught her scent as she closed the distance between us and dipped her feet into the water beside me, sending a ripple out across the surface. She was sweet mixed with sweat, an aroma I had grown accustomed to in her time spent working out and training. It was a strange mix that only she could make desirable, and my cock stirred at the thought.

Violet came around and straddled my legs, her core mere inches away from my growing length. She might have been tossed around a few times, but the beauty she exuded from her post-training frame was a sight. My hands gripped her thighs and I let one hand skim her leg and drift toward the base of her spine. I waited for her to take the lead, to control what came next. I would be at her mercy.

"I don't want to talk," she stated, and I could feel our bond igniting with a passion that made my blood race.

"Understood," I acknowledged as she wrapped her hands around my submerged cock. The feel of her hand stroking me from root to tip elicited a moan, and we stared into each other's eyes at full force. I was afraid to blink, fearful that I might lose the connection that I and my body so desperately needed from her. She rose up slightly and positioned herself to take me inside, and I moved up a step as I eagerly awaited to be granted entrance.

Her flesh formed around me and my grip on her tightened. Her muscular body had a new firmness that I admired under my touch. She had a dedication, I'd give her that. Violet used the steps to lift and lower herself on me, and my fingertips dug into her.

I wanted to kiss her, to taste her, explore the mouth and body that I had missed so much. For even when we were in each other's presence, she remained apart from me. I longed for her touch and the comfort that only she could provide. I felt whole when we connected, be it by a held hand or coming together like this. I needed her like I needed air to breathe. But even though we had become distant, my love and desire for her never wavered.

She moved with a calculated ease that had me building quickly. Afraid that I might come too quick under her unrelenting stare and slow movements, I began to circle her clit, and it was then that her face softened. She caved at my caress and her lips parted. She picked up speed and so did I, the water lapping around us. She bounced faster and faster until I came inside her. I fought through the urge to stop her and gritted my teeth as I let her chase after her pleasure. I began to throb inside of her as she collapsed and I captured her mouth with mine, taking her cry of release as I tasted her. I kept circling her clit until her hand stopped me and her body spasmed, riding out the aftereffects of our exchange.

My tongue explored her mouth as hers did mine, and our hands roamed each other's bodies in a gripping frenzy. I sought the comfort that she provided, but it quickly faded as a sadness overcame her and her cheeks became wet, causing me to pull back. We still had no explanation for her black tears, but it didn't make seeing them hurt any less.

"What is it?" I brushed back the stray hairs that were plastered to her face, and she shook her head.

"I'm sorry." She choked back another sob as more tears rolled off her face and hit the water with a plink. I attempted to swipe them away with my thumbs.

"You don't need to apologize for anything—"

"But I do. I feel like I'm walking this fine line between what I know I should do and what I want to do. My mind is a constant battleground that I can't seem to turn off, and I'm taking it out on everyone else. Either by fighting—and losing terribly—or by distancing myself. I hate the coins and how weak they make me feel and the effect they have on you. And I just have this anger and this sadness that I can't get rid of. I don't know how to make it stop."

I knew she had been bottling things up, and it pained me to hear it all coming to a head. But I was still grateful that she was finally letting down the wall she had put up between us.

There might be hope after all.

"Violet, you don't have to hide this. I am here for you no matter what, no matter what you need. I don't want you to ever be afraid of this battleground inside that head of yours, because I am on it with you. Beside you."

"But the things I dream about, the things I envision and want to do…" She searched my eyes as she fought for the words to say. "I'm afraid you wouldn't love me anymore if you really knew me. This new me. I'm not the human you first fell in love with. I love you too much to let you think I could ever be her again, because I can't."

It hurt that she would ever think such a thing. Perhaps giving her some space was the last thing I needed to do— maybe she needed me now more than ever. As a friend, a companion, a lover, and any other box that needed checked. I would see to it that I never let her doubt my love for her ever again.

Love.

Wait a second.

"What did you say?" I blinked at her, disbelieving. It had been a while since I had felt it from her, and I was second-guessing whether or not I had really heard her say those words in the first place. She had only uttered them one time before, and only while on the verge of sleep. I never brought it up in fear she might not remember, or might deny it had ever happened.

Her mouth opened for a moment but closed again.

"Say it again," I urged her as I leaned forward, my cock twitching inside of her at the movement.

Her breath caught as she tensed, her tears ceasing. "I...I love you." The intoxicating sensations that flooded through the both of us was overwhelming. I could get high off of the immense gratification of hearing that, and feeling the connection between us. It was like sparks were igniting from my extremities and I was itching to touch her and consume her once more.

She spoke again and this time, more sure of herself. "I love you, Kade."

I didn't doubt her for one moment. Her feelings were true and I returned them with equal ardor.

"I have always loved you, Violet. Nothing could ever change that. I love you as a demon, a banshee, a fury and all." Her face faltered as if relieved by my acceptance, and our mouths collided once more.

I knew she was troubled, and by her own admission. She feared herself and what I might think of her. But right here and right now, we were united as one. And I would strive to remind her of that every day, no matter what the future may hold.

ACKNOWLEDGEMENTS

Self-publishing is no easy task. Some might think that writing the story might be the hardest part, but there's so much that happens after the first rough draft that it makes my head spin just thinking about it. That being said, I wouldn't be at this point without the help and support of others.

Just for giggles, I'm going to call my husband 'Jackson' for now. Thank you for all of your behind-the-scenes work. I honestly can't shout your praises enough. From the formatting, to the cover design, the website, and so on. I literally couldn't have done these things without you. All of the time you have poured into helping make these books happen, means the world to me. Thank you for believing in me.

A huge shout-out goes to Rebecca, my editor, who I was so incredibly grateful to have in my corner again for this book. Her attention to detail saved me in a few areas and her kind words are always a pleasure to hear. I am not a fan of editing to begin with, but she makes things a little more bearable. Thank you so much.

Fun fact, seamstress Rebecca in Altering Me was named months before I had the honor of getting to work with editor Rebecca. I'm not sure what the chances are of that, but dang, what a coincidence.

When I released my first book in December of 2023,

nobody besides my husband and a select few knew about my self-publishing start. Even then, I wasn't providing any details as to the book title or my author name. I was scared out of my mind putting my work out and into the world.

But slowly, some family members, coworkers, and friends have begun to find out my little 'secret' and have been wonderfully supportive of this hobby of mine. I'm so thankful for each and every one of them.

I can't end without thanking you, the readers. Thank you for diving into this book, turning pages, and giving this author another chance. I hope you'll stick around with me a while longer.

ABOUT THE AUTHOR

Krystal Kae lives in the corn-filled Midwest with her husband, children, and pets. Her love of reading and writing started back in high school, but it was over a decade later when she decided to put her overactive imagination to work again and began filling blank pages.

Fascinated by all things paranormal, fantasy, and romantic-you can find these topics the center of her writing universe.

When she's not working her full-time office job or buried in a story, she loves to create memories with loved ones, travel, and take long walks in cemeteries.

Get the latest updates at **KrystalKae.com** and follow @krystalkaewrites